THE BALLAD OF DAVID AND ISRAEL

Hi! I wrote this book & hope that if you enjoy it, you can leave me a positive review on Amazon. Thx, & be safe & be well!

Roderick Byron Palmer

R B P

ISBN: 150034656X
ISBN 13: 9781500346560
Library of Congress Control Number: 2014912049
CreateSpace Independent Publishing Platform
North Charleston, South Carolina

This book is dedicated to God first, who allows me to do all things to give Him the glory. Then my beautiful children, Sean, Nyilah and Jordan, who are the lights of my days and the lamps of my eve; my mother Dorothy, who raised me to love writing and literature and whose prayers held me up during times of my life when they were most needed; and my wife Zandra, my friend, my rock of support and the person without whom you would not be holding this book in your hand if not for her backing her man up all the way. LOVE…

PROLOGUE

Damn! He couldn't figure out how it all got to this—strapped to this chair in this room of torture, bleeding, the pain as intimate as if it were a close personal friend, ready to die, watching the monster before him readying itself to do the deed.

His mind raced back to the morning. He'd gotten out of bed feeling like a million dollars, like he had the whole world at his feet. He had a good breakfast, worked out, and went to work with some extra pep in his step. Everything just seemed *right.*

Now, it was as if twelve hours ago was a million years in the past.

He had never known such pain in his life. It was not that dull, throbbing ache, which he probably could have handled. It was a bright pain, alive and burning through every pore. And it was compounded by the fact that he knew the thing before him was about to kill him.

At least his death promised to be a quick one. He held onto that. Hell, he had to hold onto *something.*

He tried to speak to the beast, but amazingly, he could not hear his own voice. But the thing must have heard, because a smile spread across its lips as it spoke back to him.

He could not hear a word the beast said. But he knew.

The thing picked up a meat cleaver off the floor and whipped it through in his direction. The motion was so quick he could barely even follow it. But he noted what fell off of him.

There was nothing left to do now but scream, and so he did. Because a demon was laughing at his anguish as it sliced and cut him and drank in his suffering, painting itself in his blood.

PART ONE:

DAVID

1

I grew up around La Brea and Adams, just a couple of miles south of the mid-Wilshire district in Los Angeles. At the time, all you were going to see there were black faces like my own; now you'd probably see just as many (if not more) brown ones. It was not a great neighborhood, but neither was it a terrible one. Most of the people who lived there were recent arrivals from the South or Midwest, all come to California to ferret out job opportunities and make new destinies for themselves.

Israel Baylock lived around the corner from me. He moved into the neighborhood when he was in the eighth grade, fresh from the heart of South Central LA. Immediately the local kids tested him as a fighter. He had a little heart but no skills, and the former kept people from bullying him for the most part. But occasionally somebody just couldn't resist going at him. Israel was a scrawny, high-yellowish kid, small for his age, with big black glasses that never seemed to fit his face right. Something about the look of him made people want to bully him at times, and on top of that, he had that funny-ass name.

Israel was also kept relatively safe and rather popular around the 'hood by his mother and sister. They were beautiful, and I don't mean that they looked really pretty or were exceptionally good-looking. I mean they were *beautiful*—like the kind of beauty you see on TV or on the movie screen or in fashion magazines. They were the color of coffee just barely tinted with cream, and each had a body that evoked the voluptuous '70s actress Pam Grier, strong and small-wasted but overflowing in the bust and behind, with legs long and toned that seemed to stretch into forever. Their faces were as much a wonder, with seductive, exotically slanted eyes that were dark gray, noses that were pert and upturned—an obviously European trait in their bloodline—and lips that were full and lush and easy to imagine being kissed by. Their hairstyles seemed to change every week, but they mostly kept to either a bob or a short, spiky do, the style of the day for those with so-called good hair. From afar, they almost looked like twins, definitely more like sisters than mother and daughter, and instead of being snobbish or repelled by the neighborhood and the world's reactions to them, they were open and kind.

A lot of the local kids began hanging out with Israel just to get glimpses of Ms. Baylock and Ellena. Ellena was slightly more popular because she was only two or three years older than most in our crowd, and in our undeveloped minds, that made her attainable; Ms. Baylock was clearly out of our league. But that didn't stop anyone who came by to visit from going absolutely google-eyed when she walked into a room. Both she and Ellena had a presence to them and moved with such a natural grace and authority that it seemed like all you could do around them was to be stunned and amazed.

We were all bused to a school in West Los Angeles called Palms Junior High School. It was a grand experiment that began in the '70s to improve the educational opportunities of those in the 'hood by sending them to quality schools elsewhere and also to provide a meeting of cultures in a sort of human gumbo sure to be enjoyed by everyone. That was all fine and good in theory (and even in practice initially), but by the mid-'80s, when *my* crowd arrived there, the quality of education was nothing to write home about. At that time, there were more brown and black faces than there were white, and while I don't want to say that was the reason for the slow downhill roll of the education there, as a man of color, it definitely made me wonder.

Mixed crowds didn't happen too much either. Blacks stayed with blacks, Mexicans stayed with their own, and the relative few whites who dared still attend the school definitely hung strong with each other. Some people were liked by all the crowds, and for some odd reason, Israel and I were that kind.

Israel had a love of comic books that was an instant bonding agent for most of the kids at the school. He seemed to know everything about any superhero you asked him about; the kid was like a crazy walking encyclopedia on the subject. I was just popular with everyone because I was a fairly intelligent kid, at the top of my class (even above most of the white children), but I was also a big, fearsome kid known in the 'hood for fighting at the drop of a hat.

2

One day I was sitting on a bench during a PE class Israel and I were in, waiting for my turn to play tennis. I was bored, still under the impression at that stage in my thirteen years of life that it was a white folks' game. I just couldn't give a shit. Football and basketball were the sports of choice for me.

Israel was on that bench next to me talking to some white kid about why Marvel comics were so much richer in story and art and all-around content than DC comics. The white kid clearly disagreed, and the way they were going on about it, you'd have thought they were having a presidential debate on something very serious.

"You guys are worked up over some bulllllsheeeeit," I said, smirking with authority. They both looked at me as if I were insane. Their expressions made me want to burst out laughing, but I kept a straight face.

The white kid, who looked like a Caucasian version of Israel, seemed like he wanted to say something smartassed to me, but he didn't.

I said to him, "What? Y'all didn't hear me? I said, that ol' comics bullshit y'all are talkin' is about nuthin'. Like the both of y'all. Now what?"

"You're Dave Hill, right?" Israel said, trying the friendly approach. His prepubescent voice was high-pitched, almost feminine. "I think you live right around the corner from me. I always see you at the playground."

"Yeah, *and*?" I said with a menacing look. I was almost a foot taller than Israel and at least a good twenty-five pounds heavier. He was no more a threat to me than a gnat. Looking back, I'm ashamed at how much I enjoyed bullying him.

Israel's eyes narrowed, but he said nothing. I puffed my chest up a little more as I noticed that two other kids on the bench were checking me out. Some others nearby began to close in at the hint of a fight.

"What, nigga? Little Israel, Li'l Izzy's 'bout to have a little tizzy! And while we're on the subject, that shit rhymes with Lizzy? You almost got a bitch's name, fool!"

The other kids that had gathered about laughed. I was usually not good at the quick joke, so I was feeling good about myself. Israel's yellow pallor was flushed red with rage, but I knew that he would remain mute. He was as still and helpless as a fly in a web, and it was clearly fear that prevented action. But his eyes (which were red, hinting at tears soon to come) were filled with venom that threw me off momentarily.

I heard a whistle and saw the PE teacher waving us to the tennis court.

Israel turned to his friend. "We'll continue this later, when we don't have to worry about being interrupted by assholes."

The white kid nodded, seemingly surprised at Israel's boldness in ignoring me.

I was surprised too—so much so that when he stood up and started to jog over to the tennis court, I stuck my leg out and tripped him.

He hit the ground hard on his stomach and face, his coke-bottle glasses flying off of his head almost five feet. There was a collective gasp from all the kids watching. I immediately felt a little ashamed, but I didn't let it show on my face; I stayed the hard young nigga that the streets had already taught me to be.

ood up and got ready, just in case Israel surprised me by g up wanting to fight. As a warning not to go there, I gave hard kick in the thigh.

e stayed there on the ground for a moment. The only thing king him as a living being was the almost serene wheezing as reathed heavily through his nose.

The PE teacher, a strapping Mexican guy who was so cool at I'm embarrassed not to remember his name, helped Israel his feet. "What's going on over here? What just happened?"

"Nothin'," I said quickly, trying to give Israel a threatening look while seeming nonplussed to the PE teacher. "Looks like he just tripped."

"I see. Well, it sure looks like there's a lot of you guys floating around here for a kid who just tripped."

"Well, he *did*. You can ask him yourself."

The big man kneeled before Israel with an almost pitying look. You could tell he had a soft spot for scrawny, unathletic types like the young boy before him.

"Well kid, did somebody push you, knock you down?"

There was a slight pause before Israel answered in that girlish voice. "No, sir. I tripped." Two big tears rolled down his cheeks after he spoke.

The teacher sighed and stood up. He knew there was nothing to say if Israel didn't want to come clean. "Okay, okay," he yelled. "We're getting back to tennis here. I want *everybody* to the court *now*!"

As everyone converged on the tennis court, Israel gave me a look of pure hatred. I looked at him with as thuggish and hard a look as I could muster, but I have to admit, I was a little creeped out by the expression on his face. It said—in bold, Vegas-style neon letters—Payback's a Mutha.

3

And it was.

Everyone had talked about what happened between Israel and me on the bus ride home. They clowned Israel, who sat in silence with a stony expression on his face.

Philly Phil Peters, a kid who lived but a few houses away from Israel, was seated behind him on the bus. He reached over and slapped the back of his head hard several times, calling him a pussy. At one point he even knocked Israel's glasses off of his face, garnering many *oohs* and *aahs* from the other kids on the bus, hoping for a confrontation. Still, nothing from Israel.

This was the major topic of discussion for twelve-, and thirteen-, and fourteen-year-olds who had yet to worry about serious worldly issues. We talked about the incident right until the last kids (of which I was one) were dropped off the bus. Then we went on with after-school play at the local playground, which Israel was usually a part of. But not that day.

He would tell me years later that he had gone home and cried and kicked his toys and comic books around his bedroom and cursed the world. Then he'd thrown himself dramatically on his little twin bed and cried even harder.

I would have felt bad about all of it—if he hadn't done what he did the next day.

I suppose I asked for it. We were all standing at the school bus stop the next morning when we saw Israel approaching. I started talking crap again, thinking that this would probably become a daily habit. He was completely expressionless, like a dead man walking.

I was actually kind of disgusted with his attitude; in the 'hood, you didn't let anyone punk you like I was doing him. I figured I would look bad now if I didn't keep on him, if I let him off the hook.

He had a backpack full of books that weighed him down. He walked past me, and I gave him a little shove on his shoulder. He stumbled forward a little and then stood in place like a statue, his back to me.

I clicked my tongue. "It's a shame you such a li'l punk. We could give the people here a little entertainment...by lettin' 'em watch me whup yo' ass!"

Everyone started laughing and oohing and aahing. Israel reached into his backpack and laboriously pulled out something. I was too busy enjoying the other kids' reactions to really notice or care what it was.

He suddenly dropped his backpack, spun, and made a mad dash toward me. I was so surprised at his motion that I didn't move; I just stood there wide-eyed. He was holding a big black cast-iron skillet tightly with both his little hands. I had just enough time to wonder what he was doing with it before he swung it, striking me squarely in the jaw.

I actually don't remember the pain of the blow; I remember being flat on my back and looking up at the sky, feeling like I couldn't move at all. I seemed to be looking down on myself, as if I were disconnected from my body, but at the same time I had a perception of looking up. I watched in mute, paralyzed amazement as Israel went for Philly Phil Peters.

Philly Phil had forewarning, having seen me go down. When Israel rushed him, he sidestepped, sticking his foot out at the same time, and tripped him, almost the same way I had the day before. Israel went down hard with the force of his forward motion, the skillet flying away from him and striking the ground with a loud clang. The kids, who were initially in shock at the suddenness of it all, closed in a tight circle to whoop and holler and watch Phil (who was, like myself, a foot taller and much heavier than his opponent) beat up on Israel.

Philly Phil was a mean cat when he was mad, and it was clear that he was not going to give Israel any slack for the slightness of his form. He pulled Israel to his knees and scowled at him. "You wanna fuck with me, nigga! Okay, here you go."

He hit Israel in the jaw several times, each blow seeming harder and more potent than the last. The crowd was eating it up, egging him on. He unleashed a blow on Israel's nose, which surely would have broken it if the smaller kid hadn't pulled his head back a little at the last second. But the blow still made enough impact to send blood gushing from his nostrils. The crowd went even wilder at the sight of it.

Phil pulled his opponent to his feet. Israel had a blank, noncommittal look on his bloodied face. Phil drew back his fist in a dramatic display to impress the crowd with his next blow. But before he could loose that cannon, Israel casually stepped in, grabbed Philly Phil by his shirt, and brought his knee up into his balls.

Phil backed up a step and looked at Israel in an almost bemused fashion, his arm still drawn back. Then he sank to his knees with an awful moan, his hands grabbing his crotch, his face contorted in a silent agony easy for any post-pubescent male to comprehend. The crowd seemed to utter a collective *ooh* and fell silent for a moment. Two larger kids had fallen to this bleeding midget and it just seemed so... *weird* to everyone.

Israel stepped away from Philly Phil and casually surveyed him for a moment. He seemed not to notice that his nose was still bleeding a little. Phil looked up at him with a pained expression, and Israel drew back one arm, as if he had all the time in the world. He brought it around in a looping roundhouse and caught Philly Phil on the cheek with a loud crack. Phil toppled over, semiconscious.

Israel surveyed the crowd, which was now silent and looking at him as if he were some sort of grand madman, the smallest kid of them all. He probably did look a little crazy. His eyes were flat and dead looking, full of disdain and contempt and a few other things one couldn't immediately put a name to. And he looked as if he had a blood beard.

He let out a strange sigh and then turned his back on the crowd and began to walk away. Everybody watched him as if he were Clint Eastwood riding off into the sunset, none of them offering to help me or Philly Phil at all.

4

Of course it was all the talk of the school. When Phil and I got there—he with a bright red fist imprint on his cocoa-colored cheek, me with a swollen jaw—every kid looked at us like we were crazy, wanting to know what happened but not daring to ask. We were still two large kids with fearsome fighting reps, and even the kids that were as big and bold as us saw that they shouldn't be going there. The word quickly got around anyway, and then came the stares of wonderment and the whispers of kids wishing they could have been there to see Israel's amazing feat. It was incomprehensible to many, even to Philly Phil and me.

Israel didn't show up to school that day, which only added fuel to the fire. By the end of the day, the story had blown up into several different versions—Israel had brutally beaten both of us; he'd beaten both of us and a third party as well; he'd bitten a finger off one of us, and so on. Philly Phil and I bonded hard that day as we tried to figure how we were going to get even with him.

We decided we would take Israel's approach and jack him up as soon as we saw him at the bus stop the next day. There would be no talking. We would simply attack on sight. We agreed that we had to really whip him up good, bloody him up, maybe even break a bone or two.

When the next day rolled around, I was tired, not having slept much the night before in anticipation. Israel was usually one of the first few kids to show up at the bus stop, so when he didn't come, Phil and I looked at each other impatiently. We assumed he knew what was coming and opted to have his mother drop him off at school or something like that.

We'd begun plotting how we would get to him there when one of the kids shouted, "Look, there's the Baylock kid!"

Israel looked a mess as he strolled up the street toward us, holding the straps of his backpack tightly. His face was swollen and bruised and there was a fresh bandage on his nose. He looked like someone had really worked him over badly.

The slight injuries Phil and I had were nothing by comparison. We looked at each other in confusion, not really knowing what to do. If the two of us went after him in the state he was in now, we'd look like the biggest assholes in the world—two larger kids beating up on a much smaller kid who already looked like he'd been thoroughly beaten. Even for the streets, that was above and beyond cold behavior.

So we did what we had to do. We just let it go.

It kind of worked out for everybody when all was said and done. When people saw how bad Israel looked, the rumors of Philly Phil and I getting destroyed by him went out the window. At the same time, he gained a newfound respect from his peers and was never messed with again. No one doubted that we'd gotten over on him, but the way he'd gotten us back in return was still a quietly whispered legend that no one wanted to test.

Some time later, Phil and I both admitted to each other that we didn't really want to take another crack at Israel. There was no doubt that in a fair fight either one of us separately would have beat the crap out of him, never mind the two of us combined, but the thought of wondering how he'd plan his revenge for it gave us both the chills. He'd hit a homer that first time; who knew how inventive he could get given a second chance.

5

Let me correct myself; one person did try to get at Israel a few years later. This act was the one that initiated the beginning of the friendship between Israel and me—and ultimately much more.

When we were in the eleventh grade, Israel had grown a little but not too much. He still had absolutely no athletic skills at all. But at Hamilton High School, he was still a fairly popular kid, although still considered a nerd. Most of the kids we were with in junior high were also at Hamilton, so Israel managed not to get messed with beyond playful verbal jabs and teasing. He usually brushed it off. He mostly hung with a clique of fellow nerds, a weird collection of brainy blacks and whites and Asians and Mexicans who served as his support group.

As for myself, I was a pretty good student but an even better athlete. I had, as a running back on the football team, helped lead Hamilton to more wins than that school had seen in almost ten years. I was pretty much a shoo-in for an athletic scholarship if I continued doing as well as I was both athletically and scholastically. There was only one threat to that. Earlier that same year, I'd become a card-carrying member of the Playboy Gangsta Crip gang that ran my area.

Thankfully the Gs were looking at me to succeed in athletics, so they didn't let me get involved yet with too much of the dirty stuff. Most gangbangers look forward to a bleak future, and I became the living, breathing totem on which they pinned all of their secret hopes and dreams. Entertainment or athletics, at that time, seemed like the only road out for a G, and it had been a long while since one of us made it to the good life.

There was a student who transferred to Hamilton midsemester named Wade Anderson. Wade was a senior coming to Hamilton from Dorsey High in the 'hood. He was a known Blood gangsta whose home was the notorious hilly area near Dorsey nicknamed the Jungle. He was a tall kid with a dancer's build, all long torso and legs with a slim waist and broad, powerful shoulders and chest. He had a boyish, almost babyish face, but the eyes told the story. They were hard as steel, joyless, and had probably seen things no sixteen-year-old outside of Beirut should have.

It was said that Wade had an IQ of 130 and was a very good student, but he sauntered through Hamilton's halls like school was just another jailhouse he was enduring for the time being. He never carried books, and more often than not, he wore a wife-beater, freshly pressed beige or black Dickies pants (always with a red bandana hanging out of one of the pockets), and black or red Chuck Taylors. He was a golden-skinned pretty boy, with long, wavy hair that he wore in either a single braid that fell to the middle of his back or pigtails. Girls seemed both be attracted to and wary of him at once, and the guys seemed to admire and fear him in equal measure.

One day between classes, Israel was quickly scampering to another class. He looked weighed down by his backpack. As I said, he was not as small as he'd been in junior high, but he was still a short, slightly built kid. He accidentally bumped into Wade. He started to utter an apology, but Wade pushed him so hard that Israel fell and skidded across the floor into the hallway wall. He looked up at Wade like he was insane.

Wade screamed at him, "What, nigga? What the fuck you gon' do?"

All the kids in the hallway zeroed in on the scene. There were no teachers around, and it would take a second for any of them to realize something was going on in and poke their heads out of their classrooms to investigate.

I was in the hallway and saw the whole thing. A dull rage filled my heart. I was silently offended at how the enemy strolled the halls of my school daily showing his colors so boldly, but most at my school didn't know of my gang affiliation, and that was the way I wanted it. So I did not engage Wade as I normally would have on the streets.

Israel took off his backpack and stood up, looking Wade in the eye with absolute calm. He said quietly, "Before you pushed me down I was about to apologize. I didn't mean to bump you."

Wade looked Israel up and down with a cruel sneer. "Little bitch," he said, and he turned to walk away, a mocking chuckle filling the air in his wake.

Israel seemed to quietly explode at the insult. He reached down and pulled a book out of his backpack, throwing it like a Frisbee at the back of Wade's head.

The book struck home and Wade stumbled forward with the force of the blow and let out an almost feminine yelp. He spun with a murderous look on his face.

Israel stood ready to fight, suddenly not looking much like a nerd. Actually, he looked as if he didn't have a shred of fear in his little heart, his face serenely calm and focused as a samurai's.

Wade started moving toward Israel. I stepped between them. I gave Wade a short shove that sent him stumbling back a couple steps but not throwing him completely off-balance. Israel would later tell me he thought I was crazy. I didn't care; I was a little shorter than Wade, but much heavier, my young body strong and solid as a rock from hours of football drills.

Wade seemed to sense my gang affiliation. He said with an evil smirk, "What up, muthafucka?"

"Ain't nuthin', ya slob bitch!" I replied in gang speak. Most of my peers were looking at me like an alien. My gang affiliation had been rumored, but until now I had never spoken or even referred openly to it.

"Soft-ass 'ho'," Wade said, spitting out a wad of phlegm. "I put in work on crab bitches like you on the daily, nigga!"

"Then come and get it, fool!"

We were damn near shouting at each other, which brought a couple of teachers out of their classrooms to see what was up. The crowd began to disperse, and Wade and I gave each other stares that said, "We'll continue this later."

As the crowd left and Wade shuffled off, I turned to Israel. "Watch ya back, man. He probably gonna come after you before me."

Israel chuckled and shook his head. "I'm not gonna say I don't appreciate you sticking up for me, but I wish you would've just let me handle it. It's probably gonna be a little harder on me now whenever he makes his move."

I laughed. "Yeah, it looked like you was gonna throw down."

Israel smirked. "More than likely I was gonna get throwed down."

We both laughed. We had to get to our classes, so I told him in all seriousness, "Look li'l man, since I stood up for you, I'm now responsible for your ass. If dude wanna come after you again, it's on me to do something about it."

"So why'd you do it?"

I gave him a wry smile. "I didn't think you'd get as lucky gettin' even with him as you did with me."

We both laughed again. I gave him my home number and my pager number and told him that if he had any trouble from Wade on or off campus (Wade's neighborhood was close enough to ours to warrant my concern) to let me know ASAP.

6

Israel began calling me out of the blue just for nothing. I was annoyed at first, sorry that I'd intervened with Wade Anderson on his behalf. (Wade had never bothered either of us again and ended up being transferred to yet another school after he started a fight with another student.) But Israel eventually wore me down and I began to feel like a big brother toward him, even though we were the same age.

We had a couple of classes together, so we would get together at his house after school and study. I never like being at my house much. I lived with my mother and her latest wino/substance-abusing boyfriend, so I loved going over to Israel's as much as possible.

I got a lot closer to his mother, who became like a surrogate mother to me. And his sister, Ellena, was pretty nice to me as well. I had developed quite a crush on Ellena Baylock. She was now a freshman at USC and lived in a student apartment on campus but was at her mother's house more often than not. I had the admiration of half the girls in high school and was feared around the neighborhood—at times it was like I had a double life—but to Ellena I was still just a young, foolish, eleventh-grade boy. That fueled me even more to do and say little things to try to get her attention, but nothing worked.

It got so that I looked forward to going to Israel's house just to see her. To my delight, she was there most days, but those times she didn't show up filled my heart with sadness, and I worried of her safety, even when Mrs. Baylock explained why she wasn't around.

I thought with time I would figure out a way to get in the door with her, but I seemed to grow more confused, tongue-tied, and moronic in her presence. I was not a bad looking guy—chocolate-skinned, five eleven, 195 pounds of solid muscle, with a face I was told was not so much pretty as handsome. I was already having sex, and you couldn't tell me I wasn't an expert (although I would later figure out I had a *lot* to learn), and I just had a notion that if I got her into bed, I'd be able to convince her to give herself completely to me.

7

One evening, Israel and I were studying in his bedroom. We were completely silent, each of us buried in a book. I was sitting at the desk across the room; he was seated on his bed. Then, out of the blue, I blurted out, "Iz, I'm in love with your sister."

Israel pretended not to hear me, still seeming to be contemplating what he was reading. So I went back to reading my book, or at least I faked it. I was waiting for him to say something. When it seemed like he wasn't going to, I actually turned my attentions back to studying.

After thirty minutes or so, he said, "Why do you think you're in love with my sister? You don't even *know* her."

I put my book down. "Iz, what I know I love. It's that simple. I figured I oughta let you know 'cause some people can get funny about their friends datin' their sisters."

Israel laughed—a big one from the belly that was true and full of mirth. He closed his book and looked at me like I was crazy. Between chuckles he said, "First off, I don't even think your ass stands a hair of a chance with Ellena. You aren't even old enough to take her to most of the places she hangs out at. You're still a boy in her world, and I *know* this. Second, even if you did stand a chance, I'd feel funny about it just 'cause you've fucked half the girls at school. You couldn't be playing my sister like that, or we'd have to fight."

I started to laugh, thinking Israel was joking, but he was dead serious. One thing I noticed and liked immensely about the Baylocks was that they stuck together like glue, and an injury to one was an injury to all. That was absolutely *not* the case in my family at all, making it more awesome to be among them. Even as an outsider, I got much love from them, and that they would do most anything for me. I definitely would do anything for them.

I looked back at Israel just as intensely as he was looking at me. “Hey, man, I know that. But I would never touch another girl again if I could have just a crack at your sister. I think about her all the time and even dream about her sometimes. I be tryin’ to think of ways to mack to her while she’s here at your house, and whatever was in my head disappears when I see her.”

Israel just shook his head. “See, that’s what I’m talking about. The words you’re using. You’re trying to *mack* to her.” He shook his head again. “Man, you’re not ready for my sister yet.”

I was annoyed at this statement, although really, in retrospect, I think I was just frustrated because Israel was right. I blurted out, “Why you keep tellin’ me I ain’t ready for her?”

Israel sighed deeply. “Dave, men have been sniffing around my mother as long as I can remember. Same thing with my sister, at least since she was twelve years old. *Grown-ass men* were trying to get at Ellena then. With the both of them, I’ve seen all types come and go, and most just don’t get it. They’re all like you; they see the outside, the outer shell, but they don’t know anything about the women inside, and really, they don’t want to.

“I asked my mom when I was like, nine or ten why we didn’t have a daddy. Did I ever tell you how my daddy died?”

I thought for a second and realized he hadn’t. I shrugged. “I assumed he left or just wasn’t around like most of the daddies in the ’hood!”

Israel chuckled at this, but it lacked mirth. “No, he was around. He was a good daddy, too. He was alive until I was about two and a half. And then one night, he went to pick up some stuff from the store around the corner from where we lived in Compton, and he was hit and killed crossing the street by a drunk driver.”

“*Damn*, man.” I didn’t really know what to say. “Uh, sorry.”

He shrugged in an almost annoyed fashion and continued. "I asked my mom what was so special about him. In pictures, he just looks like a taller, skinnier, darker version of me—a six-foot-plus string bean of a nerd. Not a bad looking guy, but I've seen guys that look like Billy Dee Williams come on to Mom. That pretty boy from *Miami Vice* even tried a few years ago."

"No shit!" I said in genuine surprise. *Miami Vice* was still popular at that time and was one of my favorite shows, so this was a big deal to me.

"Yeah. I asked her what she saw in my dad out of all these guys trying to get with her, and she told me that he saw *into* her. He knew her from the inside out. He didn't just want her body, he cared about her soul, her true happiness. She'd never been with a guy like him before. She said the rest really only wanted her as either a trophy piece to show off or sexually or even to idolize her, put her on a pedestal that she'd stay on even when she treated them like shit. Like being beautiful put her above being a decent person, and she was allowed to treat men badly because of it, which she admits she's done *plenty* of times before.

"Anyway, I think now she might hate most men—like she's mad no one else like my father has come along. I told her my theory, and she thinks I'm wrong, but I don't think so. I certainly don't know what it's like to have him around, but I'm glad she didn't bring anyone else into the house. I like the way she and Ellena have always described my dad, and if no one could come close to being like him, I'd rather have the situation we've had."

I listen in rapt silence, fascinated by all of this. I could never have such frank discussions with my mother, and I realized at that moment I envied the closeness of the Baylocks as much as I idolized it.

Israel gave me a cockeyed look and asked, "What do you think you know about Ellena?"

After his last spiel, this caught me by surprise. I stammered, "Uh, well, you know, she's real cool…she's just…I dunno, she's just a special person!" I stood up from the desk, suddenly annoyed. "Damn, Iz, what the hell you want me to say?"

He laughed at me. "See, that's what I thought. You don't know anything about my sister. If you don't know anything about her, what makes you think you could make her happy?"

He had stumped me. It was all too much for my eleventh-grade mind to handle. I said angrily, "See, that's what a nigga get, tryna explain how he feel. You ain't gon' never catch me soft again, muthafucka!"

Israel was slightly startled. "Whoa, you don't have to get like that, man! I'm just keeping it real. Think about what I'm saying and see if I'm right."

I sat down and picked up my book again, breathing hard and fuming angrily. "Fuck this shit, nigga. *Fuck* this shit. Let's just get back to studyin'. Forget I said anything."

8

Israel and his family and I stayed close until his senior year, when he made a startling announcement. We were all eating dinner at the kitchen table when he said out of the blue, "I'm going into the marines. I signed up and took their test. It's gonna take a few days for me to get the results back, but I already know I passed it."

Ms. Baylock had prepared a sumptuous southern-style meal of fried chicken, mashed potatoes and gravy, string beans, black-eyed peas, and cornbread. We were all deep in the fruits of her good cooking and not saying much when Israel dropped that bomb. It was funny in retrospect; all of us paused either in midchew or as we were bringing food up to our mouths. It looked like a three-dimensional still shot: "People Shocked While Eating."

Israel's mother and sister were pretty even-tempered folk. I'd never seen them truly get mad—annoyed maybe, and even that was a rare occurrence. But now mother and daughter just looked at each other. "What the fuck?" they seemed to be thinking.

I ventured to speak first and ask the question that was on all our minds. "Why you wanna do that, Iz?"

He took a bite off of a drumstick. Shrugging, he said, "I dunno." At this point he was the only one still eating.

"Uh, you don't know? You don't know why you're makin' the most major decision of your life?"

Israel put his drumstick down and sighed deeply, bowing his head. Then he looked up and addressed all of us. "You know, I want to do something totally different right now. I want to live a different way, learn to become a man. And, Mom, that's not to say that living with you hasn't helped me to become a man, but it's time to step it up to the next level. I want to go different places and try some different things. I want to make a big step into being my own person."

We were probably all shocked for the same reasons. Israel was getting academic scholarship offers from universities all over the nation. He was at the top of our class and could have gone to any Ivy League school. I was getting as many offers myself for sports scholarships, and we often discussed ending up at the same school. It was very hard for us all to fathom that he would choose the military instead.

His mother, clearly furious, mustered as much calm as she could. "Boy, while you're under eighteen, *I* call the shots around here. And I am telling you that I am not letting my only son go into the damn army!"

"I am not going into the army, Ma, it's the marines. And I'm gonna be eighteen two months after I graduate. I really want to do this, and if you do anything to try to prevent it from happening, then I'm telling you now that I will *never* forget it."

There was silence again. I think everybody was kind of confused—as if we thought it would always be like that for the rest of our lives, all of us sitting in the kitchen without anybody making any grown-up decisions. I think this was particularly traumatic for Ms. Baylock, who allowed Ellena to grow up because they were more like sisters, or even twins, than anything else. Israel was still her baby—Ellena's too.

Israel finished his plate and pushed it away. "Well, is everyone gonna stay silent here?"

It sure seemed like that.

He sighed again. "Maybe it's good y'all don't have anything to say. My decision is final. I would really like your support. I mean, it's gonna be messed up for me if I don't have it."

I wanted to take the bait and tell Israel I stood behind him. But I didn't want to risk alienating the Baylock women. Inside,

I supported him in that way that young people who can't see beyond the day after tomorrow do. I thought it would be a great adventure for him, although I was sad that we wouldn't be in college together.

"Well," Ellena finally said. "You know you're my baby boy. I don't ever want you to think I didn't support you in something you really wanted to do, so…you have my blessing."

Israel looked at her like he wanted to cry tears of joy. Ms. Baylock looked at her like she was crazy, and Ellena shot her a look back that seemed to scream, "Well, what are we suppose to do, alienate him?" Ms. Baylock turned her head away with a disgusted look, wrinkling that gorgeous face. I wanted to tell Ellena I thought she was the most beautiful person in the world to me right that second.

Against the odds, though, Ms. Baylock finally caved in. It was crazy. I could see the change in her face, like a werewolf in one of those cheesy movies changing back into a human being. She let out a deep, dramatic sigh. Israel wasn't looking at her, but he was waiting for her to speak. We all were.

Tired of waiting, and suddenly feeling my manhood behind Ellena, I spoke up. "Iz, you know whatever you want is cool with me." I reached over and slapped his shoulder. Then I let out a dull laugh. "Damn, man, we was s'pose to go to college together though! We talked about it as recently as yesterday."

"Yes," Ms. Baylock added with just a fading touch of venom. "You were supposed to go to college. There's so much going on over in the Middle East now. There's no guarantee that you're going to go in and not have to pull a tour of active duty overseas."

Israel rose from the table and walked over toward his mother. She thought he was going to walk past her and keep going, but he stopped where she was and wrapped her in a big, loving embrace from behind. She looked surprised, but reciprocated. I could see her melt in his embrace almost sensuously, and then I realized that all the love she'd once given to her husband—the only man who'd understood her and whom she loved and bore children for—had been funneled into her only son. She thought her love would be rewarded with him staying at her side forever and all of them existing as they had been. Instead, he was going to leave her as her husband had so many years before.

These were realizations I really didn't want to deal with. I think I just wanted to stay the young, stupid jock/gangbanger that I was at the time. I had a firm definition of manhood, and I didn't want it altered to include being perceptive and aware of other people's emotions.

"I support you, baby," Ms. Baylock said against Israel's shirt, holding on as if he were going to disappear on the spot if she let go. "I'm just scared. I mean, who's going to take care of you?"

"Me," Israel said with a man's confidence. "I'll take care of myself. And you can take that to the bank, Ma. No doubt."

9

In his room after dinner, Israel laid on his bed. I was sitting on the floor beside the bed, just twirling a penny over and over again. Even after dinner, everyone was still a little shell-shocked. Ellena bolted right away (which was disappointing; I was hoping she'd stay a little longer and I could talk to her alone about Israel's strange decision), and Israel's mother went into her room and closed the door as he himself had done.

I exhaled, as if I'd been holding my breath the whole time. "Damn, nigga," I said. "I think I really counted on us going to the same school together. Knowin' you, your family, has kept me out of a lot of the shit that I see going down with my homies, yaknowhumsayin'?"

Israel nodded yes, smiling this weird, unreadable smile.

I said, "I mean, I think I just counted on you bein' there to help me stay on the straight and narrow. Not too many of the homies really care about me. They all make like they do, maybe a couple actually do, but for the most part, I just get the feelin' that if I didn't make it, they could care less. You, I know you're like my brother. And your mom is like my mom, and your sister..." I had to pause. I didn't want to lie on that one. "At any rate, I was just countin' on you to be there for me and to help me make the right decisions."

Israel reached under his pillow and brought out a beat-up paperback. He gave it to me, and I just looked at the cover. It was *WILL*, by G. Gordon Liddy. I looked at him quizzically. "Iz, what's this for? Isn't this book by that muthafucka that was in all that Watergate shit back in the seventies?"

Israel nodded yes. "But that book has been a major inspiration to me over the past few months. In fact, I can say that nothing has shaped my life more."

I whistled and laughed. "This must be a helluva book."

Israel sat up and looked at me seriously. "It is, Dave. It is. Right now, I need to get up out from underneath my mother and Ellena for a second. I love them, but I feel a little smothered, and there's so much out there that I want to do and see and try. You know I spend a lot of time in books, reading about different things, places, and people. Well, it's time for me to get out in the world and start charting my own destiny. If I stay in the safe zone, underneath my mom and my sister and even you—you've looked out for me as much as they have, and I appreciate it—then I know I'm just going to stagnate. And I can't let that happen."

I looked at the worn paperback closely and flipped through some of the pages. "So what's ol' G. G. Liddy talkin' 'bout in here?"

"He's just a guy that forged his own will and transformed himself from something weak to something strong," Israel said, very animated. "Like he was scared of rats, so he ate one to get over his fear of them. That kinda shit."

"Oooookay," I said, handing him back the book. "He just sounds like another crazy white boy to me."

"No, it's more than that. He created an idea of manhood for himself and became it. And now it's time for me to forge my own manhood."

I had to laugh at that one. "Nigga, you only seventeen. You s'pose to be thinking about the great adventure of college, havin' fun, gettin' pussy, and all that shit. There's plenty of time to worry about your manhood."

"No, Dave. The next day isn't guaranteed to anybody. Nobody knows how much time he or she has. Only God know that."

I couldn't argue with that. I'd already seen enough on the streets to know that was a stone cold fact. I was a little fascinated by Israel right then because he was speaking like a wise old man. I wondered who this person was I was dealing with tonight and what happened to the one I thought I'd known for the past couple of years.

"Well, I stand by what I said—I wish we were going to college together still, but I can't do nothin' but support your decision. That's what bein' a brother is all about, right?"

Israel lay back down in his bed, his hands crossed behind his head. He said contentedly, "Now you're getting it, Dave. Now you're getting it."

10

And upon graduating, that's what went down. Israel was in town for another month before they shipped him off to boot camp in Georgia. I ended up going to USC, partly to stay close to the Baylocks (particularly Ellena) and partly to stay close to the homies. I wasn't like Israel at all. I had a semiconscious fear of venturing outside the 'hood. That was not part of the master plan anyway.

My dreams of travel and adventure involved wherever a bus or plane carting whatever NFL team I was going to end up on was going to. My plan was to go through college, hope to get drafted to a West Coast team, and ask Ellena to marry me. I figured by then I would be done sowing my wild oats. As it was, I was screwing girls as if it were my job, but I knew I couldn't do that forever.

I even had a backup plan for if I somehow sustained an injury in college—I would become a gym teacher and go back to the 'hood and teach at a school there, my way of giving back to the community. But I just knew it wasn't going down like that. I'd be giving back to the community by using my riches to fund a rec center or something of that nature.

I continued my double life through college. I wasn't as good a student as I was in high school, but I was getting passing marks. My priorities as a college student were getting high, getting laid, and getting off on the field. And in my other life, I hung out with the homies and stayed involved in things that I shouldn't have been. I had the energy and vigor of youth on my side, so it wasn't a big deal to me. I thought that at the pro level I'd leave the streets completely alone. I knew that I'd have to then.

But life rarely works out as planned, particularly when you're down for the set.

I'd been hanging out with some of the gangstas one weekend evening. We were all in the living room of the homie L-Roc's house. There were about eight of us. Some were smoking weed, some were drinking, some, like myself, were doing both. I was squeaking by in my junior year of school and we had just won our last three football games, so I was feeling good. Actually I was feeling invincible, like everything was going according to plan, and nothing could alter the course of my destiny.

After a couple of hours of watching videos and an occasional Sega interlude, someone noticed we were out of booze. L-Roc, a bear of a man who was as black as midnight and had muscles like a chiseled onyx sculpture come to life, came out of the kitchen with an empty Jack Daniel's bottle. "Y'all niggas cain't jus' be layin' around my house without me gettin' somethin' out of it. Who gon' go get some mo' shit?"

One of the homies, named Shaggy-Loc, after the Scooby Doo character (and also for the Jheri-curled quasi-Afro adorning his head), said, "The nigga Sleepy down the street gots the chronic. I'll go take care'a that!"

I raised my hand and said in a slurred voice, "I'll take care of the booze. One o' you lazy asses'll drive me to the store. I needs a designated muthafuckin' driver, yo!"

Everybody cracked a laugh over this. The homie No Good, a tall cat with a weasel face, said, "I'll drive yo' stank ass, nigga. Why don't you put some gas in my car while we out?"

I stood up with a laugh and said, "I'll fart in the muthafuckin' gas tank, fool. That's as good as it's gon' get!"

No Good stood up and flipped me off to the laughter of the others. He motioned me to the door and we left. His car, which was parked in front of the house, was a beat up old '73 Camaro. We hopped in and he fired her up and pulled away from the curb with a mad screech. We roared down the street as if it weren't a Saturday night and there were no cops anywhere to be found.

"We gotta hurry up and get back," No Good said. "You *know* them niggas will smoke up all the weed quick if we ain't timely."

I just nodded with a dopey smile. I was feeling like I was the king of the world right then.

We ended up at a liquor store a couple of blocks away. I had a nice fat bankroll on me. (One of the things I used to do that kept cash in my pockets was sell crack to some of the other athletes and selected students on campus, the wealthier white kids who paid the big bucks for it.)

I told No Good to grab as much liquor as he could hold.

"Nigga, I'm'a need help," he said. "Get yo' ass over here!"

We loaded up the front counter with ten forties of Olde English and then had the little Korean guy behind the counter get us some pints of Jack Daniels, E&J, and Remy Martin. As I was pulling out money to pay, I noticed that someone had just entered the store. I glanced toward the door. I was shocked, and then a slow wave of rage rolled through me.

Wade Anderson, the Blood gangsta who went to school with me at Hamilton High, walked right past me, taking a quick glance at all the alcohol we had on the counter and then proceeding toward the refrigerated liquor case himself. He didn't seem to recognize me at all.

I tapped No Good on the shoulder and pointed at Wade. "See that yellow muthafucka over there?"

No Good could see immediately from the way he carried himself that he was gang affiliated. "Who the fuck is he?"

"That slob nigga went to Hamilton with me. Used to wear his muthafuckin' colors out on the daily."

"What? Aw, *hell* naw! He gots to know where he is. We gots to serve him up."

The little Korean counterman looked from one of us to the other, panic in his eyes. "Please, not in here! Take outside, take outside!"

The Korean was known around the 'hood for being fair and respectful with his constituents, so we gave him that respect. We loaded all that alcohol in the trunk of the car, which was parked right out in front of the store, and got in and waited. There was a cherry red, '65 Mustang with shiny twenty-inch Daytons parked in front of our car, which we figured to be his.

No Good reached in the glove box and pulled out an onyx-colored nine-millimeter Glock. I felt a slight panic, but this was the life I was in, and thus, protocol. And I *wanted* to get Wade, he was the enemy. Still, I had an ugly feeling in the pit of my stomach, like I was about to go down a road from which there was no turning back.

We waited for about five minutes in silence. No sign of Wade. No Good furrowed his brow. "There ain't no back exit outta that store, is there?"

I shook my head. "Just the one we lookin' at now. That's the only way in or out."

After another minute or two, No Good threw up his hands. "Shit, half the fuckin' house gon' be smoked out on the chronic by the time we get back. We either gots to give this fool a pass or go on in there and get 'im."

I was about to speak when Wade settled the issue for us both. He came out of the store with a Glock in one hand and a .38 special in the other, piercing the night with a murderous scream. He started shooting into the car. Me being on the passenger side, I was his immediate target.

"Ohhhh, *shit*!" I screamed as I jumped in the backseat, but I couldn't even hear my own voice. The sound of Wade's guns and of No Good's as he returned fire drowned everything out. I felt immediately wet but didn't feel any pain. I just crouched down in the backseat and waited for all the noise to end.

After what seemed like forever, it was over.

I peeked up from the backseat and saw the front seat covered with broken glass and droplets of blood everywhere. A smoky haze filled the car, as if we'd been smoking a ton of weed. I looked over at the homie No Good and jumped backward. Half his face was gone, a meaty, dripping mess, and his body was riddled with bullet holes and leaking fresh crimson. For a moment I was dumbfounded.

I realized I had to get out, that I could not stay in the car with No Good's fresh, dripping corpse. I climbed over into the front seat and opened the passenger door. I was trying to get out, but I felt weaker and weaker, like the strength was being pulled from me by some unseen force. I couldn't hear anything. I thought I was in some dream-like, soundless state but would later discover that all the gunfire had left me temporarily deaf. I had pushed the door open a little but couldn't move anymore. My mind dulled, I wondered, "What the fuck do I do now?"

Someone pulled me out of the car. I was standing, but when I tried to walk, it was too much trouble, and I just fell to the ground like a rag doll. There was a crowd around, including the little Korean man from the store. The guy that helped me out of the car, a middle-aged, stocky Hispanic fellow, was trying to say something to me, but to me it just looked like his lips were doing some kind of strange, soundless pagan dance. It seemed as if the world was slipping further away from me by the second as those lips kept flapping away silently.

I didn't care what he was trying to say anyway. I just wanted to fall sleep and then wake up to me and No Good driving the car home. Then we'd be kicking it with the homies, and I'd be thinking how I felt like the king of the damn universe as I sipped good liquor and blew out mushroom clouds of chronic smoke. But as my eyes closed, I already knew it would never be like that again.

11

I woke up in a hospital bed. Tubes were coming out of me left, right, and center. I was heavily doped up, and my vision was hazy and unfocused. I could hear my mom crying and asking the Man Upstairs where she went wrong. Some of the homies were chit-chatting about me sympathetically and praying for me at times.

Later I would discover that my football career was over, which pretty much meant that so was my scholarship. It wasn't the injuries from the bullets that entered my chest, right arm, and left leg that finished football for me; it was the brutal tear in my right knee ligaments that I sustained jumping into the backseat of No Good's Camaro.

To USC's credit, after I healed from all my injuries, they gave me a chance to rehab the knee. It was just no good. My doctor informed the school, via a written report on my progress, that he just didn't see football as a viable option for me.

The police also had a few questions for me, like why I was in the car with a known gang affiliate and how I seemed to know so many of them. My status as an athlete on the rise had protected me from John Law for as long as I had been touted as a possible contender for making it out of the 'hood, but now all bets were off. They were just getting started on me when the doctor came into my hospital room to inform me that he was going to let USC know that there was a chance that I might not be able to play ball again, at least not without a lot of rehab. After that, they took pity on me and eased up, and eventually the whole thing went away. It wasn't like the president got shot up, just a couple of 'hood niggas.

It took me almost a year to heal from the shooting. The chest wound was the worst one, the one that made it a fight for me to live. I almost didn't care about dying when I learned I might not play ball again. When that became a reality, I gave up on living in many ways.

My homeboys were there for me, satisfied to play a sympathizing, caring role. I was no longer that one muthafucka that defied the odds and was on his way off the streets. Now I was just another nigga who was no different from them. They helped me to recover, providing drink and drugs in excess to try to kill the pain and all the pussy I could handle. But after a time, they expected me to deal with it and get on with life.

When the sympathy stopped, it was initially a shock. That was my last moment of feeling special. But once I adjusted to knowing my star had fallen, I sank into life on the set with gusto.

Selling drugs was now a full-time occupation, and I became a soldier, one of the gangstas that did all of the extreme, messy, dirty work. Here I became a star of a different sort. At the drop of a hat, if there was anyone that we were going to ride on, I was the one stocking the car with the guns and making sure I called shotgun so that when we crept up on our enemies, mine would hopefully be the last face they ever saw.

With Israel gone, I didn't see as much of the Baylocks as I used to. They were there for me when I was shot and during my subsequent recovery, but after that, they began getting wind of my reputation around the neighborhood, and I was suddenly not as welcome anymore.

That was understandable. I sold powder cocaine, crack, and on occasion, heroin. I had enemies now, the kind of people who wouldn't hesitate to shoot up a house that they even thought I was in. I could easily accept the Baylocks' rejection, and at that point, it almost didn't even matter. Where once I dreamed of winning the mighty Ellena, now she was just as much a dream as my chances of playing professional ball were.

12

But it's kind of funny how life works out at times. I gave up completely on Ellena Baylock, and then the Man Upstairs turned around and dropped her in my lap.

I was at the store one summer day—the very one where Wade had shot me and the homie No Good a couple of years prior—and as I was paying for an orange Fanta and some Ding Dongs, in walked Ellena. She was still a vision, wearing old-school bell bottoms—the kind that were tight at the waist and flared almost to exaggeration at the cuff—and a black lycra halter top that looked as if were barely up to the job of holding in her considerable assets. Her hair was in cornrows, and she wore huge silver earrings that just seemed to be the icing on her look. Her doe-like gray eyes lit up with joy as soon as she saw me.

"Dave!" she screamed loudly, startling the little Korean man behind the counter. She threw herself into my arms, and I hugged her tightly as I would a sister or a good friend. She pulled back. "How have you been, sweetie?"

I shrugged and gave her a crooked smile. "Hangin' in, baby. Hangin' in."

"You still living around the corner with your mom?"

"Naw," I replied as I paid the Korean for my goodies. "Me and one of the homies live over on Orange Drive right near Jefferson."

She laughed, shaking her head. "Still trying to stay in the 'hood, huh?"

I smiled mischievously. She swatted at my arm in disapproval, but it didn't come from a smug, self-satisfied place but one of a genuine concern for me. I think that ignited a match-sized flame in me for her that hadn't been there for a *long* time.

We walked out of the store together after she bought herself a can of Pepsi. It was a hot, cloudless summer day in July, and the sun beamed heat down on Los Angeles as if from the eye of some disapproving god. I wore a tank top that showed off my chiseled physique, which I kept up by lifting weights with the homies, doing two hundred sit-ups a day, and doing semiregular five-mile runs (which was all my poor knee could take). My Bermuda shorts were big and baggy but didn't distract from my strong, sturdy legs. Ellena gave me the once over and tried her best to play it off, but I knew when I was being appraised. I thought it ironic that only a few short years before it would have filled my heart with joy to know that she could possibly see me in a sexual way, but not now.

"So what's up with you?" I asked, opening my Fanta and taking a light swig.

"Nothing. Just going over to visit Mama. What's up in your world?"

"I'm finna go back home and get out of this damn heat, that's what I'm'a do!"

We both laughed and Ellena said, "I know that's right." She paused for a second and cocked her head. "Dave, are you sure you're okay?"

I shrugged. "It's all good in the 'hood, sis. Why you ask me like that?"

She smiled sadly. "Dave, I know your life is not how it's supposed to be at all. I know that you've had some disappointments, and I'm just concerned."

I chuckled. "If you was really that concerned, you'd let me take you out on a date sometime."

She laughed with me and punched my arm. "Now, if I said I'd go out with you, you'd probably get all scared like a little girl and not even know what to do."

I took offense at that, although I kept my face slightly stony. "Hey, if that's what you want to believe, that's cool. But I think you ain't had the experience of havin' a *real* nigga in your life. Might change your perspective on things."

She was still looking at me with a lopsided smile like she wasn't taking me seriously, but then she suddenly pulled a pen and an old grocery receipt from her purse and said, "Write your number down. I definitely want to stay in touch."

As I scribbled my number, I asked, "How is your little brother? What's he up to nowadays?"

She laughed as she took the piece of paper from me and put it in the woven straw tote bag on her shoulder, but her laugh had little mirth in it. "Honey, I don't know what my brother is up to lately. Since he got out of the marines, he's just been traveling the world. We get a postcard from China, a postcard from Egypt, another one from Amsterdam. Neither me or my mom have seen him in almost a year and a half. Haven't even had a phone call in, what, like six months. When we do get one of those postcards, we get so happy we want to frame it."

We both laughed at this. I said, "Well, I don't think you gotta worry about Israel. He's a man now; he can handle his."

"You know, I've never really worried about my little brother, not one day. He's always been our little man, taking care of business. My mother is more wrapped up in worrying about him than I am, but even she knows Iz is smarter than the average cat. It's just hard for her to let go. And although I'm not worried about him, I do miss him. It was just us for so long."

"Well, I sure wish my mom would worry about me like that. We live in the same 'hood, and I think I see her ass maybe once a month. She's got some muthafucka livin' with her that she say in recovery from drugs and alcohol, but the nigga be coming to my corner just about every night hittin' me up for that rock. Tried to tell her about it, but she ain't hearin' it. She think I'm just hatin' on him."

Ellena shuddered. "Don't worry about it, David. Even though you're into a lot I don't personally approve of, I think you have a good heart. I always have."

I laughed at that one. Me with a good heart. Yeah, right. I had committed so much dirt on behalf of my gang that I felt like what little goodness was left in me had died two years ago in that car with No Good. Ellena didn't even know who I was anymore, and to be honest, I didn't either.

"Guess what?" she said. "I'm going to become a cop!"

It was so out of the blue that I just looked at her like she was crazy. Cops were the natural-born enemies of anyone who had grown up in the 'hood, even those who weren't gangstas. I couldn't fathom someone who'd been so important in my life actually joining with my worst foes.

"Ellena, why you wanna do that?"

She saw the look on my face and laughed at it. "It's something I've wanted to do for quite a while now. I know it's not the most respected job in the world, but there's quite a few financial benefits to it, and it's so far from who I am right now that it just excites me thinking about it."

I had to laugh and shake my head at that one. "Girl, between you and your brother with the military, y'all just obsessed with guns an' uniforms an' shit!"

She laughed back. "You're one to talk about being obsessed with guns!"

We chatted for a minute more about things that meant nothing and then hugged and said our good-byes. I walked back to the apartment and put on the AC as soon as I walked in the door. Smiley, the homie I roomed with, wasn't in the house, so I took off my shirt and laid my sweaty body on the sofa and just drifted away from the world with a relaxed smile.

13

Two days later, Smiley woke me up out of a dead sleep early in the morning. I'd been up selling dope at a USC frat party almost until dawn the night before, and I was not in the mood to be bothered. I reminded myself for the hundredth time that I needed to put a lock on the damn door.

I was just opening my mouth to give Smiley a mouthful when he stuck the cordless phone in my face. "Somebody named Eraina, Laina…she wanna talk to you."

"Ellena?" I said, now alert.

"Yeah, whatever, nigga. Take the phone an' find out!"

I snatched the phone from him and gave him a dirty look. He pretended not to notice as he walked out of my room. Smiley was a cocky, pretty boy muthafucka and I didn't like him much as a person, but he brought a lot of wild girls around the apartment, and he didn't hesitate to share them with me. He could, at times, be a lot of fun.

I said sleepily into the receiver, "Hello?"

"David? It's Ellena. Did I wake you up?"

"No, I was getting up anyway," I lied. "What's up?"

"What are you doing today?"

I thought about it for a second. At some point I had to freshen up my dope supply, and that was it. "Nothin'. My schedule's clear as water. Why?"

"I want to go to Venice today. It's nice out. I feel like hanging out at the beach. You want to go with me?"

I almost wanted to laugh. Ellena was asking *me* out. It was something I would've dreamed about years ago, and admittedly I was still curious about what she was thinking about me. But one thing I knew about women already was never to assume anything, to just lay in the cut and wait for them to reveal what they felt. Ellena was always like a sister to me, she may have just been asking me out as a brother—looking for a surrogate one since the real one was off cavorting in God knows what country.

"Hello? Dave? You want to go with me or what?"

"Yeah, yeah, let's go. You want me to pick you up?"

"No way," she said with a laugh. "I'll pick you up. I don't know who might follow you over to my house, shooting up the place just to get to you!"

I laughed sarcastically. "It ain't even like that, woman. But whatever, I didn't feel like drivin' no way."

"Then it all works out for everybody! Now your address, please."

I gave her my address. She told me she'd be by in an hour. I got up and showered and put on a sleeveless black T-shirt, some baggy jeans and Timberlands. I made sure that every pore on my skin was clean and smelling just right. I brushed my teeth vigorously and then popped three sticks of peppermint chewing gum in my mouth. I didn't want Ellena to find fault with me at all in any respect; I wanted her, by the time the day ended, to think that it had been a *tremendous* idea to hang out with me.

I was pacing nervously in the living room of the apartment when I heard three shrill honks. I peeked out the window and saw Ellena sitting in a shiny silver Jaguar. She saw me and waved. I waved back, wondering what she did to afford such expensive wheels.

I took my time going outside. This usually worked to show the ladies that I didn't give a damn, something I liked to establish quickly, but Ellena didn't seem fazed. She was just bopping her head to some music she had going in the car, looking at me but not seeming to even acknowledge my relaxed attitude. I thought, "Okay, baby, you moved in on me, but I'm gone figure out how to bust you open."

When I got in the car I nodded my head at her with a cool expression on my face and said, "What up?"

She laughed at the gesture as she glided the car away from the curb and down the street. "Dave, you're a funny guy!"

"Um, funny how?"

She threw a flirtatious glance at me and turned her attention back toward the road. "You come sauntering out of your apartment like you're a big shot or something, and you're just cool as cool can be getting in my car and being like, 'What up, my dog? What's crackin'?'"

I had to laugh. "Girl, you puttin' extras on it!"

"Not really! You're just too cool for me. You think I'll be able to hang with you today?"

I glanced at her and thought, "Yeah. Yeah, you will." She was wearing all white, from the tank T that clung tightly to her braless top to the white shorts that seemed glued to every curve and cranny of her southern assets to the pink and white Pumas adorning her feet. She had her long, curly hair in a ponytail. It looked nice, and I felt a surge of pride that she actually wanted to hang out with me, plus we were rolling around in that cherry little number of a car. I almost felt that old king-of-the-world feeling I had when I was in college.

As we hit the on-ramp of I-10 west, I finally asked, "What's up with this ride? It's gotta be your mom's car. Can't be yours!"

She looked at me with a cross smirk. "Who says it can't be mine? Can't a young black woman just be doing good for herself?"

I shrugged. "I guess so. But most females I know have done some janky shit to have a ride like this, and I know that ain't you."

"How do *you* know that? You know everything that's going on in my life right now? Are we talking every day or something, and I don't know about it?"

"Naw, you ain't tryna get into nothin' crazy if you gonna be a cop! We ain't got to talk every day for me to have some common sense."

She laughed again. I loved the sound of her laugh; it was like music to me, warm and sensual. I felt like I could just close my eyes and listen to that laugh, even just the sound of her natural voice.

"You got me there, Dave. I'm actually doing well for myself. I work as the personal assistant to the Channel 4 anchorman, Jim Brady."

"Word?" I was impressed. "I see that dude on the news every night! He payin' yo' ass that much, to get Jaguars an' shit?"

"I wish! No, he doesn't pay me enough to buy them, but I have enough money to rent one, for sure."

"Oh, so this is just a rental car."

She nodded her head. "I wanted to try it out to see if it would be a car I'd want someday. I have a list of cars that I am going to rent to see what I am going to get when I come up. This is the fourth one on my list."

I checked the leather interior of the car. The stereo was nice; she had it at a low volume while we were talking, but the system still had presence. I thought about most of the women I'd been dating up to this point—ghetto bitches who rolled in nice cars that were tricked out 'hood style, bought with money either they or their boyfriends earned questionably. A lot of good lookers, but with the hearts and souls of devils, which I felt suited the person I was at that moment just fine.

I looked over at Ellena. She was bopping her head to that Cameo song Candy, singing along under her breath. She had always represented something better to me, and I wondered if maybe it was still within my reach. I hadn't dared to dream about anything for a long time, and it literally felt rusty as my mind wandered into that place where you feel your goals are attainable.

All of a sudden, my mouth moved and words just started tumbling out. Thinking about it even now, I am amazed at that moment. "You know, I think I've spent so many years lovin' you that it seems strange to me now that I don't. You were a symbol of so much to me, but more than that, there's just something about you that just appealed to my soul, my spirit. So many years ago, I would'a thanked God to be where I am right now, sittin' next to you, hearin' you, smellin' you, trippin' that you actually asked me to be here with you. But whatever I felt for you was something good and pure, and I really believe that part of me died the night I was shot up. That's when all my dreams stopped, and you were a precious one of 'em."

I had my eyes closed as I said these words. I let out a deep sigh, afraid to open them. Strange, considering there wasn't much I feared those days. But I didn't want to see Ellena's face just at that second. And I wanted to enjoy the feeling of having gotten off my chest what I wished I had years ago.

I waited for Ellena to speak, but she said nothing until we got to the beach. My eyes had been closed, and I stayed silent for pretty much the whole ride.

After we parked, she said, "I think I want to walk on the boardwalk heading toward the Santa Monica Pier. Is that cool?" I numbly nodded yes, amazed that she seemed her perky, usual self, as if she'd heard nothing I'd said in the car.

14

As we walked, I decided I'd go with that flow as well. We talked of many things as we strolled, pausing to watch the various street performers that made the walk up and down the boardwalk so interesting. We stopped and checked out quite a few of the street vendors, and I picked her up a sarong from one of them. She tried it and it looked real sexy on her. From the way she was acting, it seemed, amazingly, as if there might be a chance I could see her in it again.

The day was a nice one, a typical Southern California, clear, sunny afternoon. The boardwalk was crowded with locals and tourists looking to soak up the flavor. Ellena was getting quite a few glances, fueling my pride at being with her.

At one point we stopped and got pizza slices and peach Snapples. We walked over to one of the benches lining the boardwalk and had a seat. We actually had a little appetite after almost two hours of walking, so we made short work of those large slices. Ellena wanted to just chill and enjoy her Snapple for a second before we started walking again and that was fine with me too.

"So," she said after taking a good-sized swallow of her drink, "did you really mean all that stuff you said in the car?"

I looked at her like she was crazy. "Shit, woman, why would I come at you like that if I didn't mean it? You think that's some line I just hit any ol' female with?"

"Hmmm," she said, with a thoughtful look on her face, and then she went silent. I tried to maintain a patient façade, but after a minute of watching her sip her drink, I finally said, "What the hell you thinkin'?"

"Damn, Dave," she said with a coy laugh, "can't a sista think for a moment? I hope you aren't always this impatient."

I gave her a cocky smirk. "I got patience where it really matters. You can test me on that *anytime*!"

She laughed and actually blushed a little. "Um, I'm good with taking your word on that, thanks."

"So...back to what you were thinking."

She shrugged. "I dunno. I just thought of you for so long as my other little brother just because you were so tight with Israel. I knew even back in the day you liked me, but I was in my datin'-ballas stage. And you were two years under me. At that point, the age thing made a difference, you know?"

I simply nodded, silently indicating for her to continue.

"I remember how I felt when I saw you after you got shot. When I saw all those tubes coming out of you and how doped up you were, I cried like a little baby. I reached out to hold your hand and your fingers kind of barely moved. They tried to clinch mine, but you couldn't really make them work. Do you remember that at all?"

I shrugged. "I can barely remember anything, just bits and flashes of hearing different voices and seein' blurry shapes of people. I don't really remember you bein' there, though. You and your moms told me about it later."

"Well, it was sad for me and my mother because we already felt like we lost Israel, and then it was like we lost you too—first to those bullets, then to the streets when you got back on your feet."

I didn't know what to say to that. The streets did have me, and I was completely unapologetic about it.

"Anyway, you were always in our minds and hearts. You're pretty much an honorary Baylock now, you know?"

I had to smile at that. I didn't think it was true at that point, but it sure was a nice thought.

"Well, to be honest, I don't know if you'd consider me an honorary *anything* at this point if you knew some of the shit I been in since I was shot up. Hell, even before then. I'm a whole different person, Ellena. Sometimes I wonder if I ever was the Dave Hill that your brother got tight with, a maybe not-so-straight arrow but still a good person. Or maybe the Dave Hill I am now is the nigga that I always was deep inside."

Ellena reached out and lightly brushed a hand against my cheek. The gesture was so surprising that I jumped a little. I was embarrassed, but Ellena didn't seem to notice my reaction. She had a sorrowful expression on her face. "Dave, we've always believed in you. *I've* always believed in you. And it's never too late to turn your life around and do what you want. I just don't think you know how to believe in yourself."

"Yeah, well, ain't been nobody to show me how to believe in myself. I ain't exactly workin' from no examples."

Ellena laughed softly. "Well if you look at my brother, he could've been your example. He's the most absolutely fearless person I know. Some of that he got from my mom, but this thing he's into now, all this globetrotting. I mean, he's probably seeing and doing things a lot of us never will. At least I know that I won't.

"He's part of the reason I am going to be a cop. It's something I've wanted to do for a long time, but I was just scared, and it's one of the least respected jobs a person could have. But the last conversation I had with Israel all those months ago convinced me."

"What did he say?"

Ellena looked dreamily happy as she recalled it. "I told him I wanted to do it but that Mama had just shot down the idea when I mentioned it to her. He said to me, 'Ellena, you are put here on this earth for you, not for Mom, not for me or anyone else. We aren't born to bother with what-ifs. We're here to live our dreams and follow our destinies. If you feel destiny is leading you toward being a cop, then follow your heart. It isn't the first job I would have liked for you, but just like you set me free, Mom has to set you free too.'"

She took a swig of her Snapple, and in an almost unconscious, Pavlovian fashion, I did too. “So I’m going to do it,” she said. “And I’m scared about it but also excited as hell.”

I wasn’t pleased with this, and my face reflected it. With black humor in my voice, I said, “Well, I might as well enjoy this time with you now. After today, you might be arrestin’ my ass.”

“For what?”

I looked at her quizzically. “’Scuse me?”

“I asked why would I arrest you, Dave? What have you been into?”

“You say it like it’s past tense. The gangsta life I lead ain’t somethin’ I quit when you picked me up today, Ellena.”

She looked at me with a smile curling her lips. “Dave Hill, you don’t know that. You don’t know that at all. My brother would tell you or me or anybody that anything is possible if you just believe.”

I laughed harshly. “Sounds like some ol’ Disneyland bullshit.”

“So then, I guess you stopped believing that you could get with me.”

I looked into her eyes to see whether she was kidding or not so as to quickly formulate a snappy response. But her face was wide open and earnest. She wanted a real answer, and I was so startled by her seriousness that I was stuck.

“Well, Dave? You going to answer me sometime today?”

“Um…yeah, I gave up on it a long time ago. Why you ask?”

Ellena shrugged and turned off her emotions just like that. I could feel a wall spring up between us, and I wanted to shout, “Don’t close me out!” But my heart could be hard, and my response to her shutting down was to do the same.

We finished our drinks and walked back to her car. The conversation was still there, and it was alive and vibrant, but there was still a little something missing. As we drove home, we were for silent the most part, just listening to the radio and enjoying the ride.

15

When we got to my house, I was almost sad. I didn't want the day to end. Actually, I didn't want to go back to my life, period. I wanted her to drive to someplace in that beautiful Jaguar where no one knew us and we could forge a life of our own devise. I felt my heart pulling toward what she'd said to me. And I almost felt anger at her for dropping that seed in my heart, making me believe that maybe anything actually was possible still.

She looked over at me and said, "Well, we're back. What are you going to do for the rest of the day?"

I shrugged. "Dunno. I'm sure something'll come up. I left my pager here, so I'm bettin' if I check it, there's gonna be a million damn pages on it."

"Ooooh, Mister Important." Ellena chuckled sarcastically.

I laughed with her. "Uh, well…um…we gonna be seeing each other again?"

Ellena looked thoughtful. I waited for her answer, and then she suddenly leaned in and kissed me. Her lips were soft and yielding against mine, her breath sweet as candy. Our lips initially kind of just brushed together as if they were at the beginning stage of some mating dance. Then it grew passionate, and I felt like I had fallen into the cradle of Heaven and was being rocked by the hands of the Almighty himself.

When we separated, I looked deep into her eyes. There was something in them that I couldn't put a name to. She smiled, her eyelids heavy over her smoky-gray eyes, and I wanted her so bad right that second that I would have done anything for her, to have the only name to ever leave her lips in love be mine.

She finally broke the spell and said, "Well, are you going to sit here all day or what?"

I tried to play off the moment, although I felt my cheeks flush with embarrassment. "Uh, yeah, I was just gettin' out. I'm a little tired. Sorry."

I got out of the car and was getting ready to walk the steps up to my apartment when she gave me a cross look. I was trying to figure out what that look was for when it hit me. I walked over to the driver's side and gave her another passionate, very hot kiss. We said not a word to each other as I walked back to the sidewalk and she guided the car away from my apartment and off toward the setting sun.

16

I watched Ellena drive away, and all of a sudden the old feelings were creeping back in. It felt literally like something was crawling along my skin, something disturbing. I shook my head in confusion and went into the apartment.

When I walked in the door, Smiley was sitting on the sofa with two fairly attractive, scantily clad females. They were watching television. It looked like an old episode of *Def Comedy Jam* (from the Marin Lawrence era). He nodded toward me with that engaging smile that was the origin of his street moniker and said, "What up?"

I just waved him off and went into my room. I saw the setup—he was kicking it with the women, and I could have easily joined them, which would have led to some hijinks later. But I suddenly had Ellena all on my mind, and I felt like it would have been cheating to be with anybody else—at least that same day.

I checked my pager, which was beeping on my dresser. Sure enough, there were a multitude of pages. I didn't even know where to start. I had several pages from my mother (and probably some voice mails also; I hadn't even bothered with those yet) and a few of my regular customers. I decided I'd start with getting myself some more cocaine to rock up for selling.

I went to see some El Salvadorians I dealt with. They lived around Wilshire and Alvarado, which was an intersection in a sour area close to downtown LA. There were not too many black faces around, mostly hardened Hispanic ones. I got love because

I came with cash in hand and didn't bother with useless chitchat. I paid, picked up the product, and shook the spot.

Once at home, I took the ounce I'd picked up, carefully unwrapped it, and began the process of rocking it up. I separated a sizeable amount and put it into one of those old school jelly jars with a good portion of baking soda. I then put water in the jar and sealed it up.

I put the jar into a pot of boiling water. The baking soda with the cocaine and water coagulated into a soft big lump. After a time, I took it out and let it cool off. Once cooled into a huge rock-solid mass, it was just a matter of chipping away at it to produce a number of tiny ones for sale.

After doing this, I was exhausted. It was almost eleven by the time I settled in and laid down. The pager kept going off, but I had given up on looking at it, and I still hadn't even checked my voice messages from earlier. I laid down in my bed and thought of Ellena, and sleep descended on me like a curtain falling at the end of a play.

17

Ellena and I began to hang out more. It hurt me to think that I might have to start dreaming about her again and that I was setting myself up for a letdown, so I decided to let her initiate calling me. And she did, quite often.

We did everything from movies to concerts to television tapings to just walking around the block several times talking. We dined out at nice restaurants and listened to after-dinner jazz. I never once moved on her, because we were growing close as friends, and I didn't want to do anything to drive her away. She knew of my life and seemed to accept me as I was, which to me was a gift from God. She actually gave me good advice on a lot of things, and I felt she was there for me. I didn't try to repeat that kiss we'd shared after our beach date, and she didn't seem to mind one way or the other.

Her mother welcomed me back to the fold, but warily. I think she saw Ellena and I were getting closer than we should have been, and it seemed a little like incest to her. Ms. Baylock, who once treated me as if I were a brother to her son, another egg seeded and nurtured in her womb, now regarded me as someone to be tolerated simply because her daughter had great affection for me. It saddened me greatly that we couldn't have the closeness we once had, the closeness that had once filled the void of nurturing and mothering that I never felt in my own home. But I had grown used to life's curveballs at that point, and I don't think I really expected any good to come out of anything I was involved in.

One night Ellena and I had gone to a movie in Santa Monica. Our times spent together often involved getting out of the 'hood and going to hang in areas where we didn't have to worry about any stupid bullshit going down. We went to a theater at the Third Street Promenade, a walkway that stretched about two miles, filled with clothing stores, furniture shops, toy stores, and just about any other kind of store you could think of. As on the neighboring Venice Boardwalk, the Promenade (which was scant blocks from the Santa Monica beach) was also rife with street performers of different kinds, and it was cool to know you could be entertained there—at times literally every five feet or so.

We were talking about something when out of the blue Ellena asked me, "Dave, why haven't you kissed me since that day in Venice?"

I halted midstride. Not a smart thing to do on the Promenade on a Saturday night in August, as it is densely packed with locals and tourists that time of year, but I was severely thrown off by the question. "Ellena, what the hell are you talking about?" I said with a laugh. "I just thought you didn't want me to go there. I been trying to show you that I ain't tryna play you like just some piece of ass."

She laughed and looked at me like I was a moron. "Nigga, please. I've been dealing with you silly-ass men since I was thirteen years old. I think by now I know when a man wants to just try to get into my panties and when he doesn't. You didn't have to exaggerate the point."

We began to walk again. I said to her, "Damn, you ain't gotta get smart with me. I just wanted you to know how special you are, what our friendship means."

"David, I've known all of that since you first came into our lives. Even for that brief period where we didn't communicate, you were always in me and Mama's hearts."

I had nothing to say about that one. Somehow I didn't think I was in her mother's *anything* after I'd gotten shot, and for sure not now.

"You know, I have really strong feelings for you," she said. "I've been putting that out for you to look at for almost six months now, and you're just kind of fronting me off."

I was very surprised at this, but I said nothing to give that away. My heart filled with joy and something else—a kind of weird, perverse sense of triumph. I thought of all those nights as a youngster in high school when I was fantasizing about being with her, dreaming about it constantly, and it made me feel good to know that I might now have a shot.

"Well? Do you have anything to say?"

I shrugged almost casually. "Damn, girl. I was just kinda diggin' on how things were working out with us. We got us a nice li'l friendship, and I don't want to fuck it up. Trust me, a nigga like me is no one you wanna get involved with, particularly if you tryna be down with John Law."

"David, I don't think you've ever had anyone in your corner to make you believe there might be something else out there besides all the bullshit you're into now. You *must* know that I can't be involved with anyone doing drug selling or whatever you're into. I wouldn't even trip off of you if you hadn't told me you've been thinking about leaving the streets behind and getting real with your life."

I had told her this on more than one occasion. I probably meant it too. But I knew right at that second I was not ready to leave the streets alone, and I didn't even want to lie to her about that, so I opted to change the subject. "You know what, Ellena? I'm suddenly ready to get outta here. It's too crowded in this mugg, and I cain't even think. What do you say?"

"We've seen our movie. We can go."

18

Ellena and I walked back to her car in silence. It was a beat-up old '72 shit-brown Mustang that her mother had purchased as a graduation gift. She tossed me the keys and said, "You drive. I'm a little tired. I'm going to lay down if that is cool."

"No problem. Get ya beauty rest—not that you need it."

I guided the car out of the parking structure and onto the 10 Freeway on-ramp a couple of blocks away. As I got onto the freeway, I looked over at Ellena. She had let her seat back and her eyes were closed. She was wearing a blue jean skirt with a tight white T-shirt, and laid back like she was, she looked completely defenseless and open. I felt my dick stiffening up on me as I struggled to keep my eyes on the road ahead and look at her at the same time. Up to that point, I had carefully controlled what I said to her, how I acted around her, and how I felt about her. Her words while we were on the Promenade had unchained a beast that now wanted to run rampant.

My free hand drifted to her thigh, casually brushing it to see what kind of reaction would come. She didn't move, and nothing about her even, steady breathing changed. She seemed to be honestly asleep, or at least on a quick road there.

After a couple of minutes, I let my hand rest on her thigh. Still no reaction. My mouth was dry, as if someone had stuffed a big wad of cotton in it. Despite what she'd told me, I still had this fear that if I moved on her physically, I would be met with rejection. What I was doing was scaring me and exciting me in equal proportions because I knew that, for better or worse, I was going somewhere with her that there was no coming back from.

I began to ease my hand up her thigh. She still didn't react. My heart was beating so fast that I could hear the blood pounding in my ears. I felt like I was out of breath, and my creeping hand may have been trembling ever so slightly.

I felt the lacy crotch of her panties at my fingertips. I waited for her to pop her head at any second and ask what the fuck I was doing, but still nothing. I let my fingers linger there for a moment, and then I deftly eased them past her panties into that special place they kept safe and covered. It felt like there was but a little hair there, but that patch was soft and downy.

I found her pussy and let my fingers trail up and down her lips. They seemed to unfurl like a flower at my touch, immediately wet and hot. I took my time, massaging and teasing them expertly. As the heat and wetness increased, so did her breathing, which was slowly but surely becoming labored and ragged.

There was much fear and excitement coursing through my heart, making me more animal than human. Not all of it was from what was going on and the ramifications of it; it was also getting to be a chore to drive properly and still concentrate on what I was doing. I didn't even feel like I was seeing the road ahead, just some patch of black illuminated by street lamps that whizzed by, dream-like, as I sped down the highway. My dick felt like it was ready to explode out of my pants, and nothing in the world meant anything to me at that second but what was going on in that car.

I finally worked my probing fingers to Ellena's clit. She let out an audible gasp as my index finger brushed it. It was soaked in her juices, so I was able to manipulate her precious pearl with the greatest of ease. She was still struggling to stay with the game of feigning sleep, but her hips seemed to involuntarily move to work with my fingers. I found myself wishing I could manipulate my own dick as well to join her in the orgasm I could clearly see mounting within her.

As I continued to manipulate her pearl, a couple of my fingers still working the lining of her sweet box and on occasion diving into the hole where my penis longed to nest, she was getting to the point at which she could no longer hide her excitement. Her hips were now raised off the seat to move in conjunction with my fingers. I was really trying hard not to kill us both as I continued to navigate the car down the freeway, but it was getting tougher and tougher. A couple of people in other cars noticed our shenanigans, but I didn't care. I was just too damn excited.

The labored breath graduated to low moans. The low moans eventually became sensual purrs and growls. Her eyes were still closed but no longer because of mock sleep; we were both going to a place outside of this world, as if the car were a spaceship or a time travel machine, although she would get there far quicker than I.

Her body was moving as if it had a will of its own, but my fingers were still keeping time with her undulations. I felt so in tune with her in that moment that when her orgasm began to roll through her, I could feel it, and it was powerful and frightening at the same time because I knew she was in some place I might never reach while I was stuck trying to focus on the highway as I hurtled down its endless stretch at no less than eighty-five miles an hour.

She cried out, "Oh, shit!" Her body stiffened for a moment, and it seemed as if all time ceased. I was still working my fingers when she finally growled, "No, no, stop. It's too much!" Her body stayed like that for a moment, like some still life statue, then she relaxed as the sensual poltergeist that had seized her fled from her body into the wind.

I slowed the car down to the legal limit, letting out a burst of breath as if I'd been holding it. I noticed then that I was sweating a little, and my armpits felt damp and hot. She was looking at me in what seemed to be wonder. I took the fingers that had brought her to that special place and put them into my mouth, licking the juices, savoring them.

She brought her seat up, laughing as she did it.

I said to her with a smile, "What's so funny?"

"You," she said softly. "You know, if I knew you could make a woman cum like that, I might've given you a chance back in the day."

"Naw, I cain't front, I didn't have it like that then. But yes, indeed, I am the man now. You betta recognize, baby!"

She laughed and punched me in the arm. I was laughing, but for a different reason. "Um, Ellena, you know, I passed our exit about six miles ago."

She shrugged without a care in the world. "And? Is something bad gonna happen because of that?" She leaned in and put her head on my shoulder, a move that surprised me. Then I was caught in the middle of feeling like a strong, secure man and a frightened little boy all at once.

"I don't care where we go right now," she said in her husky voice, head against my shoulder, her slender arms wrapping around my free arm securely like vines on a trellis. "Take me anywhere you want to take me."

I had no idea where that was. I just let the car hurtle along the dark highway, the passing street lamps flashing like neon in Hollywood, and decided to let fate guide the way.

19

I drove aimlessly for a while, eventually ending up back at my apartment. Along the way, Ellena had actually fallen asleep. I nudged her awake, and she groggily sat up and looked around, as if she'd been asleep all night instead of an hour or so. She asked sleepily, "Are we back at your house?"

I nodded. "Wanna come in?"

She nodded.

When we got in, I noticed Smiley wasn't home. This was most certainly a rare occasion. I thought it was an excellent sign that I was going to have at least one of the major dreams of my life come true that night.

I silently led Ellena to my room. I closed the door and just stood looking at her. She sat on the edge of my bed and began taking off her clothes. I tried to look nonchalant, but I could not wait to see her naked.

She was just as I imagined, voluptuous in all the right places, slim, strong, and sturdy everywhere else. Her belly was flat, faintly hinting at a six-pack. I thought again of the '70s actress Pam Grier, who had been my first major crush as a youngster.

She laid that lush, rich body down across my bed and said in a husky voice, dripping with raw sex, "I want you to come over here and make love to me, David Hill. Give me everything you've got."

And that is exactly what I did.

20

They say there's nothing like your first drink, when the colors of the world seem to brighten and become flashier and more alive. Or that first hit of weed, when you just sit back and relax and float as if you're in a waking dream. Or even when you turn twenty-one and go to the club for the first time legally, feeling that hot glow of satisfaction when the doorman actually lets you through without looking over you and your ID six or seven times.

That is how it was with Ellena, except that feeling seemed to last for months. We hadn't officially classified ourselves as a couple, but we were together every moment that we could be. I still sold dope and gangbanged, and her personal assistant job kept her busy, so when we would hook up, we did all we could to just be with each other and shut the rest of the world out. Her job was rarely discussed and we *never* talked about the things I did. And that was just the way that I liked it.

One night we had gotten a room at the Bonaventure Hotel, downtown. We had ordered dinner in the room and then just spent most of the evening making love. We had taken a break at one point and were laughing and joking about various things, just having an all-around good time. I got up from the bed and went over to the dresser, where I'd thrown my pants while we were in a rush to get our clothing off. I reached in the pocket and brought my hand out wrapped tightly around something. As I walked by the bed, Ellena stared intently at my hand, trying to figure out what was in it. I sat on the bed next to her and gave her a long, passionate kiss.

After a moment, she broke the kiss with a laugh and punched me in the shoulder. "No fair trying to distract me! What's in your hand?"

I unfurled my hand and let her see the little black velvet box resting like an egg in my palm. She squealed with delight and snatched it from me. She looked at the box with wide eyes and a slack jaw, and I laughed. She looked at me ruefully and said, "What's so damn funny?"

"You!" I imitated her facial expression and she laughed and hit me in the arm. I said, "Are you scared to open it or something?"

She looked at me as if she was silently saying yes, but she opened the box anyway. Her eyes went even wider and her free hand flew to her heart as a breath left her body with a loud whoosh. I had bought the two-karat diamond earrings earlier that day, thinking I hadn't gotten her even one gift since I'd known her. I had carefully picked the gift because I wanted it to be something she'd always remember and treasure and associate with the time we were having then. It ate up a lot of my money I had saved but I didn't care.

She stared at the earrings for a moment as if in a trance, then she began to cry. I took the little box from her and put it on the nightstand, and then took her in my arms. I shushed her and told her that it was okay.

"No, David, it's not okay," she said against my chest. "I can't keep those earrings."

I pulled her away from me, suddenly confused. "What, you don't like 'em or somethin'?"

"Noooo, they're beautiful. Damn, they are so beautiful. I don't think anyone has ever given me a gift like these before."

"Then what's the problem?"

Ellena took a deep breath and looked down, then she looked up into my face. Her eyes and cheeks were damp and streaked with tears, but her expression was steely and resolute. "I'll keep the earrings if you can tell me how you got the money to pay for them. And that's the only way I'll keep them."

I jumped off the bed laughing, but I was really upset. "What do you mean, how I paid for them? I paid for 'em with cash. What the fuck?"

"No, I said, how you got the money to pay for them, not how you paid for them. Don't play stupid with me, David."

I puffed up my chest. "Don't call me stupid." I felt like I wanted to slap her. I was still confused as to how a moment I had planned on being magical for us both was now turning out so messed up.

"I didn't call you stupid, I said..." She shook her head dismissively. "Don't try to dodge my question. Did you get me this gift with legal money?"

I laughed harshly, looking at her like I thought she was an idiot. "Sweetheart, there ain't no such thing as legal money. If you knew anything about how this world really works, you'd know that."

She shook her head at me, clearly getting upset. "Negro, you have done everything but answer the damn question. You think I might get one today?"

"You sure you want the answer?"

She picked the earrings up off the nightstand and looked at them. There was a heavy silence in the room. We were both kind of charged up with anger, but her's was leaving her.

She put the earrings back on the nightstand and waved for me to come sit next to her.

I scoffed. "Woman, I ain't no gotdamn dog. You want me next to you, you betta ask me the right way!"

"Will you please sit next to me?"

I did as she asked, satisfied with that small victory. But the look on her face crushed that feeling quickly. It wasn't a look that I could place and it scared me. I had never opened myself deeply and completely to anyone before, and there were still fears and doubts in my heart about that whole process.

Ellena took my face in her hands and said, "Tell me something. We do a whole lot of sexing, talking, and hanging out, but we haven't really talked about the future. I mean, we've talked a little about my future, but not yours. Definitely not ours.

"I *know* love, David. And I know you love me, even though you have yet to say the words. You're a man, so I don't expect you to say them to me anytime soon, because y'all are so full of fear in that area it's not even funny. But like I say, I know.

"I can never take a gift from you that legal money didn't pay for. That's just me, my morals, and my values, who I am. It doesn't mean that I don't care for you as much now as I did before you gave it to me. It just means I appreciate the gesture, and I appreciate how you thought so much of our relationship to make it, but I cannot take it.

"I don't believe in any of the things you're into right now. And I still plan on becoming a police officer, so if we plan on having any kind of future, you'd better have that straightened out by then. I'm not threatening you; I'm telling you a simple truth. Even if I wasn't going to be a cop, I would not be having that in my man. At least if he planned on staying my man." She shrugged. "That's the way it is."

I lowered my head. I couldn't look her in the face. I wanted to leave the other life behind, but it was just so much a part of me that, in a way, I *didn't* want to leave it alone. Being a gangsta defined me, especially since athlete-on-his-way-up-from-the-ghetto no longer did.

"Damn, Ellena," I said quietly, unwanted tears stinging my eyes. "I don't know what the fuck to do if I ain't slangin' and bangin'. I ain't never had no real job. I ain't never tried to do it the right way. The closest I've come was takin' that scholarship and I was still sellin' dope in college."

"Jesus Christ, David." She wiped the tears from my eyes and once again took my head in her delicate hands. "Look, you don't have to worry. I'll be twenty-five in a couple months, and I want to be a cop. Do you know how hard it's gonna be for me to give up this comfortable gig I have with Mr. Brady now?

"You're only twenty-two years old, Dave. Twenty-two. You have your whole life ahead of you. And I'll help you in every way I can."

In a voice that sounded more childlike and insecure than intended, I said, "You will? You'll be there with me?"

"David, I love you. It's an honor and a privilege for me to stand by you and help in every way I can…if you really want to change your life."

"Okay, but I just want to ask you one thing."

"What?"

I looked deeply into her eyes and said, "Please keep the earrings. Please. I won't every buy you anything with…dirty money again, but just keep this one gift. Let it be…I dunno, a symbol of my changin' over to the straight life or whatever."

She was silent for a moment, and then she smiled. "I'll keep them, David. But only because I love you sooooo much."

I leaned into her ample bosom and began to cry like a baby. She was shocked only for a second, but then she crushed me tight against her and rocked me and told me to get it all out. I didn't even know why Ellena had such a profound effect on me, but she did. Even though I had yet to voice it, she was the only woman I'd ever loved, and the only one I believed could actually help me change my world.

21

A week after that evening, Ellena's boss, Jim Brady, got a job offer from a major network. He wanted to take her with him to his new gig in New York. She was caught between wanting to stay with me and go with him, but he was offering her the big bucks.

She later told me how he pleaded with her. "Ellena, you've been with me so long now," he said. "I can't imagine starting over with someone else. There's going to be enough pressure on me now as it is. I need *you*."

We had gone out to dinner at the Hard Rock Café in the Beverly Center to talk about it. I ate my ribs and fries heartily; she ordered a salad and hardly even touched it.

In between bites, my lips and jaw smeared with barbeque sauce, I said, "Ellena, this shit here sounds like a no-brainer to me. You need to go on and take the damn job."

She looked at me with genuine concern and said, "David, I feel like we really made some headway in our relationship last week. I don't want to leave you now. Besides, I've been to New York a couple of times. It's too fast for me, and the people are rude as hell. It's no place I'd want to live. And have you forgotten that I still want to be a cop?"

The cop thing made my insides turn every time she said it, but I tried to keep a straight face. I sighed. "Look, Ellena, you can…you can still be a cop. Just stay with ol' boy long enough to stack some paper and get him situated, then help him find and train somebody new. Then you can bring yo' sexy ass back to LA and we could pick up where we left off."

"That covers everything but what you're going to do with your life while I'm gone."

I shrugged nonchalantly. "I'm'a live, girl. What else I'm s'pose to do?"

"Naw, nigga," Ellena said, the ghetto coming out in her. "I mean, what're you going to do in terms of turning your life around? And don't give me any bullshit or act like you don't know what I'm talking about."

"Shit, woman." I gave her a mean glance, but it didn't faze her. "What do you want me to do?"

"You know, I don't even want you to look at it like that. Just think of your life as if all the possibilities are wide open, and *you* have to decide what *you* want to do. It isn't at all about what I want. I would have liked to fall in love with an ex-footballin' CEO or something like that."

I took offense at that and snapped at her. "Oh, so a street nigga like me ain't good enough for you, huh? That what yo' ass is sayin'?"

She laughed as I rose from the table. She jumped up and with surprising strength pushed me back in my seat. She sat back down across from me, just looking at the anger that was straining my face as I stared unblinking at the table.

"David, look at me. I said, look at me."

Feeling surly, like a wronged child, I did.

She stroked my face. "I think we both know that if that was the kind of man I wanted, I could easily have him. And I am not bragging at all, I am just stating the facts.

"I don't have to go through all the worrying and questions and comments from my friends that I don't being with you, but I love you." She pushed my head up so that our eyes locked. "How many times do I have to tell you that? You've never said it once to me, and yet I tell you all the time and sometimes you act like it means nothing or it's not enough. But I don't let that faze me."

"Yeah, well—"

"Uh-uh, David, don't even start in with me. Cool your ass down. You know everything I am saying is true."

She was right; I couldn't deny it.

"So now that you're done pouting, please tell me what you are going to do if I go with Mr. Brady to New York."

I shrugged. "I guess I'm'a hafta get a legit job."

"Do you have any idea at all what you want to do?"

I laughed. "All I know for certain is that I don't wanna flip burgers!"

Ellena laughed with me. "I'm even with you on that one."

"I thought once about being a gym teacher, but I know that ain't something I'm just gonna go apply to schools for and they gon' give me. I'd have to go back to college for that."

"Well, with the money I'm going to be making, I could easily take care of us both while you strictly went to school, if that's what you want."

I looked at her in annoyance. "No way in hell I'm'a let you support me like some bum. I'd just as soon keep hustlin'."

"No, I don't want that. I was just making a suggestion. I didn't mean to offend you."

We were both silent for a second. The restaurant was noisy as hell, but the silence between us made it seem as if we were the only two folks in there and that nothing was going on around us.

"Okay," Ellena said after a minute. "I'm going to trust you to do the right thing, and I won't bother you about it." She shook her head and laughed. "I swear, I must be crazy, 'cause I can't see myself trippin' like this with any other man."

"Don't worry, girl," I said with confidence. "Just keep believin' in me, in *us*, and I'll get this taken care of. But you cain't stop believin' in me. I need that—now more than ever."

"I got all the faith you need and more, baby," she said with all the heart of the devout, reaching out to casually brush her hand across my cheek. She did little gestures like that all the time, and not once did they fail to ignite something in my heart and spirit.

22

Ellena left a few weeks later, but to our delight I managed to find a job before her departure. Stuntman, one of the OG homies in our gang, had a legit job as a warehouse foreman at a printing company out in Hawthorne, and he hired me on. He was happy to have me and made sure I got an hourly wage that was a little higher than most just starting out. He would like to have hired more of our compatriots, but most had felony convictions, and the company had a strict policy about not hiring felons that they'd violated so far only for hiring me.

I was good, going out of my way to work any overtime they had to offer and soaking up everything Stuntman had to teach me. I'd gotten a certificate to drive a forklift, which made Ellena laugh when I called her in New York, flush with excitement to tell her about it. There was a lot of lifting and packing going on, but I enjoyed the pure physicality of the work. I quit working out off the clock, because I was getting such a workout at the job that I didn't need to go the extra mile.

One night, after a few months of working there, I came home after a particularly exhausting day and checked my messages. A few were from some of the homies that kept calling asking where I was and what I was up to. One was from Ellena. As soon as I heard her voice, a big smile appeared on my face, and I suddenly didn't feel so tired anymore.

"Hey, baby, it's me. Had a loooooong day. Jim is going to interview Sylvester Stallone tomorrow, and he's been running me ragged. I told him that he has to take it easy on a pregnant woman. Okay, I love you. 'Bye."

Confused, I backed the message up a little.

"Been running me ragged all day. I told him that he has to take it easy on a pregnant woman."

I reran it again.

"Take it easy on a pregnant woman."

I got on the phone and called Ellena.

She was staying at a hotel, not wanting to get an apartment. She didn't want to even subconsciously have any sense of planting roots or permanence in New York. When the operator came on, I said tersely, "Gimme Ellena Baylock's room."

Her phone rang once. Twice. Three times. It went up to six times before she answered and tentatively said, "Hello?"

"Ellena, it's me."

"Hey, baby, what's up?"

"Well, you left me this funny message earlier. Seemed to hint at you being pregnant. A brotha was just curious about that shit."

A momentary silence desended on us.

"Ummm, what if I *was* pregnant? Then what?"

"I'd be real happy—unless...uh...unless it wasn't mines."

"What? Are you *serious*?"

"Gotdamn, calm your ass down. It's just the way you let me know on the muthafuckin' answerin' machine instead'a just tellin' me direct. That message wasn't even a direct hit. 'Yadda-yadda-yadda, and by the way I'm pregnant.' What kinda shit was that?"

"That is *not* how I left the message. And anyway, I was a little scared, to be honest. You're just getting things on track, living a certain way for the first time. I didn't want you feel like I was trying to trap you with a kid, like one of those ghetto bitches."

I had to laugh at that one. "Ellena, I would never confuse you with one'a them 'hood rat 'hos I used to mess with. You're my heart, baby, and now we're gonna be connected forever by blood, by a baby."

"Two things missing for me that would make me happier than I am now."

"What?"

"Well, if I were married..."

I coughed involuntarily.

"And if Israel were here. Ooooh, whenever he gets back, he is going to be *shocked.*"

"He sure is. He told me he didn't ever think I could get with you, and now we're going to have a kid together. Funny how life works out."

"Yeah, well, sweetie, it's almost eleven o'clock here, and I am exhausted."

"I know, Sylvester Stallone tomorrow. Well, get lots of rest, and tell ol' Brady not to be overworkin' you, yah?"

"Okay. I love you, baby."

"I love you too, sweetness. Sleep tight."

"'Kay, 'bye."

"'Bye."

23

Ellena was wrong about me being scared of my new life. I embraced it completely, and that's saying something, because I'm not one who deals with dramatic change well. But I was not used to the changes being good ones. At this point, I was having the most perfect life I could imagine.

I would get up every day feeling good. I loved going to work. I would shower, make myself breakfast and have a quick cup of coffee before jumping into Ellena's beat-up Mustang (I had my own tricked-out Honda Accord that I drove off the clock, but I was getting stopped too much by the police on the thirty minute drive to Hawthorne to be taking it to work) and happily trudged off for another grueling day.

When I would hang out with the homies, they were once again happy for and proud of me. The easy money of hustling drugs often kept men out on the streets longer than we had to be, and more often than not, a guy forgets the number one rule of the game: eventually, you're going to get caught or die. If it's the former, sometimes you might be able to beat the charge. More often than not, you might do a little time. But as sure as the sun rose in the east and set in the west, getting caught or dying in the dope game was inevitable.

Ellena's pregnancy at that point was about four months along. We talked every day. She was so proud of me, and I thought it was still so fresh that a woman actually really loved me for myself completely. The one thing that kept both of us from being completely happy with the way things were was that we missed the hell out of each other. I was even planning to ask her to marry me when we were both in the same city again. Everything was perfect.

I should have known it couldn't last forever.

I had a rare evening of staying out late drinking and getting high with the homies, and I got up late the next morning. Cursing as I groggily arose and saw the time, I jumped up and showered and dressed and bolted out the door, forgoing breakfast.

I took a shortcut of back streets to make that drive to Hawthorne, avoiding the usually packed 405 Freeway that most took. I was making better time than I thought I would as I drove along, so I decided to hit a little doughnut shop and get myself a cop shot (what the gangstas called a cup of coffee and a doughnut or two).

I parked in front of the shop and bounded in. I had never been late a day since I started my job and was happy this wasn't going to be my first. As I walked to the counter I made a mental note not to party on the weekdays any more. The homie Stuntman was just as proud of me, using me as an example to his bosses that a gangsta off the street like me could be as responsible as the next man, and I didn't want to do anything to mess that up. He and I agreed that hopefully with my example, the company might soften up their policy and let him hire some more of the homies that had felonies on their sheets.

As I was walking out of the shop, I saw a brotha sitting across the street at the bus stop. I don't even know why my eyes flashed toward something that far away, but they did, and that was about the end of my perfect life.

My jaw went slack. I dropped the coffee and doughnuts as if in a trance and began to tremble uncontrollably.

The nigga that I thought I was looking at was the one who killed my dreams, killed the homie No Good, and almost killed me.

Wade Anderson. Muthafuckin' Wade!

Even though he was only twenty-two like me, he looked much older and had gotten himself a slight spare tire around the middle. He was dressed in a security guard uniform, and his once long, fine hair was now close-cropped, but still smartly styled. I wasn't completely sure it was him, so I got in my car and swung around the block and drove by him, slow enough to get a look but not catch his attention.

It was definitely him.

Part of me was screaming just to drive on and forget that I ever saw him. Part of me was screaming bloody murder. I drove up a couple of blocks, pulled over and began to curse and rock in the car uncontrollably. A couple of people passing by in other cars stared at me like I was crazy, and right at that moment I probably was.

After I calmed down, I decided to drive around the block to get another look at him. As I passed him this time he noticed the car, but as he strained to see the driver I sped up just quick enough for him not to get a good look at me.

As I swung around the block again, I could feel all reason leaving me. Every molecule in my body was screaming for me to kill Wade as I remembered the homie No Good's half-disintegrated face, the pain of the wounds that almost took my life, the doctor telling me I wouldn't be playing football again.

I'd conveniently forgotten that if I'd simply gotten my booze with No Good and left the store that night, my life might have had a different course. Everything was *his* fault. That was all I could see at that moment.

I parked on a side street and walked back around the corner. When I saw Wade, he was looking away from me and toward the direction that he expected my car to come from again. I stealthily made my way behind him, using the bus bench as cover. The traffic noise covered me as well, and I felt a strange sense of power from knowing that I was going to get the jump on him this time.

When I was right behind the bus bench, I paused for a second. The strangest thing happened. I thought about Ellena and the baby that I would surely never see if I killed Wade. I thought that God was opening a window for me and that I had a chance to go back and get in my car and continue on to work and be thankful for the good life He'd given me.

In the second that I was considering all this, Wade spun around. He gave me a stare that read pure murder, and then he looked at me strangely. I was certain he was trying to figure out who I was.

After a moment, his eyes widened, and he screamed, "Oh shit, it's you!"

I have to hand it to Wade. In him, the Bloods had a true gangsta warrior. There was a .22 caliber pistol in his hand that seemed to have appeared there out of nowhere, a deadly magic trick. I made as if I were going for the pistol, which I knew would fool him and cause him to jerk his hand ever so slightly before drawing a bead on me again, and then I fired a punch that had the backing of several years of rage. It caught him in that spot between the bottom of his nose and his upper lip, and I saw his top row of teeth drop out like pieces of candy.

He fell backward almost into the street, completely dazed. I came around the bus bench and grabbed him by the throat with one hand and dug my fingers into the meat of his shoulder with the other. I dragged him onto the middle of the sidewalk, completely closing the window of reason that had been opened.

I spun him around to face me. Before I could get off another punch, he blindly put the .22 up to my left shoulder and pulled the trigger. I stumbled back a few steps and made sure that I was okay. The bullet had gone straight through the meat, touching no bone. Then I stepped to Wade and started kicking him. After the second or third kick, he dropped the pistol and tried to ball up to keep from taking the brunt of the kicks.

I was tired of him being curled up like a little punk and not being able to experience my full fury, so I stopped kicking him.

I picked up the gun, put it to his knee, and pulled the trigger. It's hard to say what was louder—the report from the gun or Wade's shrill scream and the litany of curses that followed it. He unfurled long enough for me to sit on his chest and start beating him in the head with the gun.

After a few strikes, I tired of using the gun and tossed it aside. I wanted him to feel my hands, to let him know that I was going to kill him intimately, and nothing was going to interfere with that. As I hit and hit and hit, pounding the skin off of his face and my knuckles, his blood made the whole world red. His battered face was a valentine for the rage I'd held for him all those years.

Someone tackled me off of Wade. It was a policeman. I kicked him away from me, and then all I saw was a rain of nightsticks falling upon me. Now it was I who was curled up in a ball trying to protect myself from the blows pouring down on me like acid rain, wearing me down and driving the demons away.

Eventually they got tired of beating my ass, and on top of that, they noticed that a crowd of witnesses had formed. They cuffed me and threw me in the back of a squad car. I was bruised, battered and bleeding—both from the ferocity of the policemen and the bullet hole in my shoulder, but I didn't care. I was smiling. Even though I knew that my life was about to undergo another major change (and this time, probably not for the better), I felt like I had closed the door on the past completely. Whatever came in the future, I would deal with it like a man with no regrets and afraid of absolutely nothing.

24

The first place they took me was to the local hospital to clean and bandage my wound. It was such a clean hole that there was barely any blood lost, although now it was throbbing like crazy. They gave me a shot of some painkiller that knocked me right out. I was happy, drifting off to oblivion in the peaceful comfort of a hospital bed, not caring about tomorrow or the next day or day after that.

I was at the hospital three days, and then I was moved to the Los Angeles County Jail. I damn near got a parade welcoming me there. The word had spread throughout the jail about how I'd avenged the homie No Good and my own shooting with my bare hands (a rarity at that time; this was at the height of the drive-by craze, when almost no one used their naked hands for murder anymore), even after I took one in the shoulder. I was given the utmost respect by not only my set but even by other Crip gang sets we didn't necessarily get along with that had even less love for Blood gangstas.

I was assigned a public defender, who came to see me once a week. His name was Raoul Furtado, and he was a short man that wore ill-fitting suits and had a look far more middle eastern than Hispanic—short frizzy hair, deep olive skin, a large, hawk-like nose, lips right between thick and thin, and dark, blazing eyes that saw everything.

His first visit, he got acquainted with me and let me know what I was up against.

"Mr. Hill," Furtado said in his grainy, high-pitched voice. "I'm not going to lie to you. This doesn't look good. Wade Anderson is in a coma right now, and he's not expected to come out of it. Even if he does, he'll probably be a vegetable. His doctor has told me that there's little chance of him recovering from the trauma you dealt his skull.

"Were he to somehow come out of that mentally intact, he'd still need extensive plastic surgery to restore much of his face. And there's no telling which physical functions will be impaired."

I didn't care about any of that. I was absolutely miserable that Wade was still breathing. I said nothing to Furtado, just nodding my head as he spoke.

"One good thing about all of this is that every witness who saw this event said Mr. Anderson pulled a gun on you first, in addition to shooting you before you did any major damage to him. So I might be able to make a self-defense angle stick. But it's clear that you used excessive force to, ah, subdue Mr. Anderson, and that is a punishable offense."

He took his briefcase off the floor and set it on the table. He opened it up and took out a thick yellow writing tablet and an expensive looking pen.

"I need to ask you about what happened with this event as you see it. I have a police report. I'm going to compare what you tell me with that and see what's going to make sense to a jury."

"Mr. Furtado, let me ask you a question."

"Please, ask me anything."

"You want the story I told the cops, or you want the real deal?"

Furtado thought for a second. I could almost hear the wheels clicking in his head. "Both. Let's hear the story you gave the police first."

"'Kay. I had parked around the corner to go to this hardware store that was right behind the bus stop where dude was kickin' it. He turned around and recognized me as a Crip from back in the day—we were in high school together at one point and we had, um, negative dealings then. He's a Blood gangbanger. Did you know that?"

Furtado nodded.

"The nigga pulled a piece on me, and I handled mines. That's pretty much the long and short of it."

"Okay," Furtado said, his voice sounding like he was somewhere far away as he scribbled on the tablet. "Now, let's hear the truth."

I told him the whole story on Wade. From the incident with Israel at Hamilton High, to the shooting and the cause and effect of that, to when I saw him as I came out of the coffee shop. Told him every last intimate detail about it, purging myself. He listened silently and wrote in his pad.

Finally he said, "Gosh, Mr. Hill, that was positively Shakespearean. Fascinating stuff." He chuckled.

I gave him a hard look. "I'm glad my sufferin' is funny to you."

He shook his head and held his hands up. "I think you've got the wrong idea. I mean, there are aspects of this whole thing I do find humorously ironic. "Mr. Anderson *did* shoot you and kill your friend and change the course of your life. But you were going to do the same to him, am I right?"

I didn't like having that pointed out to me. "And what's yo' fuckin' point?"

"Mr. Hill, I am a great believer in karma and God. You were going to kill Wade Anderson that night, and he managed to strike preemptively in a two-on-one situation. Was he dressed in his gang colors that evening?"

"No, but—"

"Okay, he came into that liquor store to purchase goods and probably would have left peacefully if you and your friend weren't there, and no one would have cared. As sorry as I am about what happened to you in that situation and how it changed your life, as I see it, Mr. Anderson was just defending himself."

I didn't like Furtado's take on it at all, probably because he was right.

"God gave you a second chance, Mr. Hill. This is also why, at that last moment before attacking Mr. Anderson this time, you saw what you were about to give up. I understand from the moment he pulled his pistol, you simply did what you had to do."

I nodded in grim satisfaction. He was finally saying something I could warm up to.

Furtado stared at me in silence for a moment. I was just wondering what was going through his mind when he said, "I will defend you to the utmost limits of my abilities. I think you're a good young man at heart, and I believe that if I get you out of here, you'll do something with your life."

"Yeah, well, I really feel that, at this point, I've closed a chapter on the first half of my life. I got a good situation. I mean, I don't know if I'm'a have my job when this is all done with, but I still got a woman I love with all my heart and a baby on the way. It's time for me to get crackin' with the second half of my life."

He nodded. "That's good, because I defend a lot of young men like yourself, and a lot of them don't deserve even a forth of my effort. Sometimes they even make me hate my job, to be perfectly honest with you. I know if I get them out, I'll only end up seeing them back here again at some point."

I shook my head vigorously. "Mr. Furtado, one thing I can promise you is that I never want to see the inside of a jail again. I just wanna start from this day like it's the first day of my life for better or worse. Hopefully, between you and the Man Upstairs, I'll have a good shot at makin' this half of my life better than the first one."

Furtado nodded with a slight smile. "Very good. Okay, let's get to work."

PART TWO:

ISRAEL

25

It usually didn't rain in the summer in Amsterdam, but on this particular July day in 1996, a storm dropped on the city like a hammer from God. Amsterdam was wracked with gusting winds and rain that, if you were unlucky enough to be stuck in it somehow, felt like hundreds of tiny fists striking your body.

That still didn't stop the tourists from pouring into the City Hall Café, one of Amsterdam's most popular coffee houses. You could go in there and order yourself a shot of beer, some marijuana (which was sold over the counter in most coffee shops in Holland), and a little something to eat and just chill out with the locals and tourists alike.

Holland has a large black population, so the golden-skinned black man sitting in the corner of the coffee house didn't really attract any undue attention for just being black, but he did turn heads for being an attractive physical specimen. Something about him radiated confidence and power, though he didn't try to put on any kind of image. Even sitting, he looked to be no more than five eleven, maybe six feet tall, but he had a strong, taut physique, pure power and definition in the upper musculature, a slim waist, and legs that were not too long. But if you could see them through the baggy blue jeans he was wearing, they were just as powerful-looking as his upper half.

He had huge keen eyes that were slanted at the edges, a slightly upturned European-looking nose, and lush sensual lips. His hair was cut neatly into a short afro. His face was boyish, but still, something about it radiated pure manliness.

He was having a cup of coffee and just reflecting on his life. It was fairly noisy and festive, but to him it was as if the place was silent, he was so deep in his own mind. His focus and concentration were far beyond the norm.

His cell phone rang in his pocket. He pulled it out and answered, "Dag?"

He listened for a moment. His dark brown eyes clouded over slightly; beyond that, there was no change in his face or posture at all.

He finally said, "Hoe heet jij?" He nodded after a moment. "Okay. Can you talk in English?"

He listened again for a moment. Then he said, "I need a name. Wat is de naam?

"Okay, good. You know where he lives? Uh-huh. In welke straat? Okay, you're doing fine...uh-huh…en wat is de nummer van telefoon?

"All right, listen...stay where you are, and I'll be there in exactly three hours. If I am not there, try the cell phone again. If I don't answer, try it once more in the morning." He listened for a minute and then said, "No, don't worry. Go to the hospital, but don't elaborate.

"Yes, I promise. And I never break my promises."

He hit the end button on the cell phone and put it back in his pocket, sighing deeply. He left a little tip on the table and got up and left the restaurant, his mind already fixed on his destination and filled with dark purpose.

26

"Tell me about it again!"

They were seated on a leather sofa in the living room of a flat near Amsterdam's famed Milky Way nightclub. The television was on, but they weren't really watching it. They were smoking a potent combination of hashish and weed from a huge bong on the coffee table.

Matthias, the huge bald, black man smiled. He'd just taken a particularly potent toke on the bong and felt like he was floating on a cloud. He stretched out his thick, chiseled arms until little pops and cracks sprang from them, and then he locked his hands behind his head. He said in his thick, rich baritone voice, "What are you talking about?"

Bastiian, the white fellow seated on the sofa next to Matthias, who was about as skinny as the black man was huge, laughed and said, "Tell me again about the girl, you fool! You know what I am talking about!"

Matthias chuckled sleepily. "Ahhhh yes, the giiiiiiirl." He looked over at Bastiian and furrowed his brow. "What girl?"

They both broke out into a raucous fit of laughter.

"Okay, fine, you black bastard," Bastiian said, still chuckling. "*Don't* tell me again. I suppose it was good enough hearing the story the first time around. I should probably just go on home anyway."

"No, I'll tell you," Matthias said, smiling. "I just enjoy having a bit of fun with you, that's all."

"All right, so on with it then."

"Well, as you know, the girl and I worked at the furniture store together a few blocks away from here. She did sales and also gave me the orders for deliveries. She was always such a haughty bitch, she used to piss me off—always looking at me like I was piece of black trash."

The cordless phone on the coffee table rang. Matthias growled, "Shit, who the hell is this calling at…?" He checked his watch. "One in the fucking morning?"

He picked up the phone and clicked it on. "Who the fuck is this?"

Bastiian jumped a little. Most of the time, Matthias's demeanor was cool and calm. Although they'd known each other since they were in kindergarten and were the best of friends, Matthias's occasional mood swings still gave him the chills sometimes.

There was no voice on the other end of the line. After a second or two, there was a click and a dial tone.

Matthias stared dumbly at the phone for a moment, then clicked it off and set it back on the coffee table beside the bong. He started loading up a bowl as he asked Bastiian, "Where was I?"

"The bitch thought you were a black piece of shit."

Bastiian said the line with such gusto that Matthias had to laugh. "Yeah, she thought I was a black piece of shit. But you know how a lot of you white people are. You look at me, I just look like a giant of a black freak to you. You don't care how it makes me feel when you stare at me in fear. It makes me want to give you a *real* reason to be afraid."

Bastiian didn't mind his friend venting. He was only telling the truth. Often, when the two of them hung out together, they were quite a site. Both were men almost an even six feet, six inches but it was even more of a trip, because he was so pale and rail thin and Matthias was this ebon hulk of a man. He was often regarded with fear, and if you knew him you *would* have a reason to be afraid. But Bastiian also didn't think it was fair that people assumed they should be afraid because of how he looked.

"So," the black giant continued, "I'm working with this bitch, and maybe a month or so ago, I see this other colored boy pick her up from work. A real pretty boy, a yellow bastard who thinks his shit doesn't stink, because he can get all the finest white women he wants. I can tell they're a couple. The little cunt is acting too happy to see him.

"I don't see the guy too much, only sometimes. He picked her up the day I first saw him because her car was in the shop. I don't know why, but I would get pissed off dealing with her from that point on because of him. He was some kind of hero to her, the pretty fuck. I was just this big freak who worked under her like what the Americans call a 'field nigger.'"

Matthias paused to hit the bong. He inhaled deeply and felt almost as good as he did when he was with the girl earlier that night. He laughed inwardly, knowing that Bas just wanted him to get to the good part right away. He enjoyed stretching the story out as he had the first time he told it. To him it made the climax all the more exciting and delicious.

As he passed the bong over to Bastiian, he continued. "I started following her home, watching her. I thought I would just do it once to see where she lived, but it became a weird game for me to do it every day. I was so insignificant to her that she didn't even know I'd been watching her for a month, seeing her nightly rituals, even creeping up to her bedroom window to watch her undress for bed sometimes."

"How did she look naked?" Bastiian asked, plumes of dope smoke rolling lazily skyward from his slightly parted lips and nostrils.

"Like an angel. She reminds me of the American actress Cameron Diaz, except she's a little thicker in the tit and the ass and has brown hair, not blond. She had the sweetest looking little pussy, too."

Something about the way Matthias said this made Bastiian get an erection. He had seen the woman one time, when he'd come to his friend's job to take him out to lunch. Now he wished it was him that had been spying on her, seeing her treasures openly with her completely unaware. But that was the way their relationship had always worked. Matthias always did the things Bastiian would never dream of doing, and he would be the faithful listener to his exploits.

"So what then, Matthias?"

"I saw that the boyfriend did not live with her. The bitch's mother often stopped by and sometimes spent the night, but essentially she lived alone.

"So today I'd decided I'd had enough following. It was time to do something or leave it alone.

"As usual, I followed her home. As she opened the door to enter her apartment building lobby, I came from behind and pushed her in. Oooh, you should have seen the look on her face when she turned around and saw my black ass! She wasn't smart enough to be scared yet. She was too much the haughty bitch still as she asked what I was doing there.

"I pulled out a hunting knife I'd purchased the week before. That thing is a work of art, a pure oak handle with a ten-inch blade. It was delicious to see the expression on her face when she realized that the tables were turned. I thought my cock was going to burst out of my pants, it was so hard.

"I made her take me to her apartment. I was so excited that when she opened the door, I pushed her in, shut the door, and started immediately ripping off her clothes. She tried to fight me, but it was like a gnat trying to fight an elephant.

"I forced my big cock in her little tight pussy, and I couldn't control myself. It was only a minute before I came. I shot every drop inside of her. She was still fighting me and cursing loudly, so I had to duct tape her mouth. As soon as that was done, I was hard again and ready for more."

"Why didn't you duct tape her limbs too?"

Matthias looked at Bastiian with scorn. "Because I liked her kicking and thrashing and fighting me. I don't want to fuck a rag doll just lying there; I wanted her to feel my hatred of her and her fucking snobbery. I wanted her to try to fight me and know that there was nothing she could do, that she was in my power, and that I could do anything I wanted."

All Bastiian could say was the same thing he said when he'd first been told the story: "Wow."

"I fucked her tight, sweet little pussy and came three times, total. By the last fuck, she'd pretty much given up on fighting me, so that took the fun out of it. I got up and told her I knew where she lived and that if she told anybody, I would most certainly kill her. I gave her a taste by working her over a little. I think I might've broken her pinky on her right hand. I am certain at least I dislocated it."

Bastiian took another bong hit. He was evenly divided between awe and fear of his best friend. After blowing out smoke, he asked, "How do you know she won't report you?"

"If anything, she'll call asking for more of my huge black cock!" Matthias laughed dismissively. "She won't call anyone. She was too frightened, I'm sure of it."

"And if she does?"

Matthias gave Bastiian a look that told him to kill that line of conversation. Bastiian knew that look well and quietly let it go. His friend had done so much and never gotten caught, and he was quite sure that he probably wouldn't be this time either. Sometimes he hated Matthias's cockiness and surety as much as he envied it.

Matthias got up and stretched. He yawned. "I have to take a shit. Why don't you load us up another bong hit? Then I'll probably go to bed. I have to get up early for work tomorrow." He guffawed and added, "I can't wait to see that bitch's face at work. She'll probably have to wear dark glasses, unless she takes the day off."

As he walked down the hallway to go to the bathroom, Bastiian quickly loaded up the bong. He fired it up and took a good pull. Blowing out smoke like a dragon, he let himself sink back in the couch, wishing he didn't have to go home so late—and in the rain to boot. He considered asking Matthias if he could just sleep there for the evening.

A soft knock came at the front door. Bastiian thought he was hearing things; he thought the origin of the sound might be from the storm roaring outside. But then came another knock, a little louder this time.

Bastiian suddenly wondered if it was the police. Who else would be at the door for Matthias so late? He suddenly felt a stab of fear as he got up and went to the door to check through the peephole. If it were the police, he would quickly go warn his friend so he could escape while he stalled them.

He looked through the peephole. It wasn't the police; it was just another ordinary-looking black man. Bastiian said through the door, "Who are you? What do you want?"

"I'm here to make a delivery for Matthias," said the man in a friendly voice. "My delivery is both brown and green, you know what I'm saying?"

Bastiian smiled. Leave it to Matthias to have his drugs delivered to him. As he unlocked the door to open it, he was simultaneously trying to figure out a way to take a pinch off Matthias's incoming stash so he could have a little something to smoke at home tomorrow.

As he began to pull the door open, it suddenly flew open so hard that he went flying right over the coffee table. His trajectory knocked the bong over and it shattered on the hardwood floor, sending cloudy water and glass in all directions.

The man who was smiling through the peephole was not smiling at all as he walked in and closed and locked the door. He was much shorter than Bastiian, but the man was built like a warrior, and Bastiian could already sense that in a violent confrontation, he would have no chance. The man's face was stony, but Bastiian could feel rage and hatred pouring out of him as if from a running tap. He tried to get up to run, but the stranger moved as fast as a ghost. He was at Bastiian's side that quick, grabbing him by the arm and pulling him to his feet with one hand as if he were lifting a baby.

The man looked Bastiian in the eye and said in a low voice, bubbling with menace, "Please call your friend out here."

Bastiian suddenly knew, as if a vision had appeared out of nowhere in his brain. "This is about the girl, isn't it?"

The man pressed a nerve in Bastiian's forearm that sent a bolt of pain through his whole body. He moaned and felt like he was about ready to piss on himself.

"I said, please call your friend out here. If I have to ask you again—"

That was all he needed to hear. "Matthias. Matthias!"

"What is it?" said Matthias from down the hall. "I told you I'm shitting, I'm not done yet!"

"Um, Matthias, you've got a visitor. He wants to see you now."

There was silence for a moment, then the baritone booming. "Who is it this late? What do they want?"

Bastiian looked at the man, waiting to find out what he had to say next.

He grunted, "Tell him it's about Gerda Shultz."

"He says it's about Gerda Shultz!"

The only sound came from the rain pelting the apartment exterior and the rest of the world. Then, there was the sound of the toilet flushing. A moment later, Matthias strolled casually into the living room and was momentarily surprised.

"You're Gerda's boyfriend, right?" He sniggered. "The pretty boy. I guess by now you must know what happened."

The man said nothing, nor did his stony expression change. But Bastiian felt the man's grip tighten on his arm ever so slightly.

"I just took a shit, pretty boy," Matthias said with a wicked grin. "I looked down and you know, I still have your little white bitch's blood and pussy juice on my cock." He laughed, grabbing his crotch. "I must say, it was the best piece of ass I've had in a long time."

The man looked at Matthias calmly and said, "I bet you can't get it up with a girl the normal way, can you?"

The smile disappeared quickly from the ebon brute's face. "What the hell did you just say to me?"

"You heard me. I don't repeat myself."

"You're not from here. I hear an accent. Where are you from, pretty boy?"

"Don't change the subject. I think you're impotent with women. Rape is probably the only way you can get laid, isn't it?"

Matthias was boiling into a rage. Bastiian could see it. But he could also see that his old friend somehow knew this stranger was no one to be trifled with. Anyone that would dare to speak to Matthias like this would normally have already been dealt with viciously. He'd seen that happen more times over the years than he could count.

"Yes," the stranger continued, his voice faraway as if he were thinking aloud, "I think you're an impotent little bitch, unless yor're forcing your ugly ass on someone. But see, the only problem is that today you picked the wrong woman to rape.

"Gerda is someone special to me. You left her like old trash for her mother to find. She was barely breathing. If her mother hadn't happened to have dropped in, I do think she'd be dead by now."

The stranger looked at Bastiian. "Makes you wonder how many other women your friend here has raped and murdered, doesn't it?"

Bastiian said nothing, but it did make him wonder. He looked at Matthias with something akin to shock, but he was also partially disgusted with himself. Even if he hadn't tried to kill the woman, what he did to her wasn't right, nor were a lot of things that his old friend discussed with him. Yet he embraced and endorsed him.

"Do you know what your friend did to my poor little Gerda?"

Bastiian was afraid to lie to him. "Yes…yes, I know."

"Had you any plans to report him to the police?"

"No. No, I…"

"This isn't the first time your buddy has done something like this, is it?"

"Bas, keep your mouth shut!" Matthias bellowed.

It was too late for that. Bastiian was looking directly into the stranger's peering eyes. It was like a dark well in there, a place he could not hold secrets.

"No, Matthias has done this before and much more. It never went this far though. And he is my best friend, the most longtime one I've ever had. He's looked out for me too, he has good in him."

The strange man chuckled with genuine amusement. Bastiian and Matthias looked at each other in wonder, startled.

The stranger looked the big black man in the eye. "Your name is Matthias Norton. Gerda told her mother your name before she passed out. Her mother found your name and address in a phone book. She was going to turn it over to the police, but I told her not to do that, that I would take care of everything. I promised her that. And I never break a promise."

Both Bastiian and Matthias knew that the time for talking had come to end. As they both thought it, a burst of thunder roared outside the apartment.

The strange man smiled, and said, "Matthias, I think I'm going to show you what you're in for. I'll use your friend here for my example."

"What?" Bastiian cried out, now struggling to escape the man's vise-like grip. "But I did nothing. I did nothing!"

Matthias watched in shock as the man spun Bastiian around like a top. He heard a series of thuds and cracking noises, but the stranger was moving so fast that he could not see what was going on.

When Bastiian hit the floor not even three seconds later, his left arm was broken, the bone sticking out of the skin of his fore-arm, his nose was a pulpy red mess, his right shoulder was clearly out of its socket, and his jaw was dislocated, a mixture of bubbled spittle and blood dripping to the floor. His eyes were rolled up in his head with the sudden shock of intense and widely distributed pain.

Matthias suddenly felt fear. He could count on one hand how many times in his life he'd felt that emotion. He outweighed this stranger by probably eighty pounds and had a good six inches on him, but he instinctively knew this was the most dangerous man he had ever encountered in his entire life. He suddenly wished he'd never met Gerda Shultz.

The man was still smiling, but the smile was dark and full of hate. "Matthias Norton, I want to introduce myself to you. My name is Israel Baylock. I am the man who's going to use his naked hands to cause you a great deal of pain. I'm going to hurt you in new and exciting ways you could not, in your wildest imagination, come up with, and when it's no longer amusing or feasible for me to keep you alive, I'm going to kill you. Would you like to make peace with God now?"

Matthias knew this man was not bluffing. He screamed and charged, hoping that he could catch the man by surprise and take advantage of the height/weight difference. He couldn't.

After a while he gave up on trying to fight back and, broken up and bloodied, begged for the stranger to let him live. His request was ignored as the foreigner with the strange name continued to work on him.

Not much later, he begged for the stranger to kill him. This one request was granted.

27

After Israel fulfilled his promise to Gerda Shultz's mother, he went to see her at the hospital. He had a little BMW motorbike that wasn't very fast or powerful, but he got there in fifteen minutes. He quickly parked and ran inside, almost knocking over an old woman as he boarded an elevator.

When he got to Gerda's room, her mother, a handsome woman who had clearly been the donor of her daughter's fine looks, was standing outside the door crying. She looked up, the question in her eyes.

Israel nodded and said quietly, "It's taken care of."

Mrs. Shultz nodded. But her mood didn't seem to change.

He asked her in Dutch, "Is Gerda...is she...?"

Her mother began to wail hysterically and fell into Israel's arms. He held her, and she sobbed and asked God why such a thing should happen to her baby. *Why?* She said a few more things that Israel could not understand, even with his proficiency in the language of the land. He knew nothing could be said to ease her aching heart, so he just kept quiet, held Mrs. Shultz, and tried to ignore the salty waterfalls burning trails down his own cheeks.

After a while, he went in to look at Gerda. She looked as if she had not left this world in peace. Her swollen and bruised face was locked in a permanent grimace. Her nose had been broken, and there was dried blood all over her face. This was a scene he was familiar with from a time in his past, and it hurt him to see her like this.

Closing his eyes, he wished he'd given Matthias Norton another couple of hours of pain before he'd killed him.

He walked out of the room stunned. Mrs. Shultz was sitting nearby, her head bent. He put his hand on her shoulder and she put her hand on top of his.

"Oh my poor heart," she moaned quietly. "Ten years ago, I lost my husband, Ferdie, to cancer. Five years ago I lost my son, Mikel, to a heroin overdose. I thought my heart would break losing both of them, but Gerda was my hero in those trying times. She never let those losses break her, and she helped me when she might've been dying inside too. Now all I have left is Mikel's son."

"Yes," Israel said. "Gerda told me you'd taken him in after Mikel and the boy's mother started using drugs full time."

"I did, and that boy is the joy of my heart. He is seven, and so bright and precocious. He's the only reason I will wake up tomorrow and try to keep going."

"Where is he right now?"

"My neighbor is watching him. You know, that boy and Gerda bonded hard. I don't know how to tell him she's gone. Ooooh, it is going to break his little heart. He's already had enough suffering in his young life."

She leaned into Israel's waist and began to cry again. He didn't know what to say or do. No one he'd ever known had died before. He wondered if his mother had been like this when his father had died.

He let Gerda's mother cry some of the pain out, then he knelt beside her and lifted her head so that their eyes met. Her eyes were watered but focused on him.

"Mrs. Shultz, I am going to have to leave Amsterdam. What I did to the person that hurt Gerda…well…uh, it was quite messy."

Mrs. Shultz smiled the only smile she would give for a long time as she said, "Good."

"Well, yeah, but here's the thing. There was someone with him, and I dealt with that person too. And I was too emotional to be as careful as I would have liked. Maybe the police might be able to link it to me, and maybe they won't. At any rate, I can't take that chance. I haven't seen or talked to my mother and my sister in almost ten years, and this makes me think I'd better take the opportunity to go see them now."

Mrs. Shultz wiped her tear-filled eyes and looked at Israel strangely. "You have not seen *or* talked your family in almost ten years?"

"Weeeeell, uh, actually, once I talked to them. That was about five or so years ago, I think."

This genuinely confused Mrs. Shultz. "Why not?"

"I was in the US military for some years, and then after I got out, I felt like I had some living to do. So I traveled and saw a few places and did a few things, but I ended up here in Amsterdam. Been here almost three years now."

Mrs. Shultz was still looking at Israel strangely. "You have been here three years and you could not pick up the phone and call your mother?"

He shrugged, feeling almost embarrassed now. "Uh, well, you know, I sent postcards."

"*Postcards*? Is that how they do it in America?"

"No, ma'am," Israel said with a chuckle. "I'm a special case."

Mrs. Shultz was not laughing as she looked him in his eye. "Israel, this is not a good thing you have done. Don't you know you have doubtlessly hurt your mother with this? When a child is born of your womb that you have nurtured and tried to give the best life to that you could, it is a knife in your heart when your child rebels against you, wants nothing to do with you."

Israel knew she was talking about Mikel. "Mrs. Shultz, with all due respect, it's not with me and my mother like it was with you and your son."

"And does your mother know this?"

"What do you mean?"

Mrs. Shultz sighed. "Israel, just think of how your mother would feel if she hadn't heard from you in ten years and something happened to you like…like what happened with my children." She took a deep breath to steel herself. "Do you know how much that would hurt her? Do you know that it might be something that she might never recover from, because she would not know why you would not contact her for so long?

"When Mikel died, I hadn't spoken to him in almost two years, out of anger. After he died, I struggled to remember the last conversation I had with him, and even back to the last time I'd seen him truly laugh and feel joy. I was easily able to recall those moments after not having thought about them in years. Sometimes it is pure torture for me, but it's all I have now. And it's not so bad, because I hold onto to the good things. But I think that I'd even deal with some of the bad just to have him back."

Israel never had thought about it like that. He suddenly felt a longing to be back with his family that was so strong, he wondered if it was something new or something he'd buried to allow himself live as selfishly as he had been.

"So, Mr. Israel, you say it may become very uncomfortable in Holland for you and that you have been wanting to see your family. Well, you need to get the first flight that you can back to America. I like you a lot. I think you were very good for and good to my daughter, but I think this thing with your mother and sister is unconscionable. You must do the right thing."

Israel nodded and said, "Okay, Mrs. Shultz. I'm going to do that."

He asked the old woman if there was anything else he could do, and when she said no, he gave her a long hug and left.

He revved up his motorcycle in the hospital parking lot. He stopped it and got off. His hand dipped in his pocket and brought out a cell phone. His eyes were locked on it for a second, then he began to dial.

There were three rings, and then an older female voice thick with sleep came on and said, "Hello?"

"Hey there. It's me."

"Well, who the hell is, *me*? Look, if you're calling for Ellena, she moved out a long time ago and you need to quit playing on my phone."

"It's me. Mama, it's me."

Silence. Then, "Israel? Baby, is it really you?"

He smiled and said quietly, "Yeah, Mama. It's me. How are you?"

His mother began to cry like a baby, huge wracking sobs like he'd just heard in the hospital from Gerda Shultz's mother. Israel was shocked for a moment but quickly realized that every word that Mrs. Shultz told him was true. He would have to make amends to his mom and Ellena when he got back to them.

"Mama, please don't cry. C'mon, please, Mama."

"Do you know that I've thought about you every day," she said, still sobbing. "Why just those fucking postcards? And where are you at right now?"

"I'm in Amsterdam, in Holland. And about the postcards… well, I'll try to explain that as best I can when I see you."

Even past the sobbing, Israel could hear the excitement in his mother's voice as she said, "When you…when you see me?"

"Yeah, Mama. Hopefully in no more than a few days, I'll be home."

28

"Aahh!"

He was in a cold sweat, his whole body moist with a thick sheen of it. His lover rolled over and looked at him groggily at first, then with a bit more awareness. His eyes were bugged, and his whole body was still tense, in disbelief that he was no longer dreaming and now awake.

"What is it?" his lover asked. "Jesus, you're dripping in sweat! That must've been some dream."

He looked at him and then sunk into his arms in a tight embrace. His lover looked at him in surprise, but held him tightly. He asked again, "What is it? Talk to me, man!"

"The demon is coming," he whispered, his mind still locked on the image of his dreams. "The demon…it…it looks like a man, but it has fur and big teeth. It destroys everything in its path. And it wants to destroy me."

His lover held him tight, not getting it. It was okay, though. Just the comfort of his loving embrace was enough.

The demon is coming for me. It wants to destroy everything I have built, then it wants to kill me. I will not let that happen. I will be ready.

29

"David. David, wake up!"

I grunted in annoyance into the receiver, still groggy. One pet peeve of mine was being startled awake by a ringing phone. Especially when the call was from someone I didn't care too much for.

"David, are you awake?"

"Gotdamn it, I am now," I snapped into the phone, trying to keep my voice down. "What the fuck do you want, Ellena?" I looked at the clock on the nightstand. "It's five in the morning It couldn't wait?"

I heard her sigh on the other end of the line but could not read the emotion behind it. I wanted to curse her as I almost always did when I heard her voice these days. If our son hadn't been asleep next to me, I probably would have.

"Dave, my brother is back in town."

This got me wide awake, even temporarily forgetting my hostility toward her. "Israel? Iz is back in town?"

I could hear the smile in Ellena's voice as she said, "Yes. He's been here for almost a day now. He wants to see you and Michael."

"Whoa! When?"

"He's thinking this afternoon, like one-ish."

"He stayin' with your moms?"

"Yes."

"Why didn't he call me himself?" The annoyance was starting to worm its way past the surprising news. "Does he know anything about what went down with us?"

"He knows we were together and that we had a child. And that it didn't work out. He doesn't know particulars. I didn't want him making any judgments."

"Well, he would'a only heard one side."

Ellena growled. I could feel I was getting under her skin. This made me feel good. A slight smile crease my face.

"Look, I gave him your address and phone number. It's on you guys now. He would've called you himself, but he and my mother are working through some things."

"All right, you done delivered yo' news. Now I'm going back to sl—"

"Hold up there. One last thing. When he comes to visit, he's going to bring Michael back with him. So pack up all of his dirty clothes that need washing and have them ready."

"Whadevah."

Ellena hung up without saying good-bye. I was smirking as I put the cordless on the nightstand. I felt like I'd won a round, which almost never happened with her since the restraining order.

I lay back down next to our sleeping son. I marveled at him as I always did. He was three years old now, a dark-skinned little prince who resembled his daddy, except for his startling gray eyes, which were really set off by his skin color, and his soft curly black hair, which grew half an inch off of his scalp.

He loved me unconditionally, which was something else quite new for me. Sometimes when Ellena would pick him up, he'd cry as if his teeth were being yanked out of his head. "Don't take me from my daddy," he scream. "Don't take me from my daddy!" I'd be caught between so many different emotions—Ellena seeing how much he loved me despite what she felt about me (and thankfully she never tried to discredit me in the boy's eyes), sadness deep in my heart because he loved someone who didn't even feel he was worthy of his love, deeper sadness because I would love to have loved my father the way Michael did me. It *did* feel good to be the kind of father that I had never had, and his love was a driving force to keep my own life stable and sane.

As my eyes closed, some part of my consciousness began to wander back in time, thinking about the only woman I'd ever loved and how it went bad.

30

I was stuck in the Los Angeles County Jail for almost a year. It didn't take them long to set up a trial date, but with courts being backlogged with cases, it was going to take that long to get to mine. My mother would not post the $100,000 bail they'd set for me. She didn't understand why I couldn't have forgotten Wade and just let the past be the past and move on.

"You had a good life," her shrill voice echoed in my head. "You didn't have to mess everything up by doing what you did. And now another man could be dead because of you. And what kind of father can you be in prison?"

My mother was also upset with me because it took me being in jail for her to find out that I had a serious relationship with someone and that she was going to be a grandmother. Against my wishes and will, Ellena and my mother became quite close. They commiserated together about me being in jail and possibly being found guilty of the attempted murder and assault with a deadly weapon charges they had against me. If they stuck, I would be doing a lot of time. They both took their minds off me by developing their own relationship together and preparing for my son's arrival.

In the County, I didn't really have any trouble. Wade succumbed to the beating I'd given him almost a month after my entry, which only added a new dimension to my already fearsome reputation that I'd brought in from prior street kills. The Bloods had it in for me, and there was no doubt that I would have to always keep one eye open, be it in the jailhouse or on the street. But for the most part, my time in the County was nothing. The worst part about it was Ellena's rejection of me.

She wrote me a Dear John that just about destroyed my whole world when I read it. She had come to visit me as often as she could in the first four months of my jailhouse vacation, but in the fifth month she sent my whole world crashing with that damn letter.

> Dear David—
>
> I never thought we'd be in a situation like this. I thought you'd left all of this behind and that I would never be the one calling or visiting you (or anyone) in jail. This is not what I wanted, and it hurts me that you're where you are now. I can't sleep right, I can't eat right, I can't even think right, and on top of that, my hormones are all over the place as the pregnancy advances.
>
> I'm about to have this baby, and I have to start doing all of the things I need to ensure that we have a good life. I am just stunned that you even went after this guy when you saw him. I know you said you had a last minute change of heart because of the baby and me, but by then it was too late. You never would have even been in that situation if you hadn't gone after him in the first place. Your thoughts should always have been on the baby and me, but maybe we haven't enhanced your world enough for you to have just let that guy be and go on with your life.
>
> I don't know how this trial is going to turn out or what is going to happen with you, but I need to start worrying solely about this child and myself. You are a grown man, you made a grown man's decision, no matter how stupid it was, and you are going to have to live with it now. Should you get out of jail okay, I will not deny you any rights to seeing the baby IF you continue to do the right things that you were before all of this mess started. I will not have my child around any gangbanging or any of that bullshit.

> I love you very much, David, but I can't continue this. I am sorry, but I have to move on. Your mother will keep me updated with everything going on with you and the trial so that I will stay in the know. Maybe I'll attend a few more days of the trial, I am not sure yet, but either way, please don't try to contact me. Ellena.

A lot of the homies had experienced being dumped by their significant others while in jail, so when I went into a funk that would last for almost a month, no questions were asked. I came to see that my destiny was to always fall short, to never fulfill my potential with anything outside of gangbanging. That was the one thing I'd never failed at—indeed, had excelled in beyond my wildest dreams. I figured that was the one thing I would be stuck doing for the rest of my life, especially since it looked like I was penitentiary bound anyway.

I went to trial after that long, slow year. I actually managed to beat the charges. I didn't expect to, and when they read the not guilty verdict on all charges, I felt like I could not move or speak. I had already been preparing in my head for them to take me away, and it was far more shocking to me that I was free and clear.

Ellena (who, to my surprise actually showed up for more days of the trial than not), my mother, and Ms. Baylock were all screaming and crying in joy. That would probably be the last time they would all be that happy for me. But at that second, I didn't know that, and it was just as uplifting to me to feel them embrace me in true and genuine love as it was for them to hear that verdict. I welcomed and accepted it as manna from heaven.

31

The day after I got out of jail, Ellena stopped by to let me see my son for the first time. She'd been paying the rent on my apartment while I was in jail. My mother told me Ellena wanted to make sure I wouldn't come running to either one of them if I actually managed to beat the charge.

I'd told Ellena in times past, before we even dreamed of having a child, that if I had a son I'd want him to be named Lucas, and she named him Michael instead but still made Lucas his middle name. I was touched by the gesture, although I wouldn't admit it because I was still angry at her.

She propped him up on a pillow on my bed. I was startled by his eyes, which were light gray. He was but a year old, and his skin had yet to get as dark as it would later. Still, those eyes looked like they were glowing against his cinnamon brown face. They seemed to take in everything, and I just thought he was the most amazing thing in the universe.

Ellena, who was seated in a chair across the room, laughed. I looked at her, feeling slightly dazed. "What's so funny?"

"You. You're looking at Michael like he was an alien or something."

I had to laugh. It was a pleasant release from the hostility that I felt. "No, it's just crazy. He looks just like me, but he's got your eyes and hair. He's like a perfect little blend of both of us. And… shit, I dunno, I think I just never expected to be a father, especially to a little baby so beautiful. He looks like the most beautiful thing in the world to me, Ellena."

"Well, he is to me. And it's funny because he reminds me a lot of Israel as a baby."

"Word? Why you say that?"

Ellena smiled. Her hair was down and flowing around her beautiful face, and she looked like an angel. I really didn't want to feel anything for her. She had a new man in her life now, some square she'd met working for Brady in New York who had even taken a job in Los Angeles for less money to be with her. She hadn't exposed the man to Michael yet, but I still felt resentful about the situation in general.

She looked dreamy as she recalled her little brother. "Israel was just a quiet baby, a natural born observer. He never cried unless he was hungry. Mama used to worry about him, but her doctor just laughed at her and told her to relax. She was just blessed with a good baby.

"I used to stare at my brother and just *wonder* at him. Mama and Daddy used to trip off of me doing that. Sometimes I would forgo playing or doing any normal kiddy stuff just to be with him, to help Mama dress him up, or watch him while he slept. He was just a special, amazing little baby, and I loved him as if he were mine.

"Michael is the exact same way Israel was—a little watcher, a little ol' man checking out the world he's going to grow into and deal with someday. I never hear a peep out of him unless it's feeding time." She laughed. "One thing about him that's different from Israel is that your son can eat. He's been wearing my poor chi-chis out!"

She was wearing a white double XL T-shirt that clearly looked as it was not up to the task of containing her considerable assets. Ellena had never been a small-chested woman to start with, but now her breasts looked like something from a Russ Meyer film.

I tried not to look at them, feeling that dormant monster in my pants stirring to life. Wanting to put my mind on something else, I asked, "Heard from your brother lately?"

Ellena looked frustrated. "He sent us a postcard from Amsterdam. I think that's in Germany or Holland or one of those damn places. He's living there right now, and he likes it. No mention of coming back here anytime soon."

"Have y'all talked to him—like, actually spoken to him over the phone?"

"No. And I don't get it. I don't know why he would not want to communicate with us. It makes my mother and me crazy. We have a million questions, but he never leaves us with any way for us to get in touch with him. Hell, there's no way for us to even let him know that he's an uncle now."

I shrugged and said, "Well, I'm sure he'll hit you guys up eventually with a call, unless something went down to where he don't wanna talk to you or your mama."

"David, believe me, I've thought about that. Asked my mom about it too. I can't think of a single damn reason he would have to be treating us like he is. Mama can't either."

She walked over and took my boy off the bed and put him in the little carrier she'd brought him in. He looked like he was drifting off to sleep. Sure enough, a minute or so later his eyes were closed and he was peacefully wheezing through his little nostrils and mouth.

Ellena picked up the carrier and set it beside the bed. I went to the bathroom, thinking that when I came out, I'd let her know that it was time to go. We really didn't have much to talk about, and I wanted to call the homey Smiley up (he'd moved out almost a year before) and see if he could get some females over.

When I came out, Ellena was laid out naked on the bed. I was so startled I actually jumped. "Whoa! What the fuck're you doin'?"

She smiled. "David, I haven't had *good* sex in almost a year. I'm really horny. I know you're probably still upset with me about breaking up with you, but I think we can forget all of that for a minute, can't we?"

I wanted to say, "Bitch, are you crazy? Fuck you. You left me at my lowest point to fend for myself, you stank-ass 'ho'. Don't think you can just throw the pussy at me and you gone just get me going like some little trick."

The problem was, I felt myself getting hard against my will.

I stared at the treasure between her legs. She was manipulating it, playing with it, sticking a finger inside were my hardness longed to be.

I tried to maintain my composure. "I thought you had a man. What's up with this shit here?"

She laughed, a teasing sound. Her eyes were burning with lust. It was almost as frightening as the power she had over me at that moment made me want her when all I wanted was to hate and detest her.

"David, am I gonna have to make myself cum, or do you want this good pussy?"

"You wanna get fucked? Okay, bitch, you are gonna get fucked!"

I stripped naked, and as I was doing so, I could see on her face that she saw the raw emotion all over mine. I was somewhere between light and dark, love and hate. When I pulled the last sock off, I jumped on the bed, and before she even realized what was happening, I jammed my penis right into the depth of her silken warmth.

Her mouth opened wide in a silent scream. I was fucking her like a beast, like I hadn't any sex in ten years. She started moaning and screaming my name and calling me a bastard as I violently pulled her hips into each of my thrusts. I was biting her shoulders and neck and pulling her hair as well.

I flipped her over doggy style and started pounding into her. Her head was hitting the headboard with dull thuds, but I didn't care at all and it didn't seem much like she did either. I could not get deep enough into her sweet pussy, and I was trying to go as far into her as I could so that she could feel every crazed, confused emotion in me raging against the walls of her vagina.

"You fuckin' bitch," I heard myself grunt as if from far away, like I was communicating with telepathy. "You fuckin' bitch. You left me but you love this fuckin' dick, don't you? Come on. Tell meeeeee—"

"Yeah, baby, I love it. Damn you, Dave, I love it, I love it, love it."

"You need this dick, huh? Come on bitch, say it!"

"I need this dick! Yes, Daddy, I need it!"

I had Ellena by her shoulders, pulling her hard into each drive of my dick into her. I could feel her body beginning to spasm as I pounded into her like a machine. She started wailing and it just seemed to fuel my lust rage even more, causing me to smack her ass hard in all that passion. She screamed, "I'm coming. I'm coming. I'm coooming!"

Her body went stiff for a second, but I still pumped away, piston-like. She was begging for me to stop. She couldn't take anymore, but I couldn't. The demon was still in me. I was flipping her over to fuck in different positions and she came at least twice more. It seemed that every time she reached her peak it made me angrier, made we want to rage inside of her harder despite the pain beginning to worm through my body in the form of tightening muscles and cramps.

I returned to doggy style and was giving it to her like it was nothing. I felt the hot sensation of cum racing from my prostate through the length of my penis. My whole body hurt now, but I was feeling good as well as I felt myself descending into ecstasy, something I hadn't felt in so long. I could feel the scream racing out of me despite the fact that I didn't want it to. I didn't want her to know that I was just as turned on by all of this as she was.

I pulled my throbbing penis out of her and grabbed her by her hair, pulling her mouth onto it. I felt the cum shooting out as she began to suck and lick the sensitive underside of my dick and rub my swollen balls. I screamed as if I were being murdered. At that point in my life, that orgasm was the most intense one I'd ever had. Ellena doubled that intensity by continually manipulating all of the sensitive areas of my dick, and I wondered dully, "How is she swallowing all of this cum? I'm still spurtin'."

When I couldn't take it anymore, I collapsed on the bed. The demon in me was gone. I looked over at Ellena, who was just as sweaty and out of breath as I was but smiling. I could not help but smile back.

"Damn, girl," I wheezed. "I see you still capable of wearing a nigga out."

"And I see you can still make me cum like nobody else." She laughed. "Goddamn you, no matter what I didn't miss about your ass, I couldn't stop missing the sex."

"Likewise. I didn't think we were ever gonna fuck again, but that sure didn't stop me from imaginin' it."

We were both starting to get our breath back. The room was growing calm and still again. I looked down at the baby. He was still sleeping in the carrier as if nothing went on, and I said in admiration, "Damn, he still knocked out. Is it normal for him to sleep that heavy?"

She smiled and rubbed my face. It was an intimate gesture I wasn't quite ready for, so I backed away from her reach casually. It didn't seem to faze her.

She sighed contentedly and said, "I told you, he's like my brother was. When he sleeps, nothing can wake him up until he wants to get up. The next time will probably be for some dinner."

I looked at her breasts. They really were huge. I didn't think it would be possible for them to get that much bigger than their normal state, but that's nature for you.

On a whim I said, "Lemme try some breast milk."

She looked at me like I was crazy and laughed. "What? You are out of your damn mind. You're kidding, right?"

I shook my head. "I am serious as a heart attack. The homies in jail was tellin' me breast milk is some of the tastiest shit you could ever have."

She laughed. "David, this is your son's food. I can't let you take food out of his mouth. No way."

"Ellena, look, you gotta be pushing damn near a triple D cup. There ain't gone be no shortage of milk for my li'l man. And I ain't talking about suckin' your titties dry. I just want a taste. Quit fuckin' around, and just give it to me."

She sighed and motioned with her head for me to go ahead. I took one of her fat honey brown nipples into my mouth and began to suck. She winced. "Gentle, be gentle. They're super sensitive right now."

I sucked the nipple for a few seconds and then backed off. I smiled. "Damn, the homies wudn't bullshittin. That shit *is* good."

She laughed and said, "Well, I know Michael sure can't get enough. He wears my titties out sometimes, and occasionally I get frustrated because I feel like I'm not giving him enough somehow."

I grunted, staring at her huge, melon-like breasts. "I don't see how he could ever drain those bad boys. If I was to judge just by the size'a yo' titties, you should have enough milk in there for two babies."

She play-slapped my arm and got off the bed. She started putting her clothes back on. I suddenly felt the anger creeping back into me. "So I guess all I'm good for is a fuck now when ya man can't give it to you right, huh?"

Ellena gave me a look that seemed to be equal parts annoyed and pitying. "David, I never said I didn't love you still, that I didn't desire you. I am just mad you made the wrong choice. I'm still in disbelief about that."

I felt my temper swell like my dick had earlier as I snapped, "I didn't have a choice, don't you understand? That nigga robbed me of everything!"

"And left you with what?" She put on her shoes and hefted the carrier. "Out of all that came us getting together—and you starting a new life—and this beautiful little baby boy, our beautiful creation together. But none of that was enough. You couldn't have simply called the police?"

I looked at her like she was stone cold crazy. "Call the police? Call the muthafuckin' police? And then what? I can't be on the set and snitchin' like a li'l 'ho', that ain't in the rule book, Ellena."

She shrugged casually. "Then we aren't what you wanted. You could have just left him be and we'd be someplace totally different then where we are today. As far as I'm concerned, you turned you back on us."

"Stupid bitch, you don't understand."

Ellena's yellow pallor went deep red. I saw anger I'd never seen on her face before as she said in a low voice close to a growl, "What did you just say to me? Did you call me a bitch? Did I hear you right?"

All of a sudden the anger I felt at her dumping me rose completely to the surface. I jumped off the bed and got in her face, screaming, "That's right, bitch! I didn't stutter, ya stupid-ass stank 'ho'. You's a bitch! Ya didn't seem to mind bein' called what you are while we was fuckin', didja?"

She said nothing, just looking me in the eye in a deep rage. I spat on the floor beside her and scowled. "Thas right, nigga. You betta not had said nuthin'. Tired'a yo' shit anyway. Get yo' ass outta my muthafuckin' apartment."

I turned away from her to get dressed. As I slipped on some pants I felt good. I had played her like I used to play some of these street 'hos I was quite used to messing with. I thought I might even have a permanent shot at the pussy again. I always thought a high-and-mighty little yellow bitch like Ellena wanted someone like me, with my true attitude. L7s weren't ever going to do it for her.

When I turned back around, Ellena had the baby carrier on the floor and a Glock pointed straight in my face. I froze dead in my tracks. I smiled at her, but her face was stony. It was completely emotionless.

"What the fuck you gone do, Ellena? You gon' shoot me? Just 'cause I called yo silly-ass the bitch you are? Is it that serious?"

Ellena said in a voice almost completely devoid of emotion, "David, I want you to listen to me and listen carefully, because I am not going to repeat myself. Six months before I met you, I had been dating a man for almost two years named Rafael. He was a cop. He was good as hell to me at first, enough for me to want to move in with him even, but in the last part of our relationship he turned out to be a real shit.

"He beat me a couple of times over nothing—some dishes that hadn't been done, me being late from working with Jim Brady. He called me all kinds of bitches and 'hos while he was doing it. After the fourth time, I stabbed his ass. And that was the last time anybody called me out of my name or laid a finger on me, and I swore nobody after that was going to do either again."

Oddly enough, I felt no fear at all. I smiled. "Well, you betta pull that trigger, cause you a bitch to me and you gone always be a bitch. You left me at the worst time in my life and destroyed me, and then you come over here today to break me off and you think that shit is gone make me forget how you did me." The smile disappeared and I looked at her with a heart overflowing with rage and pain. "Fuck you, Ellena. Fuck you."

She dropped her gun hand to her side and smiled. "I know you're still hurting. And I don't blame you. You're never gonna do any better than me. Of course you're going to call me a bitch because you're never going to get the love of a good woman like me and you are definitely never going to get this good pussy again. Damn, that's gotta hurt!"

Her words stung. I was getting afraid that I was going to hit her. "Ellena, please, just get your ass outta here. We can work out arrangements for how I'm'a see the boy later."

She put her gun in her purse and picked up the carrier again. "Fine, David. I hope that you do better for yourself than you did before me."

And with that she left.

32

I'd like to say that was the end of that, but we continued on a pattern like that for several months. She would bring my son to see me and we would more often than not end up in bed together. Each time she used me I would swear never again, but then she would come through and take off her clothes and it was right back to the usual. She had worked off her pregnancy weight within three months to prepare for her entry into the police academy so she was looking very good.

I would occasionally ask her why she kept coming back to me and breaking me off, but I would get no answer. I knew that it wasn't just the sex, but I knew also that if she'd decided not to tell me the truth I might never know it. I wondered about the square from New York and how he was dealing with it all, or if he even knew about me. I asked about this and was again greeted with no answer.

One day she came by with Michael. I played with him on my bed for almost an hour and a half, marveling at the way he had gone from being stationary, wiggling his little arms and legs like a fly in a spider web, to crawling around like an amped little crab. Ellena sat in a chair across from the bed as always, not moving. She watched us with this mysterious little smile on her face that gave away nothing.

He tired after a while and fell asleep. I put him in the carrier and went and sat at the edge of the bed. Ellena smiled and stood up, starting to remove the tight blue jeans she was wearing. I told her grimly, "Ellena, don't. Keep them jeans on."

She looked at me funny for a second, laughed, and then continued to pull the tight pants down across her luscious ass. I had in times past told her to stop, but it never deterred her.

I wasn't feeling her today, tired of her playing with me. I stood up and walked over to her. She had her pants in a puddle around her ankles. She closed her eyes, thinking that I was going to kiss her. Instead, I pushed her backward, and she fell down hard on the floor.

She looked at me like I was crazy and screamed, "What the fuck did you do that for?"

I wished I felt happy about seeing her so upset, but this day it didn't do anything for me. I sat down on the bed and said wearily, "I told you to not to take your damn pants off and you didn't wanna listen. Had to get your attention somehow."

She stood up and started pulling her pants up in a huff. She grunted angrily, "You must be out of your damn mind, putting your hands on me."

I started coming out of exhausted mode into anger mode. "No, nigga. You outta *yo'* damn mind. I love you and you don't want to be with me, but you keep coming over here throwin' pussy at me and you ain't even givin' a fuck about how it's killin' me inside."

"You should'a thought of that before you killed that man, shouldn't you have!"

I stood up so fast she backed up a little, a look of fear on her face. I screamed at her, "I'm tired of you throwing that shit at me! I made a mistake. You said you were going to stay by me. You said you were gonna stand by me!"

Ellena screamed back, "I said I would stand by you as long as you wanted to do the right thing! Killing your little gangsta friend was stupid! And it told me that you didn't give a fuck about building a new life or trying to be the man for me and my son that we needed."

I laughed harshly. "*Your* son? Bitch, whether you like it or not, that is *our* son."

Ellena looked at me with rage in her eyes and said, "That is the second time you called me a bitch. There's not gonna be a third time."

She moved to pick up her purse and I rushed her, spinning her around so that we landed on the bed. I crawled on top of her and pinned her arms down. She was momentarily shocked, but that look quickly dissolved into an expression that was completely without fear.

"David Hill, if you know what is best, you'll get your ass off of me."

"Or what, *bitch*?" I growled at her. "You cain't shoot me. As you can see, I got the upper hand. I can do whatever the fuck I want to right now."

"Oh, so are you going to take the pussy now, David? It wasn't good enough when I was offering it to you. I guess maybe it would probably turn you on to take it, jailhouse style." She smiled pure disdain at me. "I can play that game."

I got up and pulled her to her feet roughly. She gasped slightly as I pulled her so close we were nose to nose. I wrapped a hand around her throat and began to squeeze tightly.

"I said I can do anything I want. Maybe I don't wanna fuck. Maybe I'd like to hurt you like you hurt me. I cain't fuck up yo' emotions, so all I got left for yo' ass is physical pain."

"That's right, David. Do whatever you want to in front of our son," she gasped. I could hear fear in her voice, but there was something about Ellena that was resolute, ready for anything. I knew even if I did hurt her she would somehow defeat me—if not that day, then another. It made my heart ache knowing I could never get to her the way I wanted to.

I gave her a little push that sent her stumbling away from me, but she still managed to keep her balance. I turned away from her. "Get the boy and get your ass outta here. I don't wanna to hear from you unless I can set up a time to see him. And I don't want you around no more when we do spend time."

"Fuck you, David." I turned around to look at her. She was rubbing her neck. My hand made a vicious-looking print on her throat.

"I ain't bullshittin', girl. You bring him by and I'll take him back home, or I'll pick him up and bring him back to wherever you live. I don't ever want to see you again after today unless I have to."

She shook her head no and spat out, "There is no way you're gonna have unsupervised visits with my Michael. You might as well forget you even said that, even thought it."

I didn't say another word to her. She took Michael and left the apartment, cursing under her breath.

I laid back down on my bed and began to think about my life. Things were actually all right for me at that point. The homie Stuntman had gotten me my warehouse job back and it was like what happened with Wade Anderson was just a temporary distraction. I had my life back—except for the part with Ellena.

I began to think for once that maybe I could just go on with my life without her. Michael more than filled the void that losing Ellena had created—helping me to deal with losing his mother. I liked being a father, and that was maybe the second thing in my life I thought I might actually be good at. I wanted little Michael's life to be totally different from mine.

My eyes closed and I began to drift off to sleep. Despite what happened with Ellena and all the feelings I still had to deal with concerning her, I was blessed. I had nothing to complain about. Life was…well, if not good, definitely okay.

33

A week later, I pulled up from work in front of my apartment exhausted. That day had been a long one and I felt like I just wanted to get inside and collapse. The traffic coming home had been terrible as well, making my already bad mood worse. This was the only lament I had about the straight life; hustling at least afforded me my own hours and dealing with traffic or other everyday annoyances was not even a remote consideration for me.

When I got to my door, I paused. All of the exhaustion fled right out of my body and I was suddenly wide-awake and feeling like an animal.

The front door to my apartment was cracked open. I gave it a tentative push in, cursing the fates for my being unarmed. I eased my way in and quickly scanned the living room. Nothing was out of place. Everything was as it was when I left to go to work that morning.

I carefully searched the rest of the apartment. Not a shred of anything amiss at all. I began to suspect that maybe I'd left the door open when I left for work that morning.

Relieved, I went to take a piss. Just as I was starting I heard a knock at the front door. I cursed under my breath, remembering that I hadn't closed it behind me. I yelled, "Who is it?"

"Police!" came a hard yell back. "Are you the occupant of this apartment?"

"Yeah! I'm, uh, takin' a leak. I'll be right on out."

When I finished and strolled into the living room, I saw two hulking black cops standing there. One was dark as night and had a short fade. The other one was as light as the first one was black and was bald, his head clean and shining. Neither one was an inch under six feet five, nor looked like they spent a lot of time outside of the gym.

The dark cop said, "One of your neighbors said they heard a sound like someone was trying to crowbar a door open, so we're checking it out."

"Yeah," I said, feeling something was wrong but not sure what or why. "When I came home, the door was open. Don't look like nobody jimmied it, unless they used a credit card or somethin'."

"The name on the mailbox says Dave Hill," the bald cop chimed in. He had a friendly, personable manner that immediately set one at ease. "Are you him?"

"Yeah, that's me."

"Do you mind if we see some ID?" He looked almost embarrassed as he added, "Imagine if you were actually the guy breaking in here and you were just running game. Could be real messed up for us."

I didn't mind at all. I was actually happy that they wanted to see my ID. I'd come back clean as a whistle if they checked my record.

I gave my driver's license to the bald cop. He looked at it and then passed it to the other one. The other looked at it and he passed it back to me. "You're David Hill, no doubt about it."

"Yup, that's me. So what do the—"

That was all I had time to get out before the big dark-skinned cop suckered me by stepping in and throwing a roundhouse elbow. It caught me on the side of my face like a thrown brick. As I was falling, I noticed the light-skinned one closing the apartment door. I was dazed as I hit the floor hard, trying to figure out what I'd done for him to hit me.

The light-skinned cop, who I'd felt at ease with, now had a look on his face of pure animal rage. He told the darker one, "Back up off him, Paulie. He's mine."

Paulie threw me an evil grin as he backed away. "Ooooh, you're in for it now, my nigga."

I was starting to rise to my feet when the big yellow cop yanked me up. He head-butted me twice, his head striking the side of my jaw like a granite fist, and my head exploded into a thousand stars. My legs were like Jell-O, and I fell into the couch.

He hauled me up again, and I was doing my best to stand without leaning into him. To buy some time from him striking me again, I screamed out, "Wha...what'd I do? What's this about?"

The high-yellow bastard pulled me so close our noses damn near touched. He scowled. "You know who I am? I'm Sean, nigga! Sean Cudahy!"

I shook my head in complete confusion. This seemed to make him angrier. He screamed in my face, "I'm Ellena's man, muthafucka! And I don't give a fuck if y'all got a kid together or not, she's my property now. And nobody put his hands on my property."

Even though I knew it was the most stupid and dangerous thing to do in the world, I laughed out loud. The two cops looked at each other and the dark one, Paulie, said from across the room, "What's so funny?"

I gave Sean a mad-dog stare and said, "I been baggin' yo' *property* for muthafuckin' months, nigga. She been comin' *here* for the dick. Ain't even had to go to her. I just figured it must be 'cause she ain't been gettin' what she needed from home. And now I can see I was right!"

Sean's face seemed to grow huge and red with rage. Before he could go psycho on me I head-butted him as he'd earlier done me. I connected with his upper lip, which split and shot out a spurt of blood that caught me on my cheek.

Sean let me go and backed up a couple of steps and cursing and rubbing his lip. I managed to stay on my feet for the second it took for his partner to bridge the gap and get to me.

34

I'd like to say that I kicked both their big asses and ran off into the sunset like Channing Tatum or Jackie Chan or some-damn-body, but that would just be a big ol' lie. Those boys were smart though. They did just enough for me to be checked out of the hospital that same day. I was able to go to work the next day, but I must have told ten different stories as to why I was so beat up and bruised-looking. Only the homie Stuntman got the truth as we were sitting on the dock eating some cheeseburgers during the lunch hour.

After I was done with the telling, Stuntman whistled and laughed, "This broad must have some hellified super pussy."

I shook my head in a brief remembrance. "It was the best, my nigga. Not just the pussy though, but *everythang*. Never had better and I don't think I ever will."

Stuntman looked like he was thinking. He was a large man, easily as big as the cops that had served me up the night before. He had a small head that sat on that large body, the crown of it adorned with close-cropped Jheri-curls. To cap it all off, out of all that bigness came a voice that was damn near as high and squeaky as a ten-year-olds.

"Well, look at it philosophically," he finally said. "At least you got to hit it. Niggas out there gone be jockin' and lookin' at her and wantin' her an' whatnot, and you part'a that select few that got to tap it. Even had yo' seed sprout from it. Thas gotta count for somethin'."

I had to look at the homie and laugh. He had a way of putting things that in their own weird way made sense.

"You still love 'er, homeboy?"

I felt a sadness roll through me as I paused midchew. "Yeah, nigga. I still love her. If she wanted to be with my ass tomorrow, best believe I'd go for it."

"You thinkin' at all about some gitback with them two faggots that ambushed you?"

"Naw, my nigga, I'm'a just let this shit go. I cain't afford no beef with the man. I feel like my ass was lucky enough beatin' that murder charge. How I'm'a get over on the muthafuckin' police?"

Stuntman laughed. "Sheeeeee-it, my nigga. Fuck tha got-damn police. They can be touched too."

I looked at Stuntman and marveled at him. He was out of the game, living a completely legit life and staying out of trouble, but yet he wasn't. He had completely mastered the double-life that I thought I had so many years ago. He was putting food on the table for his wife and four children, but was still down to ride and had a number of low-risk hustles on the side that brought him in extra income. Yet the homies knew never to ask him for anything, just to wait and let him volunteer himself. His family was first now, not the gang, and anything he did he made sure that it stayed far away from the home he'd carefully built.

"Naw, man. I'm'a bold muthafucka, but a nigga ain't takin' no chances with the Man, yaknowwahsayin'?"

"Yeah, nigga," he said, laughing. "I was just sayin' that there's only so much shit a muthafucka can take from them fools. They know we gots rules out here, whether they on the books or not. They show they ass, we gots to occasionally spank it."

I nodded in agreement. "You right, but I'm'a just let this shit go. Ain't really that cop nigga's fault anyway. He just sprung like I was...hell, like I still am. I ain't even trippin' off'a him, really. It's *her* I'm tryna put outta my mind an' my heart."

Stuntman sighed in sympathy. "I know what you goin' through, dawg. Last time I was on a bid, my ol' lady up and left my ass. I was at Pelican Bay, and I thought without her support

I was gone die, my nigga. I dint even care about livin' no more after she cut from me."

I looked at Stuntman in surprise. It was not his MO to be so upfront about his feelings and emotions. He was a guy that liked to appear in control at all times.

"So how'd you get through it?"

"My daughter, cuz. I focused in on her. And also at the time my old lady broke it off with me she was pregnant with my oldest son. When she told me I had a boy on the way, I really wanted to zero in on jus' gettin' my shit together so I could be a man he and my li'l girl could love and respect and not no bum in and out of th' pen and not bein' able to be a real daddy.

"My daddy was a muthafucka, and I don't know or care where he is, and don't never wanta see his ass ever again. I never wanted my kids to feel that way about me."

I had thought of this in regards to my own son when I was in jail. "I feel ya on that one, my nigga."

"I focused in on a good *man*, and when I got out the pen and my woman saw the change in me and the new focus on tryna build myself a new and better life, she decided to come on back and give my rusty ass anotha chance."

I laughed bitterly. "Well, I don't think that's gonna happen with Ellena, m'man. She one'a them broads that once they give up on you, ain't no goin' back. I'm'a just have to deal with this shit as best I can and hope the feelings just disappear on me eventually."

"Yeah, I'll say a prayer for you at church tonight." That was another thing I admired about Stuntman; he was a man that had gone from believing in nothing to having God in his life. He attended church services with his wife and kids three times a week and nothing ever seemed to interfere with that schedule, legal or otherwise.

I didn't know if I believed in anything. I hadn't seen anything in my life to make me believe in any kind of higher power. It was a source of great sadness for me.

I smiled wanly and said, "Thanks, my nigga. Good lookin' out. In fact, you been lookin' out for a nigga ever since I got this job. It really saved my ass from doin' some dumb shit, havin' this gig for me when I got out the jailhouse. Appreciate it, bruh."

Stuntman blushed, and his already high voice seemed to almost break as he replied, "Aw cuz, that ain't shit. Couldn't'a really gave the gig to any of the homies out there now. A lot of them young niggas still too wild, and most of the ones my age're rottin' away in the pen or dead. Bosses liked you and dint mind having you back, and I needed the help. So you done me a favor too, don't worry 'bout it. I work with enough a these lames, it's cool havin' a soldier off the set here."

"Yeah, well, still, I appreciate it, nigga. Fuh real."

"Ain't no thang, gangsta." Stuntman threw up the set (the hand sign that represented our gang affiliation) and then took my now-empty burger wrapper from me and tossed it with his in a nearby trashcan.

"Okay, enuff jawin'. We gots to get back t'work. C'mon."

35

I went almost two weeks without speaking to Ellena, letting my body get better. I just didn't think I could talk to her without some form of anger or bitterness surfacing while the cuts, bumps, and bruises spread all over my body still healed. I missed my son and wanted desperately to see him, but I couldn't figure out how to deal with Ellena on it. I didn't want any more surprise visits from Sean or any other cop. I knew my heart, and I knew that I would not let anyone do what those two pigs did to me again without putting up a fight they might have to kill me over.

I had a restraining order served to me around this time. I felt total disgust looking at it. It was her way of letting me know that I would never see my boy alone, and at that point I didn't even want to fight it. She called me shortly after I received the restraining order and asked me in a civil and polite tone of voice about when I wanted to see my son next.

I told her I didn't really know.

She had real sadness in her voice when she said, "Dave, the restraining order—it's nothing personal. I hope you know that."

"She's just tryna get you mad," I thought. "Don't bite."

"And that thing with Sean, uh, well..." She chuckled uncomfortably. "I...I really didn't think he was going to...do what he did. I'm really sorry."

I stayed silent. Her voice grew firmer as she went on. "I told you that you would never see our son alone, and the restraining order is just my insurance. I know you won't understand, but he is my life now and I am taking no chances with you. You once told me you were done with your other life and you let it destroy ours together. I don't expect you to take your son's life or your relationship with him any more serious than you did ours."

There was a touch of venom in my voice as I struggled to stay calm. "Ellena, that ain't fair."

"I don't care. I'm not taking any chances. You're going to have to live with that."

I wanted to scream bloody murder at her. If she were right in front of me, I don't know that I would have stayed calm. Instead I just said, "Okay."

She sighed. "Good. It's settled. When do you want to see Michael?"

I thought for a second. "How about Sunday?"

"Hmm. Is around two okay? We get out of church at twelve and then your mother wants me to stop by her house first."

I absolutely hated that she and my mother got along. My mother had been so unsupportive while I was waiting for my trial, and she seemed to think it was okay that Ellena dumped me, even pushing that action. I never spoke to my mother anymore unless it was something specifically related to my son.

"Yeah, whatever, Ellena. It's all good. I'll see y'all then."

36

As time went by our relationship graduated to being decent to each other, with an occasional fight that sprung from the same old resentments. When that first occurred she happily left Michael with me and from that point began leaving him with me for overnight visits. She told me she was letting him stay overnight with me because it was right thing for her to do; I read between the lines on all that and knew that it was because she was ready to stop being a full time mom 24/7 and enjoy a day or two off.

Ellena finally did become a cop, but other than that, our lives were pretty uneventful. I began thinking about buying a house so I could rise up out of being in the 'hood all of the time. I didn't know if I wanted to bring up a kid there, even on a part-time basis. I wanted better for Michael, and the one thing Ellena and I never seemed to argue or even disagree about was what kind of future we had in mind for him. She had already bought herself a nice house in the Encino area (I suspected with Sean's help, since that wasn't the kind of area a single working mother on a policewoman's salary could afford) and I figured the best thing for me to do was to try to move a little bit closer to her direction.

The burning in my heart for her never ceased, although words between the two of us were few and usually quite caustic. Occasionally one of us would let our guard down and it seemed as if there was love there still; yet other times one of us would let our guard down, the other would take advantage of the opening and say something evil and hurtful and then we'd be back to square one for months.

I only thought of the present now, not the past. The past just hurt me and made me wonder how I could have done things differently, playing over different scenarios in my head that could've made my life better. I hadn't thought about Israel in years, and here Ellena was, calling me all excited like it was the Second Coming. I was interested in seeing his nerdy ass again, but it really held no consequence for my existence. If I saw him, I did, and if I didn't, why then I just didn't.

37

He called me later that day just as I was getting ready to take my son to the park. The phone rang several times as I was getting him dressed to leave, so I knew I was sounding a bit annoyed as I picked it up. “Yeah, what’s up?”

“Damn, is that how you answer the phone?” He laughed. “Whatever happened to ‘hello,’ or something polite like that?”

“Iz!” I was actually happy to hear his voice, happier than I thought I would be. It was deeper, older sounding in a life experience kind of way, but it was definitely my old friend.

“Dave!” He mimicked me with a laugh.

I laughed back. “Aw, fuck you, nigga!” We laughed together and I went on. “Damn, what you doin’ back here? E’erbody was about to put an APB on yo’ ass.”

Israel sounded defeated. “Please, man, I’ve been through all of that with Ellena and Moms damn near from the minute I stepped off the plane.”

“Well, you don’t just disappear outta everyone’s world for almost eight years, show up, and expect everybody just to be like, ‘Hey, Iz. Long time no see, good buddy! How tha fuck you doin’?’”

He sighed deeply. “I *know* that, Dave. But like I said, Moms and Ellena have already read me the riot act. Can I just get a break on this subject?”

“Yeah, nigga.” I chuckled, perversely delighting in his plight. “So Ellena called me earlier. She say you wanna see me and my boy.”

"Yeah, I want to see *my nephew*," he said with a laugh. "What are your plans for today?"

"Well, I been tryna get outta here to take him to the park for the past half hour, but the phone keeps ringing. After you I'm just not gonna answer so I can finish gettin' his ass ready and we can get outta here."

"Well, it's…one o'clock now. I'm free and clear for the afternoon. I told Ellena and my mom I need minute from getting beat up by them to chill. Why don't I meet you at whatever park you're taking your boy to?"

"Rancho Cienega. It's a park over in West LA, over by the Twentieth Century Fox studio. I'll give you directions there."

"Dave, don't worry, I know where it is. I used to do a lot of my training there in high school with my sifu."

My eyebrows raised at that comment. "Training with your who? Training for what? I don't remember you trainin' for nothin' back in the day except for how to try to read three books in one sittin'!"

Israel chuckled mysteriously. "We'll talk about all that when we hook up."

"Okay, well, you just said it's one now. Let's say we meet over there in about a half hour?"

"That works for me."

I described my car and what clothes Michael and I would be wearing, and then we hung up the phone.

My son, who had been in the bathroom when Israel called, came up to me pulling up his pants and said, "Daddy, was that Mommy?"

I smiled at my precious little boy. "Naw, son. That was Israel."

He looked at me strangely. "Who is Risreeuhl, Daddy?"

"That's Israel," I corrected him with a laugh. I walked him through it syllable by syllable. "He's your uncle, Mommy's brother, Grandma B's son."

"He's my uncle?"

"Yes."

"We going to meet him today?"

"That's right."

Michael jumped up and down and screamed, "Hoooo*raaaay,* I have an uncle, I have an uncle!"

"That's right, son, and we got to meet him soon. So c'mon and let's finish gettin' you ready so we can get there on time."

38

We were actually at the park for almost an hour and a half before Israel showed up. I was sitting on a bench in front of the sandbox watching Michael play when he approached. I almost didn't recognize him, I hadn't seen him in so long. I just saw this light-skinned brotha walking toward me. He who was in excellent shape, with the languid, prowling stride of a panther. I looked at him as I would look at any other brotha at that park, as there were not too many of us there. And then it dawned on me who he was.

When he got up to the bench, I stood and hugged him warmly, exclaiming, "Damn, nigga! You don't look at all like that skinny nerd that went off to boot camp all them years ago."

He laughed as we both sat down on the bench. "Yeah, remarkable what a growth spurt, a little protein, daily workouts, and contact lenses'll do for you."

I just stared at him for a second, amazed at the man sitting next to me. He looked almost nothing like the scrawny, short young boy with the old soul I'd last seen almost ten years ago.

He laughed at me. "Lord, I guess I have to go through this shit with everyone that sees me now."

"Damn skippy you do! I mean, damn! I ain't never seen nobody in my life undergo the change yo' ass has. You taller, you built *almost* as good as me, you ain't got them funky glasses on no more, your voice done gone a li'l deeper—"

"Yeah, well, I told you before I left that I was leaving to become my own man. You're looking at him now."

"So, Izzy, you got a story for a nigga? I know you prolly done told it ten million times, but you gon' have to tell it one mo' again."

"Actually, I haven't talked to anyone about all my travels at all—well, at least not in full. I gave Mama and Ellena the cleaned up *Cliff's Notes* version, but not all the sordid details."

"Sordid details, huh?" I smirked. "Well, you gon' have t'come clean on that. Start anytime you want."

"We've got all the time in the world for that. First, I want to meet my nephew."

I slapped my forehead. "Damn, homie, I'm trippin'. Michael, get over here!"

Michael bounded out of the sandbox and right into my lap. He looked into Israel's smiling face and greeted him with a smile of his own. They made an instantaneous connection that I found at once amazing and disturbing. My boy was very particular about strangers usually. I tried to tell myself that perhaps he sensed, on some level beyond reasonable understanding, that Israel was blood.

As if he'd read my mind, Michael said, "Are you my uncle Risreeuhl?"

Israel and I both laughed as I corrected him. "That's *Israel*, son. Damn, dint we just go over this a coupl'a hours ago?"

"Yes, I'm your uncle, Michael. Can I get a hug?"

Michael left my lap and went to give Israel his hug. And it was not just a casual, polite one; Michael sunk into his uncle's embrace as if he knew this was a man who would always protect him and look out for him just as much as his mother or I would. It was really like watching bonding at some sort of unconscious genetic level.

"Mike, you're gonna come with me to go back to your mom's house later," Israel said, talking to the boy like he would an adult. "You cool with that?"

Michael nodded, a big dopey smile on his face.

"Okay, son, time to go back and play in the sandbox," I said, both anxious to hear Israel's tales of his years abroad and because

I felt a tinge of jealousy at how he had taken to his uncle with no resistance at all.

"Okay, Daddy," my boy said, climbing down from Israel's lap. "See ya soon, Uncle Israel."

Israel had a big smile on his face as Michael dashed off to the sandbox. He said dreamily, "So that is the next generation of Baylock. Wow."

I was a little disturbed by that comment, although I knew in my heart Israel meant not one shred of harm by it. The Baylocks were a close-knit group, and Michael was heralded by his mother, grandmother and now his uncle as a sort of second coming. I understood all that, but sometimes it irked me that I had to share him with his mother and grandmother (in addition to my own mother) and that they would bond with him as a family in a way that I couldn't. The Baylocks were united over Michael, while it seemed my mother and I would always be at odds, tempered by the fact that since Michael was born she cut out all her old behaviors, marrying a deacon at her church and completely changing her lifestyle like I wished she would have when I was a child.

"Okay, you and the boy got that long drive to Encino when you take him back to his mom's house. You can bond with him then. I wanna hear about you, all these years gone by."

Israel shook his head as if he were coming out of a trance and hadn't even heard me. "Dave, that little boy is a miracle. That is what it's about. Looking at him, I feel like I wasted over half my life, and I don't even know why."

I looked at him like he was crazy. "Israel, you lost me there, bruh. You wanna go back and fill me in on the part I missed?"

Israel sighed and closed his eyes. He was so still for a moment that it seemed all time in his immediate vicinity had stopped. I got the chills looking at him, wondering not just who he was but what he was now.

When he opened his eyes, he said, "It's kind of funny we're meeting at this park here. For me, this is where part of my life truly began. I used to train here weekends with my sifu—my martial arts instructor."

"Enough with the riddles, man. Get on with it!"

"Okay, well, it all started the day I whupped you and Philly Phil's asses."

39

This is the story he told me, in his own words:

I was feeling numbed by the whole thing. I had never been in a confrontation that violent before. My mother basically inspired it—she told me the day you guys messed with me that if I let y'all get away with it that one time, you would continue to get away with it, and it would encourage others. She said I had to at least try to get back at the two of you to show I had heart.

After it had all gone down and the adrenaline rush passed, I made my way home like I was sleepwalking. I didn't feel the pain of Phil's ass whuppin' until much later. My neighbor, Mr. Chin—you remember him, the old Chinese dude that lived just to the left of us—anyway, he saw me and took me into his house to help clean me up.

As we sat in his kitchen, him applying a poultice to my swelling face, he asked me to tell him what happened. I did, from the time you tripped me at school up to our confrontation that morning. He laughed at the end of the story, saying, "Good for you, young man. I suspect it will be a long time before anyone dares to challenge you again."

We had known Mr. Chin as long as we'd lived there, but beyond a brief hello, we'd never really spoken. He treated me like an equal in his kitchen that day, and I stayed there with him until six in the evening. He told me that he too had been a small, slightly built boy and that his uncle had started teaching him a martial art called toi li ho that had been in their family for generations so that he would never have to worry about being picked on. He told me he'd lost only one fight his entire life, had suffered a draw in maybe six of them, and as he told me his life story, I thought that was a pretty good record. Mr. Chin had been in a lot of fights in his life.

He told me he would like to have passed his martial art on to a son. He actually had been married when he was in his twenties, but his wife and two young sons had been hit and killed by a drunk driver. He cursed the world and almost left America, but he knew somehow his destiny was here so he stayed in the country.

I told him I wished I were his son so he could pass his art onto me, and he exploded on me. He told me I had a father and that I should always respect him, even in death. He made me feel guilty as hell that I'd said anything, but he still told me that if I wanted, he would instruct me on some fighting basics and see how it went from there.

I let my mother know what was going on, and she didn't seem to object. She and Mr. Chin had a good relationship after he'd once recommended some herbs that seemed to quell these migraines she kept having after my father's death. So every day after school, I went to Mr. Chin's house and he showed me a few little moves that I picked up with no problem at all. And on weekends and days I didn't have to go to school, we came here to this very park.

When he noticed how quickly I was taking to his teachings, he began to show me the real stuff. We moved from beyond just unarmed combat training into weapons. He taught me not only traditional weaponry but advanced me to certain concepts that allow one to make a weapon out of almost anything, even a simple piece of paper. He taught me how to breathe properly, how to meditate and clear my mind, how to tap into that part of my consciousness that translates thought into immediate action. These things were just as important as the actual moves he taught me. This is what separated me from most of these guys going to these dojos paying a monthly fee and learning whatever. He was grooming me, sharing everything he knew with me, which was quite a bit.

By the time we got to high school I was proficient enough to take on most adults, never mind a kid my age.

I heard what happened with Wade Anderson, with him killing one of your friends and shooting you up and you getting revenge on him. Sometimes I wonder if it could have all been avoided it if I had just taken care of things myself that day in the hallway at Hamilton. I was so adept at the simple violent stuff that I could have beaten ten unarmed Wade Andersons. Of course, you had no way of knowing that, David. You stepped up to the plate to stick up for me, and that endeared me to you, even to this day.

By that time I had moved beyond physical combat to the more complex areas—self-hypnosis, body control (and this is in regards to inner-body control, areas such as slowing your heart rate, controlling your body temperature and so on), and things of that nature. Learning to utilize all of my senses to their full potential. Now mind you, I hadn't mastered any of this stuff—not even close to it. Mr. Chin had to first conceptualize them to me and know that I completely understood the concepts before he took me to that next level. He said I was a much better student than he ever was, and he even once ventured to hint that he would have hoped his son would have been someone like me. That happened here at this park. We had many training sessions here, many discussions about so many different things.

The only disagreement Mr. Chin and I ever had over something was my decision to enter the military. He was just as much against it as everyone else. His personal feeling was that going into the military was a fine, just, and honorable thing to do if there was a war going on or even the threat of a war. Beyond that, he thought it was a fool's decision. But David, as you yourself know, I knew what I wanted, and not even the will of this great man could alter my destiny.

I was actually a little nervous about the marines, but that turned out to be a breeze. Four months in, I shot up to the height that I am now, from five feet four to five eleven. Coupled with the regimen they had, I was actually even bulkier and more cut up than I am now. I stayed that way all during the time I was in the marines, a little fascinated myself that I could go from being such a scrawny kid into such a completely different young man, but as soon as I got out, I trimmed down to a weight that was much more suited to the things I'd be getting into next.

Why do you want to know more about the military years, Dave? They were boring to me, straight up. I excelled at everything. They saw my potential and had me do everything from radar work to driving tanks, and it was all a breeze. As far as the physical stuff, I was the best at that too, even sharpshooting—and that's with or without my glasses on. I knew I could take the guy teaching self-defense unarmed in my sleep. I was so good that folks started approaching me about drafting me into special forces—even insinuated that they would force me to do that shit. But I managed to worm my way out of it. Being in the marines served a certain purpose for me, and I knew by my second year that I'd had enough of it. I actually forced them to give me a dishonorable discharge at that point because I knew I was just wasting time there.

I kept in contact with Mr. Chin the whole time I was in. When I got out, he knew I was hungry for more of what he knew. He advised me not to come back to him but to go to India and connect with a yogi there named Satswanda. Mr. Chin's only contact with him was that he knew this man charmed cobras all day sitting on a corner in a hill town called Almora. He received an annual letter or call from Satswanda, but he never knew at what point either of those would come.

I tracked Satswanda down, and he knew Mr. Chin had sent me. To this day, I don't know how, but he did. Almora is a beautiful hill city, one of the most calming places in India, so we had a lot of wide-open space on that mountain range to work with. He taught me real yoga—how to go so far deep into myself that the effect was like dropping a hit of acid. It was like a whole new level of consciousness. This time with him was the culmination of the inner body/spiritual control that Mr. Chin had started me on in the States.

I stayed there for almost two years. My final test before I moved on with him was curing myself of a deadly cobra bite. Satswanda himself had showed me this little trick after my first year of being there. He let himself get bitten by a cobra once a year so that he could continue to keep his skills sharp in this area.

Once bitten by the cobra, you let the venom ride you into a deep state of meditation. There you begin to…what is the easiest way I can put it…find the center of each of your seven chakras, energy centers correlating to major nerve ganglia branching forth from the spinal column. Essentially, you flush the poison out of your system and heal yourself using your own mind to completely manipulate your inner body. The whole process takes about eight hours or so, depending on your mastery of it.

This process was no fun, but I did it. I knew once I got through it that this was something I would not be doing on a yearly basis. Satswanda sent me on my way, warning me that he felt that I still had one foot trapped in this world and one in the world that people like him and Mr. Chin live in. He said eventually I would have to make a choice or risk being stuck in the middle, which would cause me emotional or physical destruction, perhaps both.

I met with some of Mr. Chin's people in China and spent a few months there training and working out with them. After all that, I just had a desire just to travel for a few years and that is what I did. I didn't feel any connection with home after all the incredible things I was seeing and doing, so I think on an unconscious level I kept my contact with everyone here to a bare minimum as not to have to worry about what effect my not coming back would have on you guys. I eventually ended up in Amsterdam and decided to stay there for a minute. I, uh, got into a bit of trouble there and decided I didn't want to chance going to prison there and never seeing you guys here again. So I came back.

I believe that brings us up to date.

40

I was slack-jawed. Israel burst out laughing at the expression on my face, and I knew that if my skin tone were any lighter he would have seen me go completely red.

"Well, what do you expect, fool?" I asked him, slightly annoyed. "You're tellin' me essentially you went off after high school to become that nigga Caine from *Kung Fu.*"

Israel shrugged. "I guess you could look at it like that."

"So you sayin' you can like, kick anyone's ass?"

Israel laughed, shaking his head. "I'm saying that I know a lot of shit, but as bad as one person is, there's always someone out there that can take him."

"Naw, nigga. Sounds to me like you sayin' ain't too many people out here could fuck with you."

Israel shrugged again but this time said nothing. That was all the answer I needed.

"So wait—let me back up a coupl'a steps here. I'm still tryna absorb all this shit. You said you left Amsterdam cause'a some trouble."

"Yeah."

After a moment of silence I asked impatiently, "Well, Iz? What kinda trouble?"

He smirked. "From what I understand, it's the kind of trouble you know all about these days."

I smirked back at him. "Nigga, please. I don't know what your sister has been tellin' you about me, but I been clean as a new bar'a soap for a hot minute now. Back in the day, weeellll…

"But I'm gettin' off the subject. What happened that you had to leave Amsterdam?"

Israel sighed, knowing I wasn't going to leave it alone. "There was a Dutch girl I was seeing over there, but I wasn't quite ready to settle down so we broke it off. We stayed friends though, and it looked like we were even headed toward getting back together again. But then she was raped and murdered."

"Damn, man, I'm sorry."

Israel seemed to ignore my comment. "Her mother, who I was also close to, found her as she was dying. She told her mother the name of her murderer and Moms managed to find out where the guy lived. I told her mother not to talk to the police about it, that I would take care of it. And I did."

I decided to leave it at that. I really wanted details, but an old code of the streets that I still held near and dear to my heart was that if a man didn't want to tell you his business, that was that. Still, even though my old friend was clearly a different person now it was hard for me to imagine him involved in the kind of dirty stuff I'd become used to years ago.

"Well, I guess that brings us up to what the hell you gone do with yourself now."

"At this point, I really don't know. This wasn't really part of the plan. I'm gonna stay with Mama for a few days, meditate *a lot* to get some clarity, and see what answers are revealed to me."

I looked at him strangely, as if he'd spoken some foreign tongue to me. He saw the expression on my face and laughed, and I play socked him in the arm.

"Man, I wish I could just lay up at my mom's house and seek clarity," I said with a joking smile. "Must be nice. Some of us got bills to pay an' shit. Hey, Mista Globetrotta, you know what a bill is?"

Israel laughed. "Fuck you, Dave. And for your information, it *is* gonna be nice not having to worry about bills and just lay up and do nothing. Now what?"

"Shit, now nothin', 'cept I wanna come and live with y'all and not pay bills either."

We both laughed heartily. It felt real good being with my old friend, and it made me realize that outside of the homie Stuntman I really didn't have any male friends I felt totally relaxed and comfortable being around.

We talked of some of the places Israel went and what the people and basic cultures were like. My son continued to play and then eventually came and sat on my lap, resting his little head against my chest. Israel continued to talk, his tone of voice casual as he described his travels in such rich detail that I could almost visualize them as if I'd been there instead of him.

Eventually we said our good-byes, and my son left with his uncle. I watched them get into the jet-black Suburban owned by Ms. Baylock and drive off. I stood there thinking for a moment thinking about the rich strangeness of life and then I got in my own car and left.

41

Israel and I began hanging out. Sometimes he would come over and we'd just rent some movies, drink a little liquor, smoke some weed, and just chill. Sometimes we would head out to clubs and picking up on women by tag team (we were quite a handsome pair together, and more often than not, they came to us instead of the other way around). And sometimes he would join me in hanging out with the homies on the set. Although Israel was an outsider, a lot of the homies had grown up with him, and they were cool with him being around. And something about him still radiated danger and power, which all of us were fascinated with on a level that none of us spoke about.

He once again became my closest friend. I even got Stuntman to hook him up with a job working in the accounting department at the warehouse. He asked me once about Ellena and myself, and I told him that I'd just as soon not discuss his sister or even have her name uttered in my presence, unless it had something important to do with Michael. He respected my wishes on that one and that only strengthened the bond between us that already existed.

We didn't talk too much about Israel's time away anymore. He seemed to be sinking into the groove of being back in America finally. It took him some months; he initially seemed to be acutely uncomfortable with being back here, as if this country and his family and friends were now alien to him and some foreign port seemed more like home. But there came a time where he'd even told me he was glad to be home and didn't want to leave for a while. And I think my son was a big part of that, which I liked. Sometimes it seemed like it was the three of us against the world.

42

One Friday night, we went up to the little mom-and-pop video store around the corner from my house to rent some videos. I had the killer chronic weed and a couple of forties at the house, and the plan for the evening was to just get high and veg. Ellena would be dropping Michael off the next day for the weekend, so that would be my only moment of chill time. I was initially thinking about suggesting to Israel that we go up to the Century Club and try to hook some women. But after thinking about it a little more, I decided to chill because Michael was an energetic young boy, and I would need my strength to deal with him for the next few days.

Before we came to the store, Israel and I had already smoked half a blunt. We were pleasantly high as we walked around the store trying to figure out what videos would be cool.

I told Israel, "See that curtained off section over there? That's the adult section. I think I'm'a grab me one'a them for after yo' ass is gone. I'm feeling like watchin' some good porno and beatin' off."

Israel laughed dismissively. "Whatever." He was not a fan of porno flicks at all. He once told me that his attitude about sex was that either he would have it with a woman or not at all. There was no strip clubs, watching pornos and masturbating, or even giving the subject of sex a thought if he wasn't feeling it.

Israel continued to look around the store for a suitable video. He saw *Goodfellas* sitting on a shelf nearby. There were two large football-player-sized guys also eyeing the video, but then they walked away from it. When they did, Israel went and got it off the shelf and proceeded to the counter, where I was already waiting with a video featuring my favorite old school porn starlet Ebony Ayes.

As the clerk rang up our videos, I heard a baritone voice behind us. "I wanted that video."

Israel and I turned around to the see the two big brothas who'd been eyeing the *Goodfellas* video earlier. Behind them was a third man, not quite as large as them but still formidable looking. The counter clerk, a smallish Pakistani fellow, looked a little intimidated by all of us.

My hackles went up, but the air around Israel was still and calm. He said, "I saw you walk away from it. That's the only reason I took it."

"Well," one of the football brothas said, "if you was really gone be cool about it, you'd let us have it and go find somethin' else."

"I could do that," Israel replied, looking thoughtful. Suddenly, his face looking like a light bulb had clicked on, he said, "But you guys could also find another video. Now there's an idea."

The third one in back of them chimed in. "The only reason they walked away from the box was to come git me to see if I wanted it too."

I laughed at that one. "Y'all are interruptin' precious time I could use to be gettin' high with. You heard m'man. If he'd'a known y'all wanted the video, he wudna fucked with it. We got it now. That's that. Like y'all suggested to us, you can go on and git anotha tape."

"What if I took that muthafucka anyway?" one of the football dudes said.

I scowled angrily. "Now I'd like to see that shit. I muthafuckin' dare you."

Israel quickly stepped between us. "Fellas, there isn't a need for all this. You want the video, you can have it."

Israel took the video off the counter and extended it to the larger of the two men. He snatched it from Israel and gave him a look that said, "Li'l punk." I wanted to do something, but I sensed that perhaps my time would still come. Israel still had that strange calm to him, yet he was not calm at all.

We paid for my porno and walked out. When we were outside the door, I said, "Damn, Iz. I feel like we punked out in there. I don't care how big those niggas are, I ain't no punk."

Israel sighed, an amused smile on his face. "So what do you suggest we do, Dave?"

"Well, it's kinda too late now. We should'a done something at least when that nigga snatched the tape from you. Wudn't no call for that, you were givin' him the damn tape."

"Dave, it's not that serious. I'll come back and rent the tape another time."

Just then the three of them came out of the store. They walked past us and the smallest one (who was about my size, so really not very small at all) said, "Damn, we was just fuckin' wit' y'all. We didn't really want that tape. But thanks, fuh real doe. We gon' enjoy this muthafucka...well, if we even end up watchin' it tonight."

As they walked by laughing, I saw Israel's face cloud over. I knew that expression—it was the same one that had appeared on his face when Wade pushed him down in the hallway back in high school.

Israel suddenly bolted for them. The shit-talking smaller fellow was the one he reached first. He grabbed him by the arm, spun him around, and all of a sudden the guy was being held in the air above Israel's head. Israel slammed him down hard, and his body hit the parking lot cement with a loud sound somewhere between a thud and a smack.

He was moaning loudly in pain as the other two spun to face Israel, looking at each other in a silent debate about who would try to get at him first. Israel was now as still as a quiet desert night, his eyes unblinking. There was nothing in him that seemed disturbed by the two of them at all, which fascinated me. I was caught between wanting to get involved in the fracas and watching to see what Israel would do next.

One of the two, who was cornrowed and had a big ugly scar on his thick neck, charged Israel with a scream. Israel didn't move until the guy reached him, and then at the last second he lithely stepped aside, sticking his foot out. The guy tripped over it and his large body went down with a hard, wet-sounding smack. Before he could get his bearings, Israel shot out a straight kick that hit the guy squarely in his ear. He rolled around on the ground clutching that ear in a silent, breathless scream.

Israel didn't wait for the third one to figure it out. He stepped to him and brought the knife-edge of his hand across the guy's nose, breaking it instantly and creating a bright crimson gush. The big man stepped back with a guttural scream but still tried to swing at Israel. He easily dodged the misguided blow and then launched a roundhouse kick that hit the guy in the ribs like a baseball bat swung at full force.

The big man dropped to one knee, wheezing loudly. Israel stepped in and hit him so hard in the face that he crumpled like a rag doll, clearly unconscious before he hit the ground.

The other guy that he had tripped was sitting up. Israel casually strolled up to him and pulled him to his feet. The guy outweighed him by fifty or sixty pounds, but to Israel it was like he weighed nothing. I heard the sound of several quick, precise blows landing, and then the fellow dropped back down to the ground barely conscious and bleeding profusely from his mouth.

The whole fracas was over in less than thirty seconds.

Israel strolled casually to the passenger side of my car while I stood there gaping in awe. He looked at me in an almost annoyed fashion. "David. David. Wake up."

I looked at him. "Uh-huh."

"See which one of those guys has that videotape. I've changed my mind, I want to watch it now."

I searched the three of them. The shit-talking smallest one had it.

We got in the car and drove back to my house without another word.

43

"Daaaaayuuuum, nigga!"

I exclaimed this after taking a big pull on a forty-ounce bottle of Saint Ides I was working on after taking a big hit on the joint I had in my other hand. I was sitting on my living room couch with Israel, and while he was fully engrossed in *Goodfellas* as if it weren't the hundredth time he'd seen it, I was still replaying the events of the video store in my head.

His eyes stayed focused on the nineteen-inch TV a few feet in front of us as if he hadn't heard me. I slapped him on his muscular arm. "Israel."

"What's up, Dave?" he said with a sigh.

I passed him the joint and he took a nice hit. I exclaimed with a raucous laugh, "You fucked them niggas *up*."

Coughing gently and blowing out a thick cloud of smoke, Israel said, "Yes, Dave. I fucked them up."

"I mean…shit!" We both broke out laughing. When I could catch my breath I said, "That was some straight muthafuckin'-ass Bruce Lee shit, nigga."

Israel shrugged nonchalantly and motioned for me to pass him the forty, which I did.

As he took a nice long swig, I said, "What's it like?"

"What's what like?"

"Nigga, you know whum sayin'—just to know that you could be able to fuck muthafuckas up like that. Do it give you, like, a thrill or somethin'?"

Israel chuckled and passed me back the forty. "Of the great things I've seen and experienced in my life, common fighting doesn't even rank anywhere near them. Defeating that poison snakebite in Almora—I was impressed with myself on that. That shit you saw tonight, that's nothing. I quit being thrilled with myself on that kinda stuff when I was in high school."

"Well, all I know is that them niggas got they asses *whupped.* I know they ain't gone forget that no time soon."

"I really don't care if they remember it or forget it or whatever."

I knew Israel spoke the truth. He just wasn't wired like that. What went on in the video store parking lot was as much on his mind as his last visit to the bathroom. Me, I was still amazed and would be for some time.

"Damn, Iz, I'm a bad muthafucka in my own right, but what I saw tonight was just on a whole nutha level of thangs. If I was that bad, I don't know that I still wouldn't be out there on the mash servin' niggas up."

"But, what you have to understand is that to be able to get to the point that I'm at, you have to let all that go. That can't be what you want out of it. You have to want to transcend who you are, transcend all the negativity and bad ideas that trap you in this world and keep you from other ones."

I sort of understood what was being said to me and took a minute to digest it. Then I said, "There was this nigga on the set named Kutty-Lee. He had a black belt in somethin' or other and could do that crazy shit. He studied the shit just to be able to fuck niggas up and that's exactly what he used to do. He wudn't on no elevated consciousness shit."

Israel laughed. "Look Dave, if you want to learn some fighting tricks, I can have you up to speed on that in a few weeks. I could show you some shit that's so unbelievably simple, you wouldn't know what to even think about it. I could take you to a certain level, but then it would be almost like hitting a brick wall. If all you want to be is a good fighter, that's so…ordinary. To teach you that is almost not worth my time."

"Naw, I don't want to learn nothin', that ain't my thang. It's just a trip that you are who you are in general these days. There's a lot about you I'm still tryna work out."

Israel chuckled. "I could say the same about you, Dave. My sister tells me you were gangbangin' like it was going out of style while I was gone. I didn't see that as your destiny when I left."

I swigged off the forty and belched loudly. "Iz, gangbangin' wudn't exactly the plan. I was supposed to be in the NFL right about now, makin' major chips and chillin' on a boat with your sister and Michael somewhere. But after that nigga shot me up, that just seemed to be all that was solid for me to hang onto. It seemed to really make sense at the time."

"So what kinds of things did you do once you got off deep into all that stuff?"

I was uncomfortable with Israel asking me that question. I still wanted him to hold me in high regard as a person. I had done some bad things, some of which still haunted my dreams at night and caught me off guard even in my waking hours occasionally.

As if he could read my mind, he said, "You uncomfortable with this subject?"

I nodded my head. "That was a whole 'nutha point in my life, man. And some of the shit I did I still gots issues with.

"One thing I *don't* mind discussin' is the amount of work I put in on our enemies. I was full'a so much rage at God and fate that I just didn't give a fuck after I got shot up. I really liked killin' niggas, Israel. I always tried to make sure that whoever I was gon' pull the trigger on had a moment to see that I was the one about to take 'em from this world into the next."

Israel was looking at me with a shocked expression. That was surprising to me because he usually didn't show his emotions that openly. I figured it must be the booze and the weed.

"You have any regrets about any of all that killing?"

I shook my head. "Them niggas was in the game. We all know that gangbangin' ain't something you might retire from. Just like I caught them slippin', they could'a caught me slippin', and they fa sho would've served me up just like I did them. So I gots zero regrets about that part of it."

"So what do you feel so bad about?"

I shifted uncomfortably on the sofa. "The dope slangin'... stealin' cars...robberies...all the shit that involved civilians gettin' caught up. I ain't proud'a that stuff at all."

"There's something else you want to tell me."

I looked at him with shock. "Yeah...yeah, there is. I ain't never told a living soul. I guess I ain't really know of nobody I could tell until now."

Israel's whole body posture changed. His whole energy seemed to have shifted and centered on me. It was not something I saw, as much as felt. It was fascinating, yet disturbing at the same time. I was getting that feeling a lot about my old friend lately.

"Go on, just tell me," he said in a smooth, relaxing voice that was as coaxing as a good pimp's.

"Okay, well, maybe a year after I got shot, I got deep into hangin' with the homies and gettin' into all kindsa shit. You already know about the warfare part of thangs I was into and some of the dirty shit on the side as well. But the thing that haunts my ass the most is this.

"One of the homies, named Dirty Lou, worked as an assistant manager at a Burger King. He came up with a plan to rob the joint. He was the guy that more often than not closed the place up, and he figured he'd set up shit to look like a robbery that he was a victim of by nobody he knew. That way he could keep his job, enjoy the spoils, and maybe even pull the same stunt again. You know it ain't unheard of in the 'hood to have yo' shit robbed more than once.

"They had cameras everywhere, so Dirty Lou was gonna have me and another homie, Mac-D, looking like we was robbin' him on-camera. We would come in through the back, make him lay down on the floor, and take all the money that he was to deposit in the safe.

"It went according to plan. But Lou directed Mac-D and me to a corner of the store where the camera couldn't catch us. We was sittin' there laughin' and countin' the cash when the daytime manager came in. She'd forgotten her cell phone earlier and had come back for it.

"She busted us *cold* countin' the money. She was about to scream and run, but Dirty Lou and Mac-D grabbed her and dragged her ass into the bathroom. I went in too, and we was all debating about what to do next.

"Dirty Lou was checkin' her out for sex. He said, 'Hell, if I'm'a go to prison, might as well get a good nut off this bitch as well.' Mac-D didn't have no problem with that at all. The woman *was* fine as hell, but all I could think was that I didn't want to go to the pen. Fuck that!

"Lou and Mac-D started tryin' to strip the broad. We had taped her mouth up, but those muffled screams sounded as loud and piercin' to me as if they was free, bouncin' off the bathroom wall tile. Them niggas was salivatin', really gettin' off on her fear. This wasn't what I wanted at all, and it seemed like things had gone from good to bad within a matter'a seconds.

"I made a decision that haunts me to this day. I took out my .45 and told them fools to back off her. They looked confused, like they thought I was going to shoot them or something. The broad looked relieved, but she saw my eyes were beaded straight on her as the homies moved away—and she understood.

"She cried like a baby and begged and pleaded for her life. Thankfully it was all muffled underneath that tape stretched across her mouth. I almost decided to let her live, but then I thought of prison, and the devil came into my spirit and sent a bolt of fire that traveled from my heart through the length of my arm and finally exploded into my fuckin' trigger finger.

"I emptied my gun into her. The homies jumped back cursin', not believing I was committin' such a cold-blooded-ass act.

Hell, I couldn't believe it either. I think that's why I kept pulling the trigger. I didn't want to stop and think about it until I had to.

"When it was over, Dirty Lou said, 'Got-*damn,* that has got to be the coldest shit I ever seen!' He wasn't sayin' this as a bad thing. The nigga was laughin' like a damn clown, like he'd just paid me a compliment of the highest order. Mac-D looked a little frightened.

"I screamed at him, 'What, nigga? You was about to rape her ass, that wudn't no more or less evil than what I did.'

"Mac-D looked like he wanted to cry. 'Yeah, but she'd'a still been alive. I mean, you just killed the 'ho' in cold blood.' He shook his head. 'Damn.'

"Dirty Lou, still laughing, chimed in, 'Yeah, that was some dirty shit, homeboy—just smokin' an innocent bitch like that. You gots major props.'

"We calmed down and all agreed that to make it all look legit, Dirty Lou would have to take a bullet. He was shakin' like a li'l bitch but cool with it. I reloaded and shot him in the leg, and then Mac-D and I got the hell out of there. Dirty Lou healed up fine and afterward loved to tell the homies about that night, but in my heart all I feel from it is shame. I see her face in my dreams sometimes and wish it was me gone and her still here."

Israel was silent, looking contemplative. Then he said, "I probably would have done the same thing if I were in that situation."

"Good to know, but how do you think you would have lived with that shit, though?"

"That's a tough one. The way I am now, I'd never do anything I couldn't live with. I think I would probably live with it the same way you do—one day at a time."

I snorted derisively. That wasn't enough for me.

"Does it get any worse than that?"

I looked at him like he was crazy and shook my head. "Damn, homie! What more you want?"

He held his hands up and laughed. "Peace, m'man. It's all good. Like I said, I was curious." He looked a little thoughtful and said, "It's just that life doesn't seemed to have worked out exactly the way either of us planned it."

"What? I thought you pretty much did everything you wanted to in your life."

"I did," Israel said with a wry smile. "It's just that I thought the result of the things I did would be a lot different from the reality."

"You wanna elaborate on that?"

"I don't know. I really don't know if I've ever had a solid plan for where my life was supposed to go, at least after I was done with Satswanda and my studies in India. I just never expected to end up back here in America. And I definitely wasn't prepared for the response I've gotten from you guys. I think I may have literally forgot how loved I was by y'all.

"I also wasn't prepared for Ellena being a mother. That was a shock in and of itself. And to add to that, there's the connection I feel with Michael. I couldn't love your son any harder than if he were my own, do you know that?"

"Yeah…yeah, I know."

"You've been a like a brother to me, Dave. And now we're bonded by blood. I really don't care what went on with you and Ellena—that has nothing to do with us as individuals. I love her no less than I ever did, but one thing that she has to understand is that I still think of you as family just as much as I always have."

"You ever ask her about details on us?"

He shrugged nonchalantly. "She's told me some vague stuff; you've told me some vague stuff. You both have probably got a lot to say about things that don't even matter anymore."

Taking a pull off the almost finished malt liquor, I thought about what he said about things not really mattering anymore. I had come to the conclusion in that moment that they really didn't. Everything seemed to have worked out just fine for everybody, despite the obstacles. Maybe that was the greatest victory anybody could hope for in life—not for things to be perfect, but just good enough to live with.

44

Ernesto Sanchez—known by most on the streets as Spider, for his daring in committing burglaries in second and third story buildings—sat on the floor of his furnitureless little Hollywood bungalow readying himself to take a hit. He was loading up the crack pipe with a sizable piece of rock cocaine, sweating and dizzy almost beyond function in his anticipation.

There was a time when he used to do his burglaries for the fun and the glory of it—and of course for the money—but that was in his youth. Now, at age twenty-five, he felt like a hopeless old man who couldn't remember how the bitch called crack had been introduced to him or at what point she'd taken over his life.

He finally had the thin two-inch long glass stem, known on the streets as a straight shooter, packed to his satisfaction. He grabbed the lighter from the floor beside him with trembling fingers. As he lit the flame he stared briefly at the white lump perched like a watching hawk at the end of the pipe, thinking he should put it down and give this up—if not for himself, for his three children by his ex-old lady.

His ex, that bitch—she loved to trumpet to the kids how their father was a bum who could not leave the streets or the dope alone. That was the painful thought that made him drop the flame onto the waiting piece of rock.

He inhaled deeply, his ears dimly registering the sizzle and pop of the disintegrating rock piece. His mind seemed to let go instantly of all that was plaguing him; indeed, it seemed almost as if his soul had fled his body for a second, racing on to some better, peaceful place where nothing else mattered. He blew a thick cloud of pure ivory smoke out and felt suddenly invigorated and ready for anything, the euphoric centers of his brain stimulated twenty times beyond their normal capacity. A wide, wolf-like grin stretched across his face and he thought of the day's earlier activities with a smile.

He had done a burglary that had been so easy that it was basically no fun. It was a second story lawyer's office. His new partners in crime, Fereal McNaughton and Orlando Flores, two LAPD officers, had come to him with the job. They had approached him in jail over a year and a half ago and offered him a unique deal: they would case out buildings for him and he would go in and get the merchandise for them (which was not always salable goods; sometimes it was paperwork or personal photos of people in compromising positions, things of that nature), after which they would pay him in cash. He didn't know or care what they did with the stuff afterward. It was nice that for once he didn't have to bother messing with a fence; he just got his money upfront and could immediately go score his drugs.

That was most certainly the case today. He'd done a couple of lawyer's offices for his cop homies before, but usually it was always for paperwork. This particular lawyer had a two-pound stash of marijuana that was hidden in a wall safe that he'd been given the combination for. If he had been really daring he would have simply told Flores and McNaughton that he hadn't been able to open the safe and given the stash to the homies on the set, taking a cut of the incoming proceeds. But another one of his homies that had been involved with the two officers crossed them up, too confident that he had too much dirt on them to be messed with. His body was found not long after in a storm drain downtown, but without the head. He was identified through his fingerprints.

No, this was a sweetheart deal. The way things were set up, if he got caught he might have to sit up in the County for a few months, but his partners wouldn't let him stay in jail any longer than that. It didn't seem like he stood a chance of getting caught though, because his boys were very good at setting him up in situations that were always low risk, high yield. He didn't know if he liked that or not because part of the whole edgy thrill of it for him was trying to see if he could do his thing and not be certain whether or not he'd be caught. But he again thought of how lovely it was just to be able to sit up and smoke his dope so soon after a score without all the extra nonsense.

He got up and went to the bathroom. He was full of energy and now had to figure out what to do with it. He thought of maybe going out and doing a job just for the fun of it, but that was another stipulation of his new partners—no freelancing or any more jobs for himself. He worked strictly for them now. They didn't want him getting caught up in anything they couldn't control or manipulate. He was grateful for their protection as anyone with good common sense would be, but there was a joy missing from his life that not even the almighty rock could fill. B and E's were about the only thing that he excelled at in his miserable existence, and he took great pride in being known as one of the best.

After he peed, he went and sat down again in the middle of the living room, loading up his pipe for another hit. The idea of doing a robbery for fun was still nagging at him. He thought sometimes that the cocaine was enough for him, and he didn't need the rush that doing a good job gave him, but the coke thrill was momentary and seemed to create a void in its wake that brought up all the pain in his life he was trying to escape from.

He once again put the flame to the tip of his pipe and inhaled deeply. As he exhaled, he could feel all common sense leaving him. "I'll go to another fuckin' neighborhood, wear some shit that covers up the gang tats," he thought. "I'll make sure it's a spot that's low risk. It won't hurt just once to go outside th' fuckin' program. Fuck those cop muthafuckers, I just wanna see if I still got it."

45

"Muthafucka!"

Fereal McNaughton was generally the calm sort. He didn't like to lose his cool. His father, a career military man decorated with honors for his service in Vietnam, often lectured him as a child barely out of diapers on the dangers of not keeping one's composure, especially as a black man. Donald McNaughton would often tell young Fereal that he had quickly learned in the hot brush of Viet Cong territory that if one lost his cool, he could not only endanger himself but even the lives of others around him. Calm in the face of danger was a lifestyle for Donald McNaughton. His only son observed early on how other people reacted to things in life that didn't even seem like a big deal while his father was a stern rudder, whether in rocky, raging seas or during simple shifts in the wind.

Fereal turned out to be a chip off the old block, which helped for a quick assent up the ladder in LAPD. His superiors praised his style and demeanor while his detractors (mostly white boys envious of a black man on the come up) called him a cold fish. He could care less about the latter. He was too busy setting goals for himself and achieving them to worry about anyone else.

He had been approached by Orlando Flores several years ago about working some side deals off the clock for extra money. It started off simply doing security at clubs. As Orlando observed his cool demeanor and as their friendship deepened, he started easing Fereal up from working the door and walking the floor to giving him access to the secret backrooms of these hot spots. That was where the *real* stuff went on, things as simple as coke-laden sexcapades to politicians cinching deals with private contractors for good contracts doing city work in exchange for a cut of the pay.

Orlando watched his new partner carefully, noting that he had an ability to absorb and retain even the most minute details of things and keep his mouth shut. These were all abilities that Orlando himself possessed, and he could not believe his good fortune that he had been partnered with such a kindred spirit. Fereal was clear on the fact that he was being tested. He was a man of extreme patience, and after a year of waiting, watching and taking his own mental notes on things, Orlando finally exposed him to a secret network of officers who had their fingers in everything from club security to dope networks with cops in other states to extortion to fixing things for certain parties who had the right kind of money. And that could be as simple as a traffic ticket and as complicated as an impatient mistress threatening to expose herself to her lover's wife.

Fereal had never been content with his policeman's salary. He felt that the very minimum one should make for risking his life daily (especially in the rough and tumble Hollywood area he and Orlando patrolled) should be a hundred thousand annually. Now he was making significantly more than that, living better than his parents had ever dreamed of, and he was helping to run the network he'd started off as a simple cog in. If he stuck with the program he'd be able to retire in the next few years. He often smiled thinking about being a retiree in his late thirties.

The only thing that Fereal didn't like about the situation was his and Orlando's occasional dependence on outside contractors to take care of certain things for them. He trusted no one by nature and he *really* didn't trust the criminal element. Most of them were liars by virtue of their activities, and despite the fact that thus far they'd operated with them quite well, he knew underneath it all they were still card-carrying members of the

Thin Blue Line…therefore, their partners-in-crime would never fully trust them. Hell, they could even secretly hate them.

He wondered about this now as he clicked off his cell phone. He and Orlando were on patrol, the worst time for him to receive news like this. They could not take time out in the middle of a shift to take care of this problem. He felt like cursing aloud again, but he was already upset with himself that he'd let the first outburst escape his lips.

"What is it?" Orlando asked, genuinely concerned. "Shit, I don't think I've ever seen you ever blow up like that, at least since I've known you."

"That was a call from Bruce Waller, our guy over in Santa Monica PD. Your boy Spider Sanchez just got scooped up over there."

"What?!" Now Orlando understood his partner's distress. "What'd they get him for?"

"He did a job in an apartment building over there. He was caught as he was coming out by a unit casually patrolling the area. Waller says the cops gave him a casual glance and were actually going to pass him up, but he started running. They caught up with him and the fool confessed to a burglary, thinking they knew about it anyway."

"Fuuuck!" Orlando was driving and almost swerved into another car. Fereal gave him an evil look that he didn't even register. Orlando's mind locked in on Spider Sanchez's imprisonment and what it could mean for the both of them.

Fereal sighed. "To top things off, he was on a severe crack high."

Orlando looked like he wanted to cry. "Does this get any better? Can Waller do anything?"

"He says he'll try, but Waller's one'a those haters I think really doesn't like a nigga and a wetback like yourself involved in this little network. He sounded almost happy about giving me the news about Spider. I could be wrong, but that's the feeling I've gotten when we've dealt with him before."

Orlando grunted in agreement. "I think you're right on the money with that puto. Okay, so where does that leave us now?"

This was a place that was completely comfortable for them. Orlando was the idea man who set up the schemes and put the pieces into place, while Fereal was the one who made sure everything went according to plan and cleaned up any mistakes that came about. This was definitely a mistake.

After a moment Fereal said, "Okay, let's see how this plays out. We'll see what exactly they charge him with. We have to get a lawyer over there to him before he starts talking out the side of his face."

Orlando shook his head and said, "I know Spider pretty well. I don't think he'd say anything about us."

"O-Dawg, when drugs come into play, I don't trust nobody. Better we stay safe than end up sorry."

"Yeah, yeah. You're right. I'll call Dave Brookline. He's a lawyer that's done some work for me before on some other shit. He's just the guy for this one."

As Orlando dialed up the lawyer on his cell phone, Fereal felt a little bit more at ease. A best-case scenario was that Spider might have to take a little jailhouse vacation that they would handsomely reward him for. He could even go back into business for them when he got out. The worst case scenario was that Spider, still high on that shit, would start squealing like a little bitch and offer up information before he found out that they were on the case already trying to get him help.

If it was the latter, that was okay too. Fereal had quite a bit of money saved up if he had to go to jail for a minute—but no, that wasn't an option. He hadn't come this far and worked this hard for some crackhead loser to send it crashing down all around him like a house of cards. No, Spider Sanchez would come to face to face with the devil first.

46

"David, I need to talk to you."

I looked at the clock. It was three-thirty in the morning. When the phone rang, I answered it first ring on pure reflex, an old habit of being on call for the gangstas 24/7 to put in work. I was so tired and groggy I could not even find the will or the strength to cuss Ellena out. All I could think was that it was lucky for her it was a Sunday.

"David, are you awake?"

"Yeah, I ain't got no damn choice but to be awake," I grunted impatiently. "If there ain't nothin' wrong with Michael, you know I'm'a be upset about this here."

"No, Michael's fine. I just want to make sure he stays that way."

All of a sudden it was if the deep fog of sleep and post-sleep had been snatched away from me. I said carefully, "Ellena, what are you talkin' about? What's goin' on?"

"Not on the phone, David. I need to talk to you in person."

"I *know* you cain't mean right now."

"Michael is at your mother's house. I could be there in twenty minutes on the 405 Freeway."

"Jesus," I snapped, raking my hand through the good-sized Afro I was sporting in those days. "This shit can't wait, huh?"

"David, believe me when I say it's a matter of life and death."

"Well, I guess you betta hurry up and get over here, then."

47

Once I splashed my face with some water, I found myself really curious. I wondered what could possibly be so important that Ellena had to come and see me at almost four in the morning. She said that it was a matter of life and death but I was comforted in knowing that Michael was with my mother, who lived but a scant three blocks away from me.

I went into the living room and plopped down on the sofa. I started watching a *Miami Vice* rerun, wondering why they couldn't have aired my favorite older show during the daylight hours. I almost fell back asleep as I was watching, but then came a soft but persistent knock at my front door. I sighed deeply, pushed myself up off the sofa and went to answer it.

When I opened the door, my senses once again became alert and open. Ellena looked a mess, her skin sallow and her eyes shadowed by deep dark circles. Her hair was pulled into a wild, uneven ponytail. She was wearing a black sweat suit with LAPD stitched in the left breast of the top. I had to note silently that even looking her worst she still looked more beautiful than most women.

I silently bade her enter, and she came in and sat down on the couch. As I closed and locked the door she smiled thinly. "You're watching *Miami Vice.* I can't believe how much you like this corny show."

I smiled back at her. "Shit, you don't know what you talkin' 'bout, baby. That's some classic shit right there."

"You know, I used to hate when you used to make me watch that show. If you weren't my man I would have made you watch something else."

"Well, it probably helped that I was puttin' this good dick on ya."

"Probably nothing—it did help. Who else would watch this under any other circumstances?"

We laughed. It was nice but strange at the same time. We never talked about our past, especially anything relating to physical intimacy. That just wasn't a topic that ever came up between us or needed to. I was really curious as to what was going on with her and why she was sitting in my living room at close to four in the morning being so open with me.

"Soooo," I said, sitting down beside her on the couch, "why ain't I sleepin' right now? Whassup?"

She sighed deeply. "I don't even know where to start, David. I could be in a lot of trouble—maybe not, maybe so. I found out about some things recently. I mean, I don't want to endanger Michael or you or anybody else, but I don't know how I can sit on all this at the same time. That is just not me, just not who I am."

"Ellena, you talkin' in circles right now. You just confusin' me."

Ellena looked up at me and it did something in me. Sometimes she would look at me a certain way and I would feel like I would do anything just to have her back again. My face never betrayed my heart. You would not have known my feelings by looking at my stony visage, but my insides would feel as if someone were twisting them around with pliers. I would have to fight those feelings with everything in me to get back to keeping her at bay in my heart and spirit.

"Well," she said, her eyes watering ever so slightly. "I've been serving the public as an LAPD officer for a few years now. I have believed in my job and what I stand for as an officer and have loved being part of the Thin Blue Line. I have simple morals, that's the way that I was brought up, and the one thing I felt was so great about being an officer was that I wouldn't have to compromise my beliefs of right and wrong for nothing.

"Now, I know that every job has a few little under the table perks. I mean, a job like this should. After all, you're putting your life on the line daily, right?" When I did not concur she continued. "I didn't even really like taking advantage of any of those little perks, because I just felt like, when do the perks stop, and how far do they go? At what point do you stop doing things when you know you have the protections of the law behind you? How far does it go?"

I was still silent. I knew she was working her way to a point and I was trying to be patient.

She sighed and continued, "You know, Sean helped me put the down payment on my house. I take care of the note, but he helped me get it. He knew the broker and got me a good deal on it. He said he'd done the broker some 'favors' in the past and he just collected on them."

She laughed, not softly at all. It was a whooping wailing sound, the kind that at four in the morning the neighbors might call the cops on me for. But I said nothing, still not wanting to derail her at this point.

"Favors, my *ass*," she went on, now frowning. "There's so much dirty shit going on, I wish he'd never tried to talk to me about it."

I finally broke in. "Okay, you talkin' about Sean Cudahy, right?"

She looked at me impatiently. "Well of course I'm talking about him, who else?"

"Ellena, you in my muthafuckin' house at four in the morning babblin' about some ol' shit that so far don't make a lick'a sense. So don't get mad at me if I'm tryna get all my facts straight, even the simplest ones."

She lowered her head and rubbed her eyes. "I'm sorry, David You're right. I haven't slept a wink in the past few days, so I'm kind of out of it."

I nodded and said, "Okay, so go on."

"Well, recently Sean and I were kicking it and he asked me if I knew how he got a lot of his money. He takes me on a lot of trips and buys me a lot of nice things. He keeps trying to pressure me into marrying him, but I keep telling him our relationship is fine how it is." I smiled inadvertently as she went on. "He likes to bring up that he does all these things for me and that I don't know what he goes through to get his money. I always used to tell him that I go through the same damn things and not to come at me like that.

"Anyway, my answer to Sean was that as far as I knew he was just another cop doing well for himself. He told me that I knew how he got most of his money and I told him that I really didn't. He kept insisting that I did and I told him to get to the point and tell me what he wanted to tell me.

"I wish he hadn't now, to be honest. He told me about some network of cops he's been involved with since he moved to LA. He'd been involved with them on a limited basis even in New York. I knew he'd hooked up doing some club security and bodyguard work, but as he laid it down to me it went much deeper than that.

"Sean told me that he has been involved with everything from drug distribution to prostitution to blackmail scams to…oh my God, I can't remember even half the things he said, I almost fainted while he was telling me."

I thought about Ellena's reaction to the earrings I'd bought her all those years ago with my "dirty money." Israel once told me that Sean was very lavish with her. I knew Ellena would be thinking about each and every last gift given to both her and Michael, every first-class vacation, every expensive dinner, even the house she lived in. The whole scenario really didn't seem like a big deal to me, but I knew it was absolutely traumatic for her.

"Ellena, did you honestly think y'all were living like that with just money from club security?"

She gave me an annoyed glance. "I went to a couple of the clubs he worked for. He was tipped lavishly by a lot of the celebrities he let in and did little favors for, and at the end of a good night he was paid upfront in cash. Between tips and his pay from the promoter, I saw him one night collect almost two thousand dollars."

I whistled. That was good money. I would not have asked any questions about his income under those circumstances either.

"As Sean was talking to me, I told him to stop, that I didn't want to hear any more. He kept telling me anyway. He said, 'You've been living this good life like I have, so you might as well know everything.' I told him that if he had told me upfront about all of this stuff we probably would not have been together today. He said...uh, he..."

She was silent for a moment. I raised an eyebrow to urge her to continue. "He said I would have looked for an excuse to leave him anyway because I was still in love with *you.* He said nobody else was going to ever take your place and he knew that, but he still had to try because he really loves me."

This was shocking to me. I laughed. "Did you tell that nigga he was delusional?"

"No, I didn't."

I looked into Ellena's smoky eyes and something passed between us. It was a quiet, special thing that hadn't been there with us for a long time, at least not in such direct fashion. I almost wanted to reach out and touch her face, but I did not want to put myself out there and get hurt. Instead I simply said, "So where does Michael come into all of this?"

She looked a little afraid. "I told Sean that I could not be with him like that. I didn't want to stay involved with him if he was going to stay involved in that. He laughed and told me I was being naïve, but I told him *he* was being naïve. He knows me, what I am about and what I stand for, and part of the whole thing of being a cop for me is upholding the basic moral code for which I try to live in my own life, no matter what."

I felt my hackles rise. "Did that muthafucka make a direct threat on my boy?"

"No, no. He didn't really threaten me or Michael at all. I mean, at least, not directly. Maybe it wasn't a threat. Shit, I don't know."

I could see that exhaustion was starting to wear away at her, but I wanted to try to keep her focused. "Ellena," I said patiently, "listen to me carefully, okay? I'm gonna ask you some questions so's I can try to get a better take on alla this."

She nodded sleepily. "Okay, David."

"After you told him you wudn't down, what *exactly* did he say to you?"

"Okay." She paused, rubbing her temples. "What he said exactly was, 'Ellena, see, I've already told you too much. Just you knowing about all this could get me killed and yourself and anyone close to you as well.'

"I looked at him like he was crazy. Then he said, 'I just assumed you knew about us. I know a lot of people in different departments talk about us, and I thought you put two and two together, but that doesn't even matter now.'

"When I asked him what that meant he said, 'Ellena, I love you. I'd do anything for you, except go to prison or get killed. If you can't hold water on this, one of those two things might occur. I don't plan on allowing either one to happen, you get what I'm trying to say to you?'"

I could feel my mood darkening. I wanted nothing more at that moment than to have her tell me where that big yellow muthafucka lived so that I could go over and kill him myself for even hinting at doing anything to Ellena and Michael. But I knew that could only open up a bigger can of worms. I struggled instead to keep my cool.

I took a deep breath. "Well, it look like if you don't say nothin', the worst thing that could come outta all this is that y'all's relationship would be over. Sound to me like he was holdin' onto that shit and wanted to get it out so y'all could figure out in yo' relationship where y'all was headin' next. And if you could get down with all this stuff, that would'a answered all his questions about the two of you."

"I've really thought about that, David—about just trying to pretend that the whole conversation never happened and just going on with my life without him. I really wish it were that simple for me. But you know I am not that kind of woman, that kind of person. I don't want my son in danger, or anybody else."

"Hold up—*anybody else*? What you mean by that?"

She sighed deeply, a sad sound like dead autumn leaves being stirred up by a passing breeze.

"David, he hinted that anybody I loved could be touched. Michael, my brother, my mother—even you. Truth be told, he hates you. He's told me on more than one occasion that he wished you were dead, and I think now the only reason he hasn't tried to kill you is because I would know he had something to do with it. I never copped to sleeping with you while I was with him, but he knew. I gave him ten kinds of hell after him and his partner beat you that time. I actually almost left him. Looking back now, that was right around the time we were talking about him helping me to get the house. I wanted a stable home for Michael and me. I think that's the only reason I didn't leave him."

That was all I needed to hear. Sean Cudahy was not a potential enemy to me, or one I'd picked up out of a need to protect Ellena and my son—now he was also a direct threat to me personally. I had not a problem in this world thinking of and treating him as such.

I looked deep into the beautiful gray eyes of the only woman I would ever love and asked, "So what're you gonna do now?"

"I have to talk to somebody about all of this, maybe Internal Affairs. That's probably about the only place I know for sure where Sean and his cronies have no pull. He told me he has people within reach even at IA, but I think he was trying to throw me off, to scare me from going there."

"Well, I'm a lame when it comes to all this cop stuff you talkin' 'bout, but I'm pretty sure that without proof, you got an uphill battle goin' on there."

"Doesn't matter. If I put the bug in their ear, they'll start watching him and whomever he associates with. And if they get together some proof, they might call me in later to testify on what he told me."

I was silent for a second. Then I said, "That nigga must have been frustrated with y'all's li'l relationship to bust out on you like that. He could'a kept his mouth shut and just let things be and you never would'a known the difference."

Ellena chuckled. "Sean has never been one for that. He's an opinionated, spoiled bastard, and if he doesn't get his way one way he'll figure out some other angle to get what he wants."

"So when he talked all that stuff about you still lovin' me, and you didn't correct 'im. What was that about?"

Ellena was silent. I felt like pushing the issue but I didn't.

She finally said, "I'm too tired to go back to the damn Valley. I would have to come back over this way anyway in a few hours to pick up Michael. Do you mind if I just lay here on the couch?" She laughed bitterly and added, "Maybe I'll have better luck getting to sleep here than I have in my own damn house."

"Yeah, that's cool. Maybe once you get some sleep, I go back to sleep." We both chuckled at that one. "Then we might get some better ideas about all this in the morning…well, later in the morning anyway."

We laughed again. I got up to get her a blanket and sheet for the sofa. I hadn't even been gone a full minute, but when I came back she was already snoring, her mouth comically open in wide *O*. I covered her with the blanket and went to the bedroom to try to get back to the Sandman's lair myself.

Sleep was a hot minute in coming. I was thinking about my life and all that had happened in it up to that point. I was all of twenty-seven years old and felt sometimes like I was fifty. And just when I thought things were at a calm and peaceful level in my life, now some more shit was about to get stirred up.

That was okay. I could deal with it, I always had. This situation was no different than any other that had been dropped in my path. I'd roughride it through and deal with whatever consequences occurred, although at that moment I didn't know that would include the ending of my life.

48

At five thirty in the morning I finally conked out. The sleep was a hard one; I felt like I'd descended into a coma.

I was eased out of sleep maybe two hours later. Ellena was sitting next to me on the bed, looking at me lovingly. She had her hand underneath the covers stoking my penis. It was stiff and throbbing and aching in her soft hand, wanting more than it was getting.

"Damn," I moaned. "What're you doin'?"

"The last time we were about to get…um…like *this,* you pushed me down on my ass," she purred gently. "I thought I'd see your reaction first before I just got into bed with you. I don't think I could handle rejection from you today."

"I don't think you gonna get it, either," I said, pulling her into a kiss. And what followed was like a dream awake after a long dark sleep.

49

A few hours later I woke up with her in my arms. She was in a deep sleep like I'd been in earlier, an occasional loud snore belching past her slightly parted lips. She looked so beautiful to me that I knew right then that I would do anything for her. The past was meaningless, almost as if it had never happened in the space of a few hours. Only the present mattered, and maybe tomorrow as well.

I wondered if this was just something casual for her, despite the little hints she dropped about still having feelings for me. I decided that I would not dwell on that right then. I disentangled myself from her comatose body and went into the living room to use the phone.

I called up Israel. He now lived in North Hollywood, a little closer to his sister and my son than I was. He picked up on the third ring and said groggily, "Yes."

"Iz, dis me."

"Dave, what's up? I got to sleep late last night, I'm still kind of out of it."

"You need to get your ass up and get over here. Your sister got some problems, fuh real."

He came awake instantly as I'd done earlier. "What's wrong with Ellena?"

I felt such déjà vu as I said, "Not over the phone, nigga. Didn't I just tell you to get on over here?"

"Okay. Give me about thirty minutes and I'll be there."

"Cool. See ya then."

50

When Israel arrived I woke Ellena up. She was surprised that I had called him but didn't seem particularly upset. I had her retell her story again. Israel listened in rapt silence, not even giving polite acknowledgements as she spoke.

We were all in the living room. While Ellena spoke I went into the kitchen to make some coffee for everyone. When I came back she was just finishing up. Israel, who sat facing the sofa in a folding chair I'd brought out for him, was the first recipient of my potent brew. His sister was next. After pouring myself a cup I sat down on the sofa beside Ellena.

"So," I said to Israel as I sipped from my cup, "what's your take on alla this shit?"

"I just hope it lasts this time."

Ellena and I looked at each other, then at Israel. Ellena said, "Uh, what are you talking about? You hope what lasts this time?"

Israel smiled like a Cheshire cat. "The two of you. I haven't seen you guys together intimately as a couple ever, and I really didn't think I would. It's pretty cool, actually."

My skin was too dark for Israel to see my cheeks flush. Unfortunately, Ellena's was not.

"Say, brah, what makes you think me and your sis here are at it again?"

"Your body language, the closeness between the two of you right now. Even if a complete stranger walked in right now, he'd sense the intimacy between you. And your apartment smells like two people that have been fucking."

We all laughed at Israel's brazen directness, Ellena also blushing even more.

"Um, okay," Ellena said as the laughter died down. "Now can we deal with my little problem here, baby boy?"

"Well, are you certain you're going to go to Internal Affairs?"

She nodded her head. "I'll compromise my job, my basic beliefs, for nothing. I'm scared shitless, but I have to do this."

"You ain't got nothing to be scared of, Ellena," I said. "*I'll* die before I let anything happen to you."

The look that she gave me lifted me to heavenly heights. I still had a chance to be her hero. I wish I could describe how good that made me feel, but I really don't think there are words for it.

Israel said, "And you know I am not going to let anything happen to my big sister. That's a promise. And if there's one thing you know about me, I *always* keep my promises."

Ellena said with a little chuckle, "Yes, you do. That's always been true about you."

Israel looked thoughtful for a moment. "Can you give me Sean's address?"

Ellena was wary. "For what? Why do you want to know where he lives?"

"I just want to do a little recon, go check him out. I won't confront him."

"Israel, I don't believe that for a minute, not even for a second. I don't want you going over there to mess with Sean. If he did anything to hurt you, I don't know what I would do."

I laughed out loud and Israel smiled broadly. Ellena looked at both of us and said, in a tone of voice bordering on annoyance, "What'd I miss?"

"Ellena," I said, trying to suppress my chuckles. "If I'd be worried about anybody it'd be Sean runnin' into your brother. Believe dat."

Ellena, who knew I knew what I was talking about in matters like these, took a good look at her brother. He was still smiling.

She looked at him like she didn't think he was physically capable of handling a bull of a man like Sean Cudahy.

She shook her head. "I don't think that's a good idea. I can't take a chance with you, Israel. I won't."

Israel shifted modes. It was eerie to watch. He came over to the couch and sat on the other side of her. He said in that smooth, warm voice he could affect at his leisure, "Don't worry, big sis. I don't plan on making any direct contact with Sean. I just want to observe him, have a look around his place while he's not there. Maybe I could come up with something concrete you could use."

"Israel, are you *crazy*?" Ellena was looking at him like an alien instead of the brother she'd help nourish to manhood. "I don't want to chance you getting hurt. There's just too much that could go wrong."

Israel's aura was still smooth and coaxing as he said, "Ellena, watch this."

"Watch what?"

Israel held out his hand. There was a silver ring in the center of his palm. Ellena gasped and then looked at both her hands as if they were alien appendages of some sort. I looked at both them strangely, trying to figure out what the big deal was.

"That ring was just on my finger," Ellena gasped, looking at her brother with amazed eyes. "How did you do that?"

"I pulled it off of your finger, big sis. Just as sure as you're sitting here."

"No, that's not possible, not without me feeling it. You…you must've gotten it off the coffee table or something. I mean, I don't remember pulling it off."

"You didn't pull it off. It was on your finger like both of those earrings are in your ears now."

Ellena checked her ears reflexively. Her earrings were still there. Israel and I laughed.

"Okay, let me ask you this. If I can get one of your earrings off of your ear right now without you feeling it, will you give me Sean's address?"

"Oh, yes," Ellena said with a smirk. "What do you need me to do? Do I have to move a certain way or get in a position or something?"

Israel stuck his hand out again. One of her earrings was in the center of his palm. Both her and I were silent and goggle-eyed.

"I want Sean's address," Israel said, his demeanor now aggressive and authoritative. "I know you'll give it to me. Just trust me to handle the rest."

Neither Ellena nor I said anything. I think we were both still trapped in some strange place between wonderment and, as strange as it is to say it, fear.

51

After Ellena had given her brother Sean's address, she excused herself to the bathroom. I told Israel that I wanted to go with him on his little recon mission.

"No," he stated emphatically. "I don't want you getting involved in what I'm going to do."

"An' what exactly is that?"

Israel smiled and said, with almost feminine coy, "No need to concern yourself with it. That's grown folks' business."

I smirked. "Well, grown folks bidness or not, I'm goin' along with you. I won't get in yo' way if you tell me what's up, but I want to be in on everything goin' on with this shit. You forget, that nigga hinted at gettin' at me and my son too. I gots to help bring 'em down."

Israel looked at me like he was trying to exert that great will of his, then suddenly eased up. "Fine. I'm not going to argue with you."

"Excellent, my nigga. So when we gon' do this?"

"Ellena said he has a shift from ten tonight until six in the morning. I'm going to go home now, and I'll come back here at around nine. That sound good to you?"

"Hell yeah," I said with a wide grin, not knowing why I was so into this all of a sudden. I was really excited.

"Okay, it's a date."

I smiled broadly, thinking about the gun I planned to bring with me. I hoped to myself that somehow we would run into Sean. If we did, I knew that I would not hesitate to shoot Cudahy first and worry about the consequences later. I found no need to worry Israel about that little detail, though.

52

Israel was at my apartment at nine on the nose. He was generally so punctual that you could set a clock by him. We were both dressed almost identically, he in a tight long-sleeved black shirt and loose black jeans, me in a short-sleeved black T-shirt and black Dickies and Chuck Taylors.

He rented a black pick-up truck for the occasion. As we got into the car he told me that Sean lived in Long Beach. We had a good little ride ahead of us, and neither of us was too talkative. Seemed as if we both had a lot on our minds.

As we cruised the 405 Freeway headed to Long Beach, I felt a sense of giddiness, yet I was calm at the same time. It was the feeling I got when I rolled out to do some soldiering for the set. Sometimes I wondered if I needed that feeling. I thought I was satisfied with my role as a father to my son as a hard-working, productive member of society, but at that moment I felt more alive than I had in years. I shook my head, trying to push the thought away.

Sean lived at the border of Long Beach and Signal Hill, a fairly nice area. His house sat right in the middle of the block on a quiet, peaceful looking street. It was strange, because only a blocks away was one of the worst sections of Long Beach.

I looked at Israel. His eyes were fixed on looking at Sean's house, almost as if he were sizing it up. It was like I wasn't in the car. It made me wonder if all this stirred something in him as it did for me. I couldn't imagine what, but I knew that there was still quite a bit about my good friend that I still didn't know. He seemed to operate on a need to know basis and that was cool with me, since I knew (or thought I knew, anyway) everything that was important about him.

"Okay, Dave. You ready for this?"

I nodded my head, my expression grim.

We drove by the house slowly. It was a modest, two-story white affair, nothing that stood out. The whole street was kind of dark, and then I realized there weren't too many street lamps on it. I thought this was perfect. If I wanted to come back and kill him later, this was a good environment to do it in.

Israel parked the pickup right across the street from the house and killed the engine.

I asked, "So, what now?"

He thought for a second and then said, "Did you bring your cell phone with you?"

I pulled it off of my waist holster and said with a smirk, "C'mon, Iz. You know I don't leave home without it."

He smiled. "Okay. Here's what you're going to do. I'm going to put my cell phone on vibrate and you do the same. If anyone looks like they're approaching the house, call me, let it ring once and then hang up. If the police come and look like they're about to approach the house, two rings. If the police just happen to pass by and are looking at you hard enough to make you want to drive off, three rings. If the latter is the case, when I get out of the house I'll call you and we'll figure out a spot for you to pick me up at."

"Straight."

Israel got out of the car, and I shimmied over into the driver's seat. I didn't expect any problems. If anything, I was hoping that Israel would hurry up with whatever he was doing and I wouldn't have to sit by myself for too long. I found it slightly ironic that at times like these there were certain homies that you let do the watching from the car, sometimes because they were excellent drivers—good for the quick getaway if anything went sour—sometimes because you knew they didn't have the heart for the hard, dirty stuff, and sometimes for all of the above reasons. I had never been in that position before and it felt kind of like a demotion.

Israel casually approached the front of the house. He surveyed it almost as if he were a prospective buyer checking the exterior for any flaws. His eyes went to the left, fixed on something. He then removed his cell phone and rapidly punched in a number.

I was trying to see what he had fixed in on when my cell phone buzzed. I clicked it on and said tersely, "Yeah?"

"David, the top left window is open. There's a storm drain line next to it I think I can use to get up there. I am going to go in that way, and then when I'm done checking the house I am going to leave out the back door. If I switch up with anything different I'll call you."

"Okay."

I clicked my phone off and watched intently as he strolled over to the spot where the drain pipe was. He looked around both ways and then tugged and jerked at the drain pipeline to see if it was solidly connected. Something about his motion seemed to hint to me that he might abandon the idea and figure out another way in.

I looked down at my cell phone, waiting for it to buzz with an update from him. It didn't ring as expected. When I looked back up my jaw fell and the cell phone slipped from my hand and hit the seat with a soft thud.

Israel was scurrying up that drain pipe line with a speed and agility that seemed more than human. He actually looked like a human cousin of an arachnid in his movement, and I think that's what gave me the chills. It didn't seem as if he were applying any extra effort to do what he was doing; his motion seemed as fluid and natural as any insects.

"Gotdamn," I whispered aloud. "What the fuck is up with yo' ass, Baylock?"

When Israel reached the top of the drain pipeline, he swung himself effortlessly to the open window and vanished, as if it had sucked him in. I knew I had that same goggle-eyed feeling as when I saw him take those guys on in the video store parking lot.

I needed to talk to someone about what I was seeing. I picked up the phone and dialed Ellena's number. She answered on the first ring.

"Ellena, do you know what the fuck is up with your brother?"

There was confusion in her voice as she said, "What do you mean?"

I chuckled deliriously. "He ever tell you about this fight he had at the video store I go to down the street from my house? Naw? Sheeeee-it, well let me start there."

53

Israel's senses were alert as soon as he entered the bedroom. He heard thumping and moans in the next room. Two people having sex. He tried to figure out how this could be. Ellena said Sean drove a Lincoln Town Car, which was not in the driveway, but who? His sister told him that Sean lived alone.

No matter. They were clearly busy. He would not worry about them unless he had to. He was still busy taking in the bedroom. It was huge and was as lavish (almost to the point of garishness) as the exterior of the house was plain, decorated largely in black and gold tones. There was a huge bed covered over with a black velvet top cover with a huge golden sun on it. In one corner of the room was a minibar setup, which looked fully stocked. In another corner there was a huge big screen TV, which sat atop a black lacquer case that housed a VCR, a music stereo system, and a video game unit.

There was a huge desk right across from the bed facing it. Israel thought it interesting because he knew that he personally could not sit behind a desk and get things going looking directly at his place of rest. He went and sat down behind the desk, enjoying the feel of the big leather chair contoured around him. He thought that Sean's activities must be good to him beyond reason; the chair and desk set had to have cost five thousand dollars at least.

He tried to open a couple of the right side drawers but they were locked. He tried the left drawers and one was also locked but another pulled right open. He carefully went through the drawer and found nothing worthwhile. The most interesting thing in it were pictures of Sean and his sister in different vacation settings posing and mugging like complete tourists.

He opened the center drawer and went through it. Mostly just pencils and pens and little receipts here and there for meals and gas and things of that nature. He knew one was prone to write all kinds of things on the backs of receipts, so he checked the back of each one. They were all clean, except for one that had a name on it: *Fereal McNaughton.* No number, no other info, just the name. Israel committed it to memory and put the receipt back.

The moaning and thumping in the next room stayed steady and consistent. Israel listened for a second and then decided whoever was going at it didn't seem like they were getting ready to quit any time soon. He wanted to continue to go through the room at a leisurely pace, not knowing if he would have the chance to again.

He went to the closet and opened the door. For a room so lavish the closet was fairly small, with not too many clothes in it. There were suits in it too large to be anything but tailor made and some other nice casual gear as well. Israel concluded that Sean Cudahy was a man who liked to dress and look nice.

There was a small, rather ornate chest in the corner of the closet. Israel pulled it out of the closet and opened it up. Enclosed were gold-plated handcuffs and a knife that had a shiny, twelve-inch blade and a golden, bejeweled handle. Israel studied them carefully for a second, thinking to himself that if he had to guess, these might be some sort of tools used for kinky sex. He didn't dare wonder if they'd been used on his sister.

Shuddering, he put the chest back in the closet. As he was closing the closet door he noticed that the moans and thumps had ceased. He stilled himself and opened his hearing up, trying to catch the conversation. It came to him faintly:

A female said, "I can't believe you just ignore your brother and bring me up in here to fuck."

The man grunted. "Fuck that nigga. I hook him up with all kinds of connections an' shit, and he don't wanna share the wealth. As far as I'm concerned, I paid for half this muthafucka so I should be able to do what I want in here."

"You *know* he doesn't like me. I don't know if this is such a good idea."

"Fool, what're you talkin' about? We done fucked already. It's too late to be worryin' about Sean now!" The both of them laughed.

The man said, "'Sides, as sprung as he is over his bitch, he got some nerve to be pokin' his head in mines, tellin' me how you ain't no good for me. He don't know shit about what's good for me. I know I'm his li'l brother, but he don't always have to treat me like a kid."

"Well, even if he treats you like a kid, I'm gonna be there to remind you you're a man." They both chuckled.

"And you do that *so* well, baby. I ain't got no complaints at all with you."

His brother. So Sean had a little brother, and a resentful one at that, it seemed. Resentment was often the sire of disloyalty, which made Israel wonder if Sean's sibling could be used somehow if things got deep.

"Well, I can't stay here all night anyway," said the female. "My cousin has my son, and she's already told me she can't keep him late, she's gotta get up early for work."

"Is that right? Well, I guess you betta g'on ahead and at least suck my dick one more time before we up outta heah."

The female laughed. "Marvin, you are so nasty!"

Marvin. Marvin Cudahy. Or at least Israel hoped it was Cudahy. In the urban community his last name could be anything, if his mother was one of loose morals or bad choices in men.

Apparently Marvin's request wasn't too nasty for his female companion, as she seemed to begin to comply. Marvin was making light moaning noises and saying, "Yeah, baby, suck that muthafucka. Oh, yeeeah." Israel decided that now was a good time to get going.

As he was moving back to the window, he heard the girl say, "Marvin, what are you doing?"

"Stop for a sec. Sit up and look out the window. No, not there. Look right across the street."

There was silence for a couple of seconds, then the girl said, "Is he looking over here?"

"If I had to guess, I'd say yeah. Ain't really no niggas around this neighborhood, so seeing one sittin' outside my brother's house lookin' gangstaed up makes me feel a li'l cautious. I think I'm'a get my gun and go downstairs and have a talk with his ass."

"Oooh, Marvin. I don't know about that. Maybe you should call your brother and see what he says."

Israel could hear the annoyance thick in Marvin's voice. "Fuck that nigga, I ain't gots to call him every time somethin' seems wrong. I'm'a man too. I know how to handle thangs. I got this one."

Israel sighed. It looked like this might get complicated if he didn't do something. It only took him three seconds to decide what.

54

I had gotten off the phone with Ellena quite a while ago. She had been shocked at what I'd told her. She wanted to know if everything was okay, and I told her it was, that I would call her in another thirty minutes just to check in. By the time we hung up, she seemed shell-shocked at all this new information about her brother.

A little time had passed and then I saw another curtain part in one of the windows upstairs. I eagerly peered at it, thinking it would be Israel. Instead it first was somebody that looked a lot like Sean, then a white, very pale looking blonde female. I immediately became alarmed, wondering if they'd perhaps overpowered Israel and had discovered somehow that I was outside waiting for him. I didn't think this was likely and decided to just wait, although my patience was on the verge of disappearing.

Just when I was debating on whether or not to go in after my old friend, my cell phone buzzed. I snatched it off the seat, pressed the On button. "Israel, what the fuck is going on in there? I just saw some nigga and some white chick looking out the window."

He chuckled lazily. "Well, damn, David. Your concern is touching, but the situation is under control. In fact, I think you should come on in here and join the party."

I hung up, got out of the car, and walked up to the front door, cautiously pushing it open. There was nobody in the living room, which was dark but still looked nicely furnished. I immediately felt a pang of envy that Sean had been able to do things for Ellena and my son that I could not. I thought it was so ironic that he had taken care of them with money gotten through dirty means while I struggled on the straight and narrow through Ellena's inspiration.

Israel called from upstairs, "David, is that you?"

"Yeah, I'm comin' up now."

"Okay, hit the second door up here to your right."

When I got up to the room that Israel was in, I was slightly taken aback. The man I'd seen in the window was naked and hog tied with an extension cord on the floor, as was his woman. They were both gagged with washcloths and duct tape. Israel was sitting beside the king-sized bed on the floor lotus-style, looking relaxed and almost serene.

I looked the man over. "That's the nigga that was looking at me from the window. I thought he mighta been Sean."

"Nope, he's Sean's brother."

"Oh *is* he now?"

Israel looked carefully into my face, trying to gauge it. I was looking at Sean's brother and feeling myself go into gangsta mode, all reason quickly falling prey to the rage that was filling my heart in a dark flood. I didn't have Sean here, but I had somebody connected to him that I could hurt. This was the way of the street. If you couldn't get at the muthafucka that caused you harm or trouble, why then, anyone from his team would do.

I stepped in and kicked Sean's brother in the head. The kick was so hard that his whole body rolled over with the force of it. His light skin went red and his hazel eyes blazed wildly at me as he screamed curses completely swallowed up by his gag. His lady friend seemed too scared to scream into her gag, overwhelmed by shock and fear.

I laughed deliciously and readied myself to kick him again, but Israel was up in a flash and between us before I could launch it.

Looking my best friend in the eye I said calmly, "Israel, I suggest you get the fuck outta my way. I don't care how much of that chop-socky shit you know, you gon' hafta use it on me if it gets down to it. This nigga's brother put a hurtin' on me before, and now it look like he a threat to my family, includin' you. I got to touch him and let him know it ain't goin' down like that. And this fool is the key."

Israel actually considered this for a moment and then said, "David, I hear where you're coming from. But we need information first and foremost. That's the main reason we're here. Can you let me ask him some questions first?"

I nodded, but then I said, "After you done, then *I* gets a piece of him. Understood?"

"Understood."

Israel removed the gag from the man's mouth. He spat out a phlegmy wad of spittle and blood and screamed at me, "You muthafucka! Yo' ass lucky this nigga got me tied up, or I would kick yo' ass."

"I don't think so," I said coolly, a wicked smile twisting my lips. He was a big mutha, almost the size of his brother, but I already knew looking at him that I could take him. "I think I'd whup your ass even worse. Bein' tied up and havin' my friend here is savin' you some grief. Well, for now anyway."

Israel kneeled beside him. "Marvin, I'm going to ask you some questions. All I want is info, and I won't let any harm come to you while I am here. If you answer all of our questions—and we actually *believe* your answers—then this will be all over with before you know it. It'll be like we were never here."

"Well, except for the fact that your homeboy just loosened up half the teeth in my head. That's gonna remind me you were fuckin' here."

Israel had a regretful look on his face. "Well, I have to apologize for that. Your brother did him bad a while back, so he's a little emotional about that still. But nothing else has to happen beyond that."

"Fuck the both of y'all. My brother is gonna kill you and that faggot over there and anybody connected to y'all. I'll be dancing on your graves, on your family's fuckin' graves.

Israel was too close to Marvin for me to get to him, so I went for his woman. Kneeling beside her, I picked her up by her hair and slammed her head against the polished hardwood floor with tooth-rattling force. She cried out loudly as I raised her head up again. It was a pained, frightened sound that her gag could not stifle. Marvin looked at me like I was crazy and I gave him an evil stare back.

I said in a clear, detached voice, "Nigga, I will rape the shit out of this bitch. I'll start with my dick, then after I bust my nut I'll find a broom handle or somethin' else to use on her until I can get hard again and do her some more. I'll do her pussy *and* her mouth *and* her ass. Then I'll strangle her to death right in front of you. When I'm done with her, it'll be your turn to die, and best believe I'll take my time about it. Your brother will come back here and find pieces of y'all all over this house.

"We are not fuckin' around here. My friend's questions betta get answered to his satisfaction, 'cause if not..."

I hit the girl as hard as I could on the nose. She loosed a muffled yelp as it squished and broke from the power of my blow. I let her head go and it hit the floor with a dull thud. She was barely conscious, and blood was dripping liberally from the busted, meaty mess that was quite a cute little nose just a few seconds before.

Marvin was easy to read. I could tell by the expression on his face that I had his attention. Israel gave me a look that I could not fathom at all, though I was sure he was annoyed at how I was handling the situation. He had to be. I didn't care. I knew I had far more experience in situations like this than he did, and judging by the look of terror on Sean's brother's face, my style was effective.

Israel turned back to Marvin and said, "I have one name for you. Fereal McNaughton. Who is he?"

Marvin was still looking at me. "He...he's one'a Sean's runnin' partners, another cop. They into a bunch'a shit together. He, Sean, another cop nigga named Mike Mettigan and this Mexican cop named Orlando Flores run a crew under 'em that's into all kindsa thangs."

Israel raised an eyebrow. "Like what? Specifics, Marvin."

Marvin looked frustrated. "Man, I don't know what the fuck they into. I know I've helped them out on some insurance scam shit—settin' muthafuckas up in cars with fake names, gettin' insurance on they car and then stagin' accidents and car thefts to get the insurance to pay off. Other than that, I know they got they hands on a bunch'a different shit but I don't know details."

I smiled darkly. "Well, I'm not likin' your answers, m'man. So you better give us some shit we can work with so I don't have to hurt your lady no more. Otherwise, I'm actually more than ready to forget her and get started on you."

Israel gave him the good cop look. "My friend here is serious. I don't know that I can contain him. And honestly, I'm not sure I'm going to want to if we don't get what we need. Now I need to know some specifics about some of the things your brother and his boys are into."

"I know…I know they workin' with some of the Compton Crips in the dope game. They also tied into that with the Nutty Block Crips and some'a them Neighborhood Crips too. I don't know contacts or names or nothin' like that, so don't ask. I know they hooked up with some big wigs up at city hall, but I don't know no damn names. Uh, um, what else? Shit, man, I really don't know that much. My brother thinks I'm a fuckin' moron, and he don't tell me nothin'."

Israel and I looked at each other. We both instantly knew that this man *was* a moron and that his brother probably really didn't tell him anything.

Israel finally said, "Okay, Marvin. I believe you. That leaves us with one thing to think about here. What happens when your brother comes home? What are you going to tell him about our little visit here?"

Marvin looked frightened as a child waking up from a nightmare. "Nothin', man. I swear on my mama, it's gone be like y'all wudn't even here. Hell, *I'm* not even supposed to be here."

"Hmmmm." I looked thoughtful for a moment and then continued. "Now why do I somehow feel that I can trust you less than a hunnerd percent?"

Poor Marvin looked like he was going to cry. "Fuh real, man. I don't know nothin', I ain't gone say nothin', and all this is about nothin'."

Israel saw a pile of clothes in the corner of the room and walked toward it. He rifled through the garments and walked back over holding driver's licenses aloft.

"We know where you live now, you and your girl. I know you're going to tell your brother we were here. But our little compromise is that you're going to tell him we wore masks, broke in here, stole a few things, and left you and the young lady here a little beat-up and hog tied. If I think anything else has been said other than that, I'm going to personally pay you a visit. And my friend is going to pay your woman a visit."

Marvin grunted and looked away.

I smiled and added, "And just so's you don't forget a nigga…"

I reached down and grabbed Marvin's naked balls and gave them a tight squeeze. His eyes rolled back in his head and he moaned loudly. I grabbed his head and took my time dealing him several vicious blows. When I wanted to give my hands a rest I kicked his hog tied body until it began to turn purple. I thought that Israel might step in and stop me but he did nothing.

When I was done I put the gag back in Marvin's bloody mouth. Slightly winded, I stood and took a deep breath and rubbed my bruised and scraped knuckles. Israel said, "We've got to find some stuff here to take to make this look good."

"Lead the way, my nigga," I said merrily, feeling an ugly joy that I knew I should be ashamed of. "As far as I'm concerned we could take this muthafucka's entire house."

55

As we drove home on the freeway, there was silent contemplation. Then I finally said, "So what next?"

"Well, we give Ellena the names he gave to us and see what she can do with them in regards to her trip to Internal Affairs."

"And that's it?" I snorted derisively. "Seems like we all still open for whatever that nigga wants to do with us, particularly since Ellena will be makin' it clear that she don't want to be with him."

"You think Sean is still going to make a move?"

I shrugged. "I dunno. He seems to be sprung on her hard. Love makes a man do funny things, makes him forget about bidness and all the things he has goin' for 'im. He may not wanna let her go."

Israel thought about this in silence.

We drove on for a few minutes and then he said, "You were pretty savage back there. Kinda interesting to see that side of you."

I laughed. "Hey, you gots to have a savage side ya own damn self. Imagine how wild it was for me to come into that room and see that big nigga and his 'ho' hog tied like that."

"Yeah, but I don't know I would have handled that way if you weren't there. I probably would have used pain to draw information out of him. I can torture a man, and he might answer me out of the fear of that pain, but you made Sean's brother truly scared, like afraid of the dark scared."

"Well, he ain't the first nigga that I done put in that kinda work on. I hope he'll be the last though. I enjoy that kinda shit too much, and that's not the way I want to be. I want to be the best example I can be for Michael.

"Some of my homeboys is raisin' their kids up to be on the set when they get of age. That don't make no damn sense to me. Little three-, four-, five-year-olds throwin' up signs and callin' out the set. This ain't the kinda life you want your kids involved in. At least I don't want mines involved in it or nowhere near it."

"You think you're going to tell Michael about your past life, even about things up to tonight?"

"Iz, I honestly don't know. I got some homies that's been down since day one that's like godparents to him, so I'm assumin' at some point he'll be able to work out that we ain't your average Joe Blow type'a cats. He ain't asked no questions so far. I really haven't figured out how I'm'a handle that yet."

"Well, getting back to tonight, I guess we're going to have to see what Ellena's going to do over the next couple of weeks and what Cudahy's response will be to it."

"Yeah, I guess, but I'm a preemptive kinda nigga, myself. I don't like waiting for someone to make the first move, particularly a muthafucka that got the resources of the LAPD behind 'im. I still feel like we should take it to 'im, force his hand."

Israel thought for a second and then said, "The gang sets that he mentioned, is your set affiliated with any of them?"

"Not really, but we ain't beefin' wit' none of 'em either. Why?"

"Well, it may not even get to that. I've got a few ideas."

"Okay, well, let's have 'em."

Israel shook his head no. "Not yet. What I'm thinking may amount to nothing. Let me turn it over in my head a little bit."

I sighed impatiently. "Y' know, if you bounce some shit off'a me we may be able to come up with somethin' together. I done told you everything that's on my mind."

"David, when the time comes, I will let you know what's up. I can promise you I won't make a move without you knowing what's going on, okay?"

I looked away from him, slightly annoyed. I knew this was the best I was going to get from him. I simply said, "Okay."

56

A couple of weeks went by and life seemed to go back to normal. I pretty much figured that we weren't going to hear anything from Sean. The only thing different was that Ellena and I started dating in earnest again. I would like to say that we took up right where we left off, but it was a slow process. We slept together once more and then agreed just to take our time and just get reacquainted. It was a little frustrating for me on the sexual side, but emotionally speaking I was happier than I was during the first run of our courtship.

I wanted to spend an evening with Michael so I asked Ellena if I could pick him up from school. She agreed with no problem. I took off work early the next day to go get him, thinking we would spend some time at a park a few blocks away from the school and then go home and log in some time on the PlayStation. I drove up to his school in a good mood, parking my car in front just as the bell rang and all the little children poured out. I watched them as they went to their various parents in cars parked in front of and behind me.

After five minutes I began to wonder what was holding my son up. I carefully scanned all the children and parents and teachers still floating about and didn't see him. I sighed deeply, trying not to get paranoid. I decided I would give him five more minutes and then go in and see what was going on.

I lasted only three minutes before I got out of my car and raced up the steps into the school foyer. I went to Michael's class and found the teacher there all alone as she was packing up her things to leave. She was an older white woman, a kindly lady that I'd met previously at a parent/teacher mixer the school had held a few months before. She spoke so highly of my son that she earned a permanent soft spot in my heart.

I leaned in the doorway and said, "Mrs. Lutz? Hi, my name is David Hill. Do you remember me?"

She smiled broadly. "Now how am I going to forget you? You're the father of one of my best students. How are you today?"

"I'm good," I lied, trying not to let the worry I suddenly felt crease my voice. "I'm just wonderin' where Michael is. I've been waitin' for him out front, but so far I don't see him. I was just wonderin' if everything is okay."

Mrs. Lutz looked at me strangely. "I guess his mother didn't tell you. The police officer that occasionally comes to pick him up took him straight out of class today, not even fifteen minutes ago. He said that Michael's mom wanted to spend some extra time with him before she went on a sixteen hour shift."

My heart sunk, although I kept my face calm and composed. "This'd be Sean Cudahy, correct?"

Mrs. Lutz nodded her head, now looking slightly worried. "Yes, Mr. Cudahy has come to school to pick up the boy quite often and is in fact listed by his mother as one of her emergency contacts for him. Is there something wrong?"

I smiled. "Naw, it's just some miscommunication between me an' his mom. I was supposed to pick him up and take him out either today or tomorrow. I couldn't for the life of me remember exactly which day. I guess I know now."

Mrs. Lutz was studying me closely as she said, "Are you *sure* nothing is wrong?"

"Mrs. Lutz, he's wit' the police," I said with a chuckled. "And on top of that, he's a cop we all know. If you cain't trust the police, who can you trust?"

Mrs. Lutz still didn't look like she was buying it. I excused myself quickly and left the class. I raced out of that school and got in my car, screeching away from the curb.

Once I was on the freeway, I picked up my phone and dialed Ellena. She answered on the first ring. I told her the situation and she was very calm and collected about it. Her only concern was with what my plans were.

"You're going to call Sean and find out what the fuck he is doing with my boy. Then you're gonna call me back and let me know what's up. We'll figure out the rest then."

Ellena sounded worried. "I'll do that, but, Dave, *please* don't fly off the handle. I know Sean. He's not going to hurt Michael. He's probably trying to make some point from you guys breaking into his house. Let me handle him, okay?"

I said brusquely, "Call me after you've talked to him. I'm cool until I know exactly what the fuck is going on."

I hung up the phone, satisfied that Ellena bought that lie. I already knew I was on my way to Cudahy's house. I hoped that he had my son there and if not I knew I'd do whatever it took to find out where he was, if he was safe or not. After that, I was going to be the one to let Sean Cudahy know he could cancel Christmas.

57

It was about a forty-minute drive to Sean's house from where I was, which was not a good thing. That was too much time to seethe, to barely be able to concentrate on the simple function of driving because I was so concentrated on what I was going to do to him if he had done any harm to Michael, my beloved little prince. The sky was an ugly gray, looking as if it might spit out rain at any moment. The weather did nothing to help my foul mood and was in fact fodder for it.

When I got there, I didn't see a car in the driveway. I parked across the street in almost the same spot I was in during my visit two weeks before. I decided I would wait there for him for a while, and if he didn't show up I would simply break into his house and wait for him to come back. I wouldn't be doing a Spider-Man up any drain pipes; I would just go around to the back door and kick it in if I had to.

As I was turning this over in my head, my cell phone rang. I clicked the On button. "What up?"

"David, it's Israel. Ellena just called me. She told me what's going on."

"Israel, I am going to kill that muthafucka just as soon as I get my boy back," I said tightly, trying to control the fury I felt. "I'm in front of his house now. His car ain't here, but if I got to wait at this bitch all night for him to get back, then I will."

"David, that's not the answer. At least not the way you're about to go at it. Let me meet you over there, man. Please don't do anything rash."

"I'll wait for you while I'm just kickin' it, but if that muthafucka shows up before you get here I can't make that promise. Did Ellena get a hold of him?"

"No. She's left messages for him on his cell phone and pager. She thinks he's just trying to build up our anxiety levels before he makes a move. I actually think that too."

"He ain't makin' me anxious. He just makin' me want to kill him even more. And that is exactly what's gonna happen, brah. I ain't bullshittin'."

"Okay, Dave. Like I said, just try to hold tight until I get there. I'm leaving now, okay?"

"I suggest you hurry up. If he get here, I'm not holdin' out for you."

I ended the call and put the phone back in my waist holster. I was literally seeing red. I already knew I would not be satisfied with just getting my son back. I wanted Cudahy's blood so bad I felt like I could taste its bright, coppery freshness in my mouth.

As I was thinking this, my cell phone rang again. As I clicked it on and said hello, I was hoping that it wasn't Israel calling and telling me there was something delaying him. I would need his guiding calm. I knew I had a fuck-the-consequences frame of mind just then, and I wasn't giving a shit about anything logical in regards to Sean Cudahy.

"Hey, my nigga, what's up?"

"What's up," I said cautiously, not recognizing the voice.

"Well, what's up is that it seems we have a little problem here."

My mood darkened even further past the point of reason. I knew now that I was speaking to Sean Cudahy himself.

I tried to keep my voice even and calm as I said, "We sure do have a little problem. You got my son. I want him back. And after I get him back, me and you gots issues to resolve."

Sean Cudahy chuckled. "Well, we *do* have issues to resolve between us. One of which is you and that other fool breaking into my house and messing with my brother. The other's about

Ellena. But we're going to get to all of that. The first thing we need to do is negotiate getting you your son back, yes?"

"Muthafucka, if you have harmed a hair on my son's head, if he say you even *looked* at him cross-eyed—"

"Now, now, we both know that this is not about Michael. I just wanted to get your attention. And I got it. So now we move on to the next level."

"And what's that?"

Sean sighed dramatically. "Well, it seems like that little bitch Ellena has shot her mouth off to some people about a thing or two. Now people are casting a hard eye on me and some of my friends. We need to make sure that if people start asking questions that they never get answered. Ellena has to forget everything she thinks she knows about my people and me."

"So why you calling me? Why ain't you talked to her about alla this?"

"I *have* talked to her. That's how I got your cell phone number. She's ready to fall into line. The only question marks now are you and her brother."

"I cain't do nothin' to you, bruh."

"Well, to use a tried and true old cliché on you, you know too much. We have to guarantee our safety. It's a simple matter of survival of the fittest, and you're at the bottom of the food chain."

"Enough'a all this bullshit, nigga. I want my son back."

"Where are you at now?"

"I'm right outside yo' house, m'man. Just waitin' fuh you."

There was silence from Sean on the other line. I could feel his silent rage burning through the receiver. Then he said slowly, "I want you to take a good look at my house. 'Cause that's the last time you're ever going to see it.

"I'm going to give you an address for a place deep in the Valley, up past Northridge near Devonshire, close to the mountains. You'll have an hour and a half to get there, tops. If you're even two seconds past that, well, I guess how fast you get there will determine how much you love your son, won't it?"

A rage filled me that was a deep and black as a bottomless well. I said tightly, "Gimme the address."

Cudahy read it to me and I wrote it down on a piece of paper. After repeating it back to him, I told him again, "If *anything* is wrong with my son, bitch—"

Sean Cudahy chuckled and then hung up in my face.

I twisted the key in the ignition and pulled the car away from the curb with a cloud of smoke from the burning of tires. I raced toward the freeway, which was thankfully pretty close to Sean's house. Once I was on the highway and cruising I called up Israel. He asked me what was happening, quickly adding that he was now halfway to Sean Cudahy's house.

"Don't bother. Cudahy just called me up. He talked to Ellena, got my cell number from her."

"What'd he say?"

"He think he's won the round on this one. He gave me this address up in the Valley and told me to get my ass up there in an hour and a half if I wanna get Michael back."

"What is the address?"

I gave him the address. "You got any ideas?"

"Not right off the top, but if you make it there in good time I am again going to ask that you wait until I get there."

"Now, Iz, you know I cain't do that. I just wanna make sure Michael is okay, and then whatever happens is gonna happen."

"Dave, we both know they're trying to get you up there to kill you. You have to keep your cool on this."

"I'll see you up there, my nigga—or not. Good-bye."

Israel started to say something and I hung up. I shut the power on my cell phone off. I was on autopilot as I cruised. I had but one thought in mind: "I will kill Sean Cudahy. Even if it costs me my own life, that nigga is breathing his last breath in this world today."

58

It took me barely forty-five minutes to make it to the address I was given by Cudahy. I had sped and rode the car pool lane and violated just about every traffic statute to make good time. I thanked God that I wasn't spotted and pulled over by the police, and then chuckled at the irony.

The house was a fairly nice two-story affair that sat on a piece of wide-open land in the middle of nowhere. It looked as if the closest neighbor was maybe half a mile away. There was a long driveway that led from the street up to the front door of the house. I debated whether or not to park somewhere else and try creeping up to the house by foot, but my impatience regarding Michael and my fuck-it gangsta attitude got the best of me. I drove up and parked right in front of the door.

Getting out of my car, I surveyed the house. I wondered dimly if it belonged to Sean, and then quickly decided I didn't care. I was still thinking about trying to go in the back door or something like that but I knew they had to have heard my car pull up. I decided to just walk up to the front door and ring the bell.

It took but one ring to get the door answered. When the door opened, the very bastard I'd pledged to kill was looking at me with a deranged smile. Sean Cudahy was as big as a Brahmin, but I thought nothing about the size of him as I launched a punch that caught him flush on the cheek.

The blow was far from anything that could knock a man of his size out, but it did stun him. He stumbled back in past the doorway and was on his way to getting himself back together when I jabbed at him and caught him again on the same cheek. This time he ignored the pain and swung at me, but I easily dodged the misguided blow. I was reaching into my waistband to pull out the snub-nose .38 stashed there, when I heard the door shut behind me and felt two powerful arms wrap around me in a bear hug, lifting me off the ground.

Sean stepped in with a looping roundhouse punch that caught me on the same cheek that I'd struck him on. My head exploded into a thousand flashing lights and I felt my legs lose all feeling. Cudahy pulled the pistol from my waistband with a hard jerk. The powerful arms released me and I dropped to the floor in a heap, trying desperately to hold on to consciousness.

"Stupid nigga," Sean said with a scowl, kicking me in my ribs. This was a new pain, and I was sure he had seriously bruised or even broken a rib or two. I moaned loudly against my will, and I could hear two satisfied chuckles. I wanted to see who was with Cudahy, but my eyes were sealed shut with the hurt.

Rubbing his cheek, Sean kneeled beside me and chuckled. "You got me a coupl'a good licks, you li'l fuck. Congrats to you. I guess you had to, seeing as how I beat the shit out of you before... say, I guess this makes two times in a row I've taken your manhood from you!"

I said nothing, still battling the pain. He continued on, "I know you're too messed up to say anything right now, but I wanted to give you some good news and some bad news. Which news do you want first?"

I managed to groan out, "Fuh...fuck you."

"Okay, I'll take that to mean you want the good news to come first. Michael is back with his mother. I made that call as soon as we saw your car coming up the driveway. She's pretty relieved, as you can imagine.

"The bad news is that you are in a world of shit, my friend. Yes, you are. I don't think you are going to get out of this one in one piece. The minute you decided that you wanted to get involved in this—especially when you broke into my house—is the minute you decided you were tired of living."

Sean instructed the other guy, whom he called Mike, to bring me to "the room." Mike, who seemed easily as large as Sean, picked me up with ease and brusquely slung me over his shoulder. My rib and my head were screaming with pain, but I managed somehow to keep my mouth shut. We walked down a long hallway and turned into the last room on the left. He dumped me onto the hard wood floor and I hit the side with the damaged rib. An involuntary yelp escaped my lips and I heard multiple voices laughing.

I knew that it was imperative that I force my eyes open. I felt helpless without knowing what was going on around me.

Through squinted eyes I looked up to see seven large men looking down at me, all of them black except for one Hispanic and one white. Two of them were clad in police uniforms. The expressions on their faces ranged from amused to curious to evil looking to noncommittal. My eyes involuntarily closed in pain, but I heard their voices loud and clear.

"Well, what are going to do with this muthafucka?"

A bemused snigger. "Kill him, of course. What did you think, we were going to take 'im out to dinner or something?"

Laughter and then a voice trying to hide its annoyance: "Well, I *know* we have to kill him, Mr. Comic View. I *mean*, are we just going to disappear him, or are we going to make him an example or what?"

"I don't see the need to make him an example. There's only one principle that is going to survive this mess and that's Sean's ex. She's not going to say a word—especially after the man she loves most disappear from this earth. She's going to want to protect that kid, her brother too, for that matter."

"Sean, are you sure we shouldn't get rid of your ex and her brother too?" This I could tell was the white man's voice. "I mean, I am *not* one for leaving loose ends. As long as someone is still breathing, there is abso-fuckin'-lutely no guarantee that they're going to stay silent."

I heard Sean say with confidence, "She's about as much a problem as this nigga here is about not to be. You don't have to worry about her, she's gonna be my responsibility. The brother, I think for his sister's sake he'll be calm and collected too."

"I don't know about that, my friend," said someone with a powerful, authoritative voice. "She is about to lose one of the only things that matter to her in this world. Maybe she might want to start making loud noises to get revenge. Who knows, maybe she might just pick up a gun and come after us herself. And I don't know enough about her brother to know what his reaction to all this might be." There was a pause, and then the man said, "I'm with Handy, I think we ought to just get rid of everybody."

Sean laughed uncomfortably. "C'mon, I told you Ellena's not going to be a problem. Just trust me on this one."

The person behind the strong voice ignored Cudahy and said to me, "Hey, m'man, I want to show you something. Please open your eyes and look up."

The pain had backed off of me enough to comply with his request. The man was large and chocolate-colored, one of the cops that was uniformed. He was handsome and bald, the light from the ceiling reflecting off of his freshly shaved dome. He had an emotionless expression on his face as he surveyed me. I wanted to give him a mad-dog stare back, but I still hurt too much for it to be convincing.

"Have you talked to anyone about us?" The man's voice was now smooth, and coaxing. "This is already uglier than it has to be. I don't want anyone else to get hurt. I don't want to lie and say that you're going to get out of this, but maybe we can keep your woman and her brother and your son safe. You just have to be honest with me."

"Hell naw," I grunted. "Ain't nobody else involved in this shit. We thought maybe once y'all knew what was up, that we had info on you, y'all would just go away, and I had plans to kill your boy there at some point anyway, so I didn't want to tell anyone about this."

"You didn't tell anyone else in your gang set?" This came from the lone Mexican in the room, a handsome crew-cut man who was wearing a muscle T-shirt, baggy jeans and the latest Air Jordans. "We know you're gang affiliated. And I can't see any reason you would care if anyone in your set knew or not."

"Gotdamn, how many times I got to tell you. I ain't told nobody *shit.* I ain't wanted to get the homies involved, wudn't no need for them to be. When it came time for me to get Cudahy, I wanted it to be a solo mission."

The big dark man laughed. "You really don't like Sean, do you?"

I looked up at Cudahy, who was smirking at me. "*Hell* no. And no matter what happens, trust, if I got to give my soul to Satan to get me some gitback from the grave, I'm'a do that."

The Mexican and the black man looked at each other, then back at me. The Mexican said cheerily, "I don't think you're going to have to sell your soul or none of that dramatic crap."

I looked at him in confusion. So did Cudahy. My mouth started to move to ask what he was talking about when the big black man with the smooth voice stepped to Cudahy as quick as a lightning bolt. His hand flashed out to grip Cudahy's neck and I saw his head jerk back and forth and heard a loud snap. Sean Cudahy's big body dropped to the floor in a heap quite close to me, twitching madly as his soul fled to the next life.

"Man, I wanted to have the pleasure'a doin' that," I gasped out, looking at the big man. His whole demeanor was now centered on me, and I felt the same powerful energy from him that I often felt from my one true friend in this world, Israel Baylock.

The big chocolate fellow laughed. "Sorry, m'man. Sean's mistake was that he opened his mouth to your lady. There was no need for him to do that at all. It was quite selfish, in fact. It put us all in jeopardy."

"I don't care about that. I don't give a fuck if y'all are plannin' to assassinate the fuckin' president. I wanted Cudahy and you just took care of that li'l issue for me. Now I just wanna live in peace with my lady and my son."

"It's too late for that, friend," said the Mexican, pulling a cell phone out of his pants pocket. "Everybody concerned with this is going to disappear."

He punched in some numbers on the phone. Everyone was silent in the room, watching him. He finally said into the receiver, "Dirk, you still outside of the Baylock girl's house?" Silence again. "Okay, I want you guys to go on in there and take care of her and the kid."

"No!" I screamed, finding a sudden burst of adrenaline. I started to sit up and two of the men pounced on me, pulling me to my feet and dragging me over to a metal chair that was bolted to the floor in the center of the room. They handcuffed my hands and legs to the chair as the Mexican continued to speak into his cell phone:

"*Yes,* Dirk. The child, too." Pause. "Well, the alternative is me, you and anybody associated with us doing some hard time. You've already spent over half of your life in the joint, and now you're making money and doing great. You want to give that up for this?"

I struggled in the chair, feeling unwanted tears sting my eyes. I had made a mistake again in anger and left my precious heart and soul defenseless. I didn't care so much about dying, which in retrospect was probably why I had acted so foolishly in dropping myself in the hands of these men. In my anger I had not thought about protecting my family, and now Israel was on his way to disaster as well.

"Okay," the Mexican concluded, "call me when you're finished." He clicked off his cell phone. "Dirk is going to call me when the deed is done. Shouldn't take more than ten minutes."

I struggled in the chair, weeping uncontrollably. I cursed every man in the room and his family and swore on everything I love that I would come back from the dead and avenge my family. The men in the room were unaffected by my dramatics. When I was done cursing and struggling I just settled down and started crying like a baby outright. I knew that there was no chance I would see my family again and that I had failed completely in protecting them.

As if he could read my mind, the Mexican walked over and put his hand on my shoulder. “Don’t worry about your people, bud,” he said consolingly. “You’ll be joining them soon enough—one big happy family in heaven.”

59

Ellena laid Michael to sleep in his bed. She was satisfied that he had been treated well. When she'd asked him what the men he had been with all day had done with him, he simply said that they had taken him to McDonald's and the park and he had played for most of the afternoon. She breathed a sigh as she watched him drift off to sleep, glad at least she'd been right about Sean on this one thing. He could never hurt Michael.

She went to the living room and parted the curtains slightly. The car with the three men in it that returned Michael was still sitting out front. She wondered what they could possibly want still—not David, Israel had already told her that he was on his way to some house in the Valley where Sean was. That was a whole other subject she didn't want to think about.

The car in the front of the house was a shiny black Acura with tinted windows and gold Dayton's. She could not see into the car at all to know what the men were up to. When the three of them came to the door with Michael, all of the men looked cold, emotionless. She could not imagine how Michael could have enjoyed himself so with them.

She let the curtain fall shut and went to the kitchen to get her purse. She brought it back to the living room and sat on the sofa. She pulled her nine-millimeter Glock out of the expensive Gucci bag and checked the pistol's magazine to make sure it was full. If these men had anything else planned or seemed like they were going to make another move of some sort, she'd shoot first and ask questions later.

Ellena's mind strayed to Dave. His temper was leading him right now and she'd already seen that all that led to was disaster. She knew Sean would relish his chance to be able to get to Dave without worrying about her feelings and emotions. Maybe that's what he wanted all along. They'd experienced a good time or two over the years, but no one would have her heart and spirit as completely as David Hill did. Sean had done so much for her. She'd honestly tried to love him like he wanted her to, but the heart follows its own path.

She wondered often over the years why she loved David Hill so much. He was unremarkable as a person and his accomplishments as a human being on the planet earth were limited to things that had no positive value at all. But she seemed to have gotten through all of that to the heart of him, and his heart was essentially good. And she could not imagine her son with a more thoughtful, attentive father than how David turned out to be. The zest and vigor in which he attacked fatherhood was a shock to her. She hoped that he would show that same attitude in their renewed romance and thus far he hadn't let her down.

"God," she thought, "please let him be okay. You just gave him back to me, please, don't take him away. We've wasted enough time and I love him so much."

She shook the bad thoughts from her head. There would be time to be weak later. That was how it had been since her father died, and she almost had to be the rock for the entire family. Now was the time to take care of keeping her son safe. Later she would weep over all that happened, hopefully while wrapped in David's strong arms.

She got up and peeked out the living room window again. The three men were once again getting out of the car. Her heart racing, she went to grab her gun off of the sofa. As she was picking it up the living room door shook with force, as if someone were trying to kick or shoulder it in.

Without a moment's hesitation she flipped the safety off of the Glock and fired two shots into the door. She heard a pained yelp and then the pounding on the door ceased. She eased toward the living room window and tentatively peeked out to see if anyone was still on the porch. There was no one in sight.

She thought quickly about the back door. As she did she heard a loud crash; clearly someone had smashed the window in the door and was unlatching the lock. She didn't want to make a stand in the living room, neither did she feel secure that all the men were coming through that door. There were multiple windows in the house, none with bars on them, including—one in Michael's room.

She raced to her son's room. She would have to hide him somewhere, but where? The house had a basement, but she would have to go through the kitchen to get to it. Maybe the bathroom in her bedroom.

As she opened the door to Michael's room, she thought her heart was going to stop completely. The window was wide open, a late afternoon breeze causing the curtains to flutter gently. The man sitting on her son's bed was gently stroking his head and watching at him sleep with a loving expression on his face. She was about to speak, but he silenced her by raising his index finger to his pursed lips.

"Don't worry, Ellena," Israel said quietly. "Nothing's going to happen to you or Michael. That's a promise. And you know I *always* keep my promises..."

60

Dirk Benton was generally a happy man these days. He had been in and out of state and federal institutions for most of his twenty-six years, but after hooking up with his homeboy Orlando Flores and his crew he was now living the good life. There was a steady stream of good money—Orlando had him on retainer. And there were women galore as well. He had never been good with them growing up, usually getting their attention by hurting them and taking what he wanted from them. But that was not the case at all now.

His crew consisted of his Aryan Nation buddies who he'd taken from the pen and trained as he had been trained. The good life was now addictive to them all and they'd do anything to maintain it. When Orlando Flores told them they would have to kill the kid along with the mother, they flinched uneasily for a moment. But they were all sold on this life now, and nothing or nobody was going to do anything to jeopardize it.

He had Friedman, the largest of the bunch take the front door. Friedman was six feet eleven inches tall and 375 pounds of mostly muscle. Dirk knew it would not take Friedman but one or two good shoulder shots to get the door down. Dirk and Shooter, partner number two who'd earned his name for his speed and accuracy with any kind of pistol, would take the back route in. Freidman would take care of the girl while Shooter grabbed the kid and he searched the rest of the house to make sure that no one was there.

No one had counted on the bitch actually shooting through the door, which was a stupid slip on their part since she was a cop. From the back of the house he had heard Friedman's high-pitched yelp. As he busted in the center window framed in the back door he was already thinking that someone, perhaps a concerned next-door neighbor, would call the cops. This was a quiet neighborhood, fairly well-to-do, so it wouldn't take the police long to respond. They would have to move quickly.

As he unlatched the door and strolled in, he wondered if his third man had made it into the bedroom. Shooter was also a career burglar, so he would place odds he was safely in. He thought he'd also heard the crunch of the front door giving way to Friedman's power. They all had Nextel phones with walkie-talkie features if they needed to communicate, but before they all had taken their places Dirk had instructed them not to use them unless an extreme situation called for it. Hell, it was only one woman and a kid. He didn't see how it should take that long to do the deed and get the hell on out of there.

"Shooter!" he shouted, throwing caution to the wind. "Make some noise. Lemme know you're in."

"I'm in. I'm in the master bedroom."

Dirk nodded and yelled out, "Friedman! Acknowledge!"

"I'm here," came Friedman's gruff yell. "I'm okay—the bullet just fuckin' grazed my cheek. Hurts like a mutha, but I'm still good. I'm posted in the living room."

"Okay," Dirk shouted, satisfied. He clicked the walkie-talkie. "I'm heading to the kid's room. If you hear gunfire, stay where you are. If there's a break in the gunfire and you call me on the Nextel and I don't answer, get the fuck outta here. Same with you guys if either of you run into the broad."

They didn't verbally acknowledge. Dirk knew they understood their directions.

As he left the kitchen and proceeded down the hallway, he wondered who would get the house when everyone concerned with it was dead. It was a nice place. He'd have to talk to his cop homies about a possible hook-up.

He got to the first open door to the right in the hallway. Hopefully the child was not in that room; better that Friedman got to him. Friedman was a pure prison-honed savage and could probably do the deed he and Shooter might not have the stomach for.

He paused, readying his Glock. He was not going to get caught like Friedman had. The bitch clearly was not afraid to shoot and that was not a plus in this situation.

He took a breath and vaulted himself into the doorway, swinging the gun in all directions in the room. It was the child's room and it was empty. There was one more room at the end of the hallway. If they'd gone down there Shooter would have caught them. Maybe they were in the hall bathroom?

As he was pondering this someone jerked him from behind. His reflexes were sharp and he tried to swing the gun around to fire, but it was swatted from his hand as if he were a helpless child. It went flying down the hallway with a clatter.

Whoever had him from behind seem to have inhuman strength. Dirk was not a small or weak man in the slightest, but he felt totally powerless as he was grabbed by his shoulders and ushered down the hall toward the living room. A voice from behind grunted in his ear, "Tell the other one to come into living room too. Now!"

Dirk had no problem with that. He would need numbers with this one. That was clear. "Shooter, get into the living room, ASAP."

When they got into the living room Dirk was given a hard shove that sent him across the room into Friedman's arms. Friedman caught him effortlessly and scowled, "Who the fuck is this guy?"

"I'm Ellena Baylock's brother," Israel said in a quiet voice that was still powerful and menacing. "And you signed your death warrants by being here today."

"I don't think so, brother," Shooter said with a smirk from behind Israel, sticking his pistol straight into the back of his head. "I think you just added an extra body for us to deal with. But that's okay, 'cause…"

That was all Shooter got out as Israel spun, ducked underneath where his pistol seemed frozen in midair and struck him with a straight punch that hit squarely in his bladder. He simultaneously knocked away Shooter's gun as he had Dirk's only moments ago. A stain appeared at the crotch of Shooter's pants where a mix of blood and urine was shooting out of his penis. Shooter was overcome with an agony he had never felt before in his life and a scream that seemed as if it would never end erupted from his mouth. Israel quickly silenced the scream by straightening up and hitting Shooter in the throat full force, crushing it. He fell hard to the living room floor jerking and gurgling and dying.

Israel looked at the other two men. He was so full of rage that he was scared of himself. He had to bring it under control, but a raging tiger was loose in him. It was hungry and wanted to feed.

"I'm going to give you fools a one-time option," Israel said tightly. "You can get out of here now—and I mean right now—or you can die like him." Israel indicated the jerking body of Shooter at his feet.

Dirk was fine with that, trying to figure out how he could explain all of this to Orlando Flores, but Friedman's face went beet red as he screamed, "Fuck you, nigger!"

The giant man charged across the room toward Israel like an enraged bull. Israel charged right back at him with a murderous shriek. The sound was like the roar of some wild animal and it caused Friedman to slow his stride toward Israel just a hair. That was all he needed as he launched himself in the air and caught Friedman with a looping roundhouse kick that landed just below his temple with a sound like a whip cracking.

Friedman went down like a wounded bull. Israel was on him quick as lightening. Dirk could not see exactly what was going on, as Israel's back blocked his view. He heard crunching and popping sounds coming from Friedman's jerking body, then a thick, gout of blood shot in the air in a single fountain stream.

When Israel stood and turned toward him Dirk was frozen with fear. The man had a good amount of blood on him and there was a look in his eyes that looked like nothing reflecting any sort of humanity. It was the look of a wild coyote that hadn't eaten in days, or perhaps of a mother lion protecting her young. It was beyond this world. Dirk knew that his escape option was done with.

"Hey man, look. I was just following orders," Dirk said squeamishly, suddenly feeling flush and hot. He knew he was sweating and looked as frightened as a child and did not care in the slightest. "It's nothing personal. You said I could get outta here. I'm just gonna start backing toward the door, and I'm gonna leave. You can handle things with your sister, make sure her and the kid are okay. That sounds good, doesn't it?"

Israel's expression and body posture did not change. Dirk tried backing up toward the door, and even felt like he could make it. But then Israel began walking toward him, locking his eyes with Dirk's. Israel's bleak stare paralyzed him. There was nothing in those eyes but the promise of the deepest, darkest sleep.

Dirk's bowels let loose on him as Israel approached him. This was death coming. "Damn, I was just starting to live, to have a little money and security," he thought. And then Israel was on him and he could not even find the voice to scream.

61

They had been trying to get a hold of the guy that they'd ordered to kill Ellena and Michael, so far without success. It seemed to make a couple of the men upset and they would occasionally slap my face and give me vicious body shots. I didn't care at this point because I had figured out two very important things:

"I am going to die today."

"Israel isn't coming to my rescue." He had already gone to Ellena's.

The Mexican cat tried to call his people on the cell phone again. He was clearly getting quite pissed. As the phone rang in his ear he said to everybody in the room, "One of us might have to head out there to check it out. This isn't like Dirk. He's the most reliable outsider on our team."

Apparently someone on the other end picked up the phone. The Mexican said into the receiver, "Hold on, I'm gonna put you on speaker." He pressed a button on the phone. "Okay, Dirk, we can all hear you. Now you can tell us what's going on over there and why you haven't been picking up. It's just a woman and a kid, for Christ sake."

"Yes, a woman and a kid," said Israel. "But the most important woman and the most important kid in the world to me. Therefore, they were the wrong ones to fuck with."

The big black cop with the smooth voice didn't sound so smooth as he grunted, "Who the hell are you?"

"My name is Israel Baylock."

"The gotdamn brother," the Mexican muttered distastefully.

"David Hill had better still be alive over there."

I piped up quickly. "I'm right here, Iz. Fuck these fools."

The white man stepped in and gave me a hard shot across my jaw. He knocked out a couple of teeth and I spit them out and cursed loudly.

"So my old friend Dave is alive. Unfortunately, none of your people here are in that same condition. I did to them what they were going to do my sister and nephew. And if you don't let David Hill go right now, I'm going to do the same to you."

"David Hill isn't going anywhere—except maybe to hell," the Mexican said, his face stony. "You want him? Bring your ass up here and get him."

"Okay," Israel said. The line went dead.

The Mexican tossed the cell phone to the ground. It broke into multiple pieces as he screamed, "That piece of shit threatened us, did you hear that? Who is this puto?"

The smooth black cop said, "That's a good question, Orlando." He looked at me. "Who is this fellow? He killed three of our best guys, cats who are the roughest of the rough. That tells me this man is somebody."

I smiled, imagining that I must have looked a sight with blood caked around my puffy mouth and a lot of my teeth missing. "He's a fuckin' magician. Moves through air, defies gravity. He's a bad muthafucka, let me just put it like that."

"I gathered," the cop said dryly. He leaned into my face with a wolfish grin and went on, "The thing about it is, I'm a bad muthafucka myself. I think it'll be very exciting for me to meet this guy."

"You heard 'im," I grunted, a giddy feeling in me trying to triumph over the pain. "He's comin'. And when he gets here..."

The Mexican laughed viciously. "When he gets here, he'll be right on time to see you die. You lucked out and got a reprieve until then."

62

As Israel drove, he struggled not to lose control of himself. He didn't go past the speed limit. He was absolutely soaked in blood, it was all over the seat he sat on, the steering wheel where his hands gripped, and it would not do for some cop to pull him over and see him like this. There was a change of clothes in the trunk so at some point he would have to pull over and take care of that.

He felt purpose but at the same time he felt like a whirling dervish spinning out of control. His whole life had been about mastery of himself and his emotions and situations. He suspected this was why he didn't want to come back to America in the first place. This was not a place he felt free in; this was a place that had held him down his whole life until he'd staked his claim for spiritual and emotional freedom.

He didn't know why that was. As much as he could think of, he hadn't had a particularly traumatic childhood. The worst that had happened to him that he could think of was the incident with David and Philly Phil Peters. He'd always missed having a father around, but his mother and sister had been *more* than enough for him. They had gone above and beyond the call of duty to make sure his was a safe, comfortable, happy life.

Mr. Chin had said almost from day one that there was another side to him, a dark side. "There is the dragon, the powerful, steadying influence that works in you, but there is also the tiger," Mr. Chin said slowly, making sure each word hit home for Israel beyond the clip of his stilted accent. "The tiger can be strong, sure and unwavering, but he can also be unpredictable and wild. He can be a creature of chaos and destruction for no reason at all. This is you."

Israel first heard these words as a young man in Mr. Chin's kitchen, sitting at the table drinking green tea as the July sun beamed on the world outside of the house. He did not understand where Mr. Chin was coming from. He was learning a lot, quickly. He hoped he was making the older man proud of him, but compliments were few and far between and he had not yet learned to know when the old man was pleased just by feeling his energy, his aura.

He wanted to ask Mr. Chin exactly what he meant, but he was scared to. He didn't want to do anything to alienate him. He had once asked the old man a question that he thought was completely reasonable and rational and he went beet red and sent Israel home without another word. Since that time he knew the best thing for him was to just keep his mouth shut and absorb all the knowledge that was being bestowed on him.

"Yeeees, you have demons within you, young sir," the old man continued, almost sounding like he was talking to himself. He sipped gingerly from his teacup. "Perhaps it is the karma from other lives that has yet to be purged. Each life brings new lessons to be learned and applied from the last life. You will continue to grow until there are no more lessons for you to learn in this plane of reality and you ascend to a place far greater than this one. Are you understanding all of this?"

Israel already knew not to lie to the old man, that he could read him like a book. He said tentatively, "Uh, not really."

Mr. Chin smiled and nodded sagely. "No, I think you don't understand me. You are still just a young boy. You are doing so well that I automatically expect you to understand everything I am teaching at one time."

Israel felt a smile light his face, although he usually knew better than to show when he was happy. He liked getting compliments from Mr. Chin, but the old man thought that the point was not to make him happy but for Israel to make *himself* happy. But Israel was still too young of mind, heart, and spirit to completely understand this quite yet.

"Mr. Chin, I'm really trying to get all of this, I really am," Israel said earnestly. "I'm a smart kid, and I think there's very little that gets by me. But y'know, I'm still a kid."

Mr. Chin's face soured slightly as he said, "I thought I'd made it clear that I understand that, young sir. But by the same token, I am a wise old man. I will know more often than not what you are getting and what you are not getting.

"You are intelligent and your spirit is almost as old as my flesh. Your being but a child is not an excuse for failure or for not trying harder. Do you understand me?"

Israel nodded silently.

The old man nodded sagely. "The tiger within you will occasionally surface. I will try to prepare you to deal with it as much as possible, but sometimes the great cat will overwhelm all sense and reason and you will be at the mercy of the fates.

"I pray that when that happens I will have trained you well and you will apply everything I have taught you to keep the tiger under control…perhaps one day you might even master it."

Israel nodded, once again reticent about speaking. He still wasn't sure what the old man meant. But there hadn't been a single thing up to that point that Mr. Chin had spoken on that hadn't eventually come to his understanding. He knew this would be no different.

He laughed aloud in the car at the memory, more than a little delirious. Right now it felt as if all of Mr. Chin's self-control training had been a complete waste of time. The tiger was raging and Israel wasn't so sure that he wanted to do anything about it. It felt good to exert his power over these stupid men, these fools that lived in some place where fear, guns and death were enough for them. There was a feeling within him that he was letting the long-dead Mr. Chin down, but this rage was something in his nature that once provoked, could not be denied.

He had to try to keep control of himself somehow before he arrived at the place that they were holding his best friend. He thought he could do it, but God help all of them if David Hill was dead when he got there. The tiger would roar and rage and destroy them all.

63

If there was a hell, I was sure I was in it. My body ached more than it ever had in its entire existence. It was hard for me to even believe that I had any coherency at all. I tried to recall if it was this bad either of the times I'd been shot, but remembered I had the benefit of medicine and painkillers to offset the tremendous pain. There was nothing like that here now, nor would there be.

I heard the Mexican say, "All right, that *puto* should be here soon. The bitch lives only about fifteen minutes from here, maybe a little more with traffic right now. Call some of our boys in Van Nuys and tell them we're going to need some support, Mike."

Mike Mettigan, the guy that had helped Sean bring me into the room, was a jet, black brute with an impassive visage. He nodded in the affirmative and threw what could be called a smile on that granite face in my direction. As he pulled a cell phone out of his sagging pants pocket and started dialing, the white cop piped in, "What about the broad? Now that we know she's still breathin', we don't exactly know if she called the cops on us or not."

The smoothed voice policeman I now knew to be Fereal McNaughton said to him, "Handy, the girl's brother said *he* was coming up here. Not that he called our brethren or even had backup with him. He made it clear he was coming to get Hill himself and damn anybody that tries to stop him. He would have made it plain to us if he were going to bring the police into it. But just to be sure, Orlando, maybe you better call your contact at dispatch and see if any calls have come in that could point to us, and also to have him look out for any calls that might come in. Tell him to contact us immediately if any even remotely point in our direction."

Orlando nodded affirmatively and sighed, "Since I trashed my frickin' cell phone, I'm gonna have to go use the house phone in the living room. I'll be right back."

McNaughton nodded and turned his attention back on me. He smiled and asked almost conversationally, "This man—this Israel Baylock. He sounds like an extraordinary guy. Tell me, has he had any military training?"

I smiled a bloody, raggedy-toothed smile. "You oughta know that one, cupcake. It seems to me like y'all ain't in the habit of not knowin' as much about yo' enemies as possible."

"You're a smart guy, Hill. Yes, I know he was in the marines, but he was discharged. I don't know anything beyond that. He seems to have disappeared off the face of the earth until he came in from Amsterdam some months back."

"Well, you don't need me to answer no questions, you got allll the answers, nigga. Anything else you need to know, maybe you can ask m'man when he gets here."

"Hill, I'm asking *you.* And I am getting to the point where I am going to quit being nice. You're right, I'm *not* in the habit of not knowing about people who could potentially fuck my life up. So you'd better start giving me some answers or this little beating you've been getting here will be nothing compared to what I'm about to do to you."

I sneered. "C'mon with it, cuz. Y'all are gonna kill me anyway. Why should I say shit to you?"

McNaughton smiled ferociously. "There are some worse things than death. There's pain." He nodded his head at the white man and he went across the room to open a closet door. He pulled out a portable electrical generator that had a long hose attached to it with what looked like a prod at the end. I understood immediately what was about to happen next.

I tried to hold a game face, but for the first time since I'd been there I was truly afraid. I could take a punch or two and had a fairly high tolerance to pain. But I was weak now and I already thought the end was in sight. I didn't know there was more to come.

McNaughton said to Mike Mettigan, "Go get the KY. It's in the hall bathroom." He looked straight at me. "We're going to lather up Mr. Hill's balls reeeeeal good. Then we're going to put that prod on him and see what he's got left."

I said nothing. My face remained stoic while my heart beat so hard it seemed to damn near be the only sound I could hear. I wanted to tell them to go fuck themselves ten ways to hell, but I knew I would need every ounce of my strength and will left for the next ordeal. I was still scared out of my mind but a stubborn part of me was still set on not letting them break my spirit before they sent it rocketing away from my physical body.

McNaughton leaned in and took my sweat and blood soaked jaw in one hand. He said in a voice that barely registered above a whisper, "You know, I really like breaking smart niggas like you. You are nothing in my world, *worse* than nothing—a low-life piece of shit. You've wasted your whole life, and when it's over nobody will know or care about you. You're nothing to the world but meat, hair and bone with a voice.

"Do you even know what your existence has been about, what your purpose has been on this earth? No, and you're going to die not knowing because you never gave yourself a chance to really live. What a fucking moron."

Even at my lowest, when survival should have been the single most important thing on my mind, McNaughton's words stung me to the core. I realized at that second that a huge part of me really believed I was everything he was saying about me. I wanted to cry badly but held on strong to those tears and kept them locked inside.

"You're not such a good guy, Hill. I've done my homework on you too. It was far less problematic than trying to get the particulars on Mr. Baylock. I don't care that you're going to die this day, and I really don't care that in less than five minutes you'll be screaming in agony and begging for your life."

Mike walked back in the room with a KY Jelly tube. He gave it to McNaughton and threw me a lopsided grin. I could not respond as I had before; seeing that tube drained what little strength I had. I knew McNaughton could sense this without even giving me a close look.

He took the cap off the tube and squeezed some of the gel on to the tip of the prod. He instructed Mike to pull down my pants and put some on my testicles. "This is going to be fantastic," he said, giving me a huge smile. "Your screams are going to be like music to m—"

A gun report slew the rest of his sentence. It was fat and bloated and echoed all through the house. Two more shots quickly followed, and then there was silence and some muffled voices.

There was then the sound of scuffling for a few moments, then a piercing scream. The sound of that scream was the sound of a man who has come face to face with the devil and realizes there is nowhere to run or hide.

Fereal McNaughton was quick on his toes. He scowled. "Mike, Handy, go see what the fuck is going on." The big black man and the white man nodded and bolted out of the room, guns drawn.

He looked more amused than concerned as he said to me, "That's your friend, isn't it? Good Christ, I can feel his energy from here."

I nodded. "I hope that Mexican dude wasn't a close friend'a yours."

"I don't have friends, but if I were to claim anybody it would definitely be him. I suppose one byproduct of killing your buddy will be avenging mine."

I felt a wave of hatred surge through me. I didn't know what motivated this man but he seemed almost sexually interested in Israel. In a strong voice I didn't know that I had left, I told McNaughton to look at me. He did so, a wary look on his face.

"McNaughton, if I survive this that means you'll probably be dead. That shit would please me to no end. If I don't survive, you're still gonna die. I'm pretty sure Israel don't have no plans to let any of you muthafuckas leave here alive.

"I say that to say that one way or another, I'll see you in hell. You understand me, nigga? I will see you in hell!"

McNaughton cocked a smile at me and said, "Well, at least we can agree on one thing. Odds are, that's where we're going to meet up again, and you'll get there first."

I heard a scream come from the living room, then a loud crash like a vase or a lamp hitting the floor. A thump and then more screams. I was thanking God that none of the voices I heard belonged to Israel.

Finally there was silence.

The other men in the room looked at each other as if they were all trying to figure out what the next move was. McNaughton addressed them all in a firm voice iron in its authority. "Everybody get out of here. Go out of the back patio. I'm pretty sure you don't want to run into this guy. I'll finish with him myself."

One of the other men said, "Yo, but what about Orlando, Mettigan, and Handy?"

Fereal McNaughton shot the man an evil look that even in my pained state gave me gooseflesh. Everybody left the room without another word.

McNaughton looked at me with that wolf-like grin again. "I'm going to go see what's going on. I'm going to break your man the way I was getting ready to break you. Then I am going to bring him back here so that he can see you die before I kill him."

I smiled. "I hope to hear yo' dyin' screams, muthafucka."

McNaughton saluted me. It was a strange gesture that threw me off. Before I could even begin to contemplate what it meant he was gone. I caught what seemed to be an afterimage, but I thought it had to be the pain that wracked my body and was now playing tricks with my mind.

Still I couldn't help but think, "Damn, Iz, is McNaughton a magician like you?"

64

Israel chose the same route of entry into the house that his best friend had earlier—only he didn't even bother to knock. He tested the door and it was unlocked. It was a thick, wooden door that opened with a loud creak, so he entered stealthily just in case. But there was no one in the living room and no responses to the sound of the door at all.

He pushed it shut behind him. It seemed to creak even louder with this motion. Still, no one seemed to have heard it. His senses were alive now, and he felt no change in the air, only a dull stillness.

He looked around the huge living room. It was furnished in earth tones, strange to him since there seemed to be nothing natural about the atmosphere of the place. There was a fireplace across the room that looked as big as a furnace oven. Mounted above it was a large Chinese sword, the kind that was so big and long you had to hold it with two hands and be in damn good shape to wield it.

In the center of the room was a plush sofa bookended with some love seats. There was a glass-topped coffee table in the middle of this setup. Israel took a casual glance at the table and noticed that there was a razor blade on it, as well as some white powder separated into several neat, orderly lines. It had to be either cocaine or speed—not that it mattered to him one way or the other.

He heard footsteps and spun around. There was an entrance to a hallway across the room. Someone was about to come into the living room. He quickly darted across the room and stood beside the hallway portal waiting for whoever was going to enter.

A well-built, casually dressed Mexican man entered the room and looked around, muttering, "Where the hell is that phone. Fuckin' cordless piece of shit." Israel immediately recognized his voice as the man he'd spoken to on the cell phone that told him to come and get David Hill. He walked right past Israel over to the couch, trying to see if he could find the phone there. Israel watched him for a moment and said quietly, "Hello."

Orlando spun quickly, a gun already in his hand. He was relieved that he could see his unarmed target. He was covered in drying blood but looking almost serenely calm. Orlando smirked. "You must be the brother—Israel, right?"

Israel said nothing. Orlando was studying him, trying to sum him up. His energy was powerful. He was reminded of Fereal, and with that thought came another: "This muthafucka is dangerous."

"We got your homeboy Dave back there," Orlando said, cocking back the trigger of his Glock 23. "We've been working on him for a minute. He's not in good shape right now...we knocked most of the teeth out of his head, and God only knows how he is internally. Not that it matters since both of you putos are going to die today anyway."

Israel smiled and said calmly, "I'm not going to die—well, at least not yet, not today. But you are, unless you put that gun away and leave right now. That's the best deal I can offer you."

Orlando's face clouded over. He put Israel in his sights and prepared to squeeze the trigger. Israel seemed calm for a man about to die. Orlando decided that really didn't mean shit to him as his trigger finger jerked back.

Israel seemed to be in one spot and then moving like a shadow, like a beam of light. Orlando had never seen a human being move that quickly, not even his partner. And Fereal McNaughton was a potent mutha indeed. He squeezed off another shot that the man who moved like a ghost avoided, then one more. He was going to empty the gun until he hit Israel, but then he was suddenly face to face with him.

Israel looked Orlando in the eye. They seemed to Orlando to glow with some unholy light. He tried to remember if he had ever encountered anybody like this in his entire life. He wanted to scream for Fereal, but his mouth was dry and he could not find his voice.

Israel snatched the gun away from him and hit him in the jaw with it. Orlando used the force of the blow to spin his body around and throw a reverse punch at his opponent, but the blow was easily dodged.

He threw out a straight front kick that Israel backed up from. Israel tossed the gun aside, looking at Orlando with disdain. He almost wanted to smile. This man was trained well. But he already knew the outcome of this match.

Orlando was in a fighting stance, trying to size up Israel. He had a black belt in Shotokan karate and was well trained in some boxing and jiujitsu, but he quickly surmised that this man was too good. There was no way he was going to take him one-on-one. Hell, he couldn't even stop him when he had the edge of having a firearm and ten to fifteen feet between them. He had to figure out a way to create another edge for himself that he could quickly take advantage of.

Israel was now between Orlando and the front door. His LAPD-issued cell phone was in the car outside. He could use that to call Fereal and warn him about this asshole. Also the shots had to have been heard so hopefully someone would respond quickly, but until then he was stuck. He tried to think of way he could get around Israel, but it was impossible. He would just have to go right through him.

He jumped high in the air with a scream and shot a kick at Israel's head. Israel almost casually dodged it. Orlando's intention was to hit the floor and start running, but when he landed Israel dug steely fingers into the meat of his shoulder and spun him around.

Orlando was not focused on getting away anymore; he had to zero in on just surviving this man. He threw a punch at Israel's head and a kick at his groin simultaneously. Israel caught the clinched fist with one hand and the leg with the other.

Orlando had one free hand, which he used to chop at Israel with. The chop was aimed right at Israel's nose; since he had Orlando's other limbs tied up, he knew there was no way for him to dodge it. Once his blow hit home and the man was distracted, Orlando already knew that he was not going to try to finish him off but simply get the hell out of there as quickly as he could.

To Orlando's surprise Israel threw his head back a little and then brought it forward. He chomped down hard on the last two fingers of Orlando's chopping hand. Orlando pulled his hand back with no resistance; surprised that Israel's bite wasn't holding it in place.

He then noticed that two of his fingers were still in Israel's mouth and a grotesque amount of blood was starting to rush out of the stumps that once held them. He looked at the gored hand and then at Israel, who looked frighteningly calm considering what he had between his jaws. He began to scream as his whole world turned dark red with pain.

Letting Orlando go, Israel spat the fingers out. Orlando was just screaming and looking back and forth between where his fingers used to be and the man who bit them off. Israel took a deep breath and then drew back in a stance. As if he had all the time in the world he set his weight and then stepped in and launched a single punch that had all the power he could muster in it.

The blow struck Orlando Flores's temple with a loud crack. He was dead before his body slumped uselessly to the floor, blood still pumping steadily from his gored finger stumps.

Israel casually wiped his mouth and picked up Orlando Flores's corpse. He quickly placed it at the mouth of the hallway entrance and stood to the side of it, waiting. Others would be coming soon. When they arrived, Israel decided there would be no conversation, no offering chances to leave. He would just start killing.

65

Fereal McNaughton eased down the hall with his .38 SIG Sauer drawn. He felt no fear—quite the contrary. He was so pumped it was like he could hear his heart as if it were right next to his ear. This was a strange sensation for him. Usually people described *him* in the terms that David Hill described his friend, and this made him excited to meet him.

Fereal's father trained him how to commit acts of violence from the time he was two and a half years old. One of his earliest memories was his father putting his pudgy little hands in his hair and showing him how to grip and control an opponent by twisting the strands. His parents had brought four girls into the world before his arrival, and his father liked to tell Fereal that he was resigned to more estrogen in his life, when Fereal arrived as a pleasant surprise. Donald McNaughton was given his son to hold shortly after birth and made a promise to him that he would help him become a man who led, never followed.

By the time he was five he was one kid the other kids on the playground knew not to mess with. Donald McNaughton narrowly avoided several lawsuits from parents whose children dared to test his son. Fereal was then lectured nightly by his father about the importance of maintaining self-control and not letting people know upfront how easy it was for him to dominate them. It would make him a target, and indirectly make the family a target as well.

On the rare occasions that Fereal disobeyed these rules he was made to stand in a corner for hours on end or was locked in a dark closet. He could take the former (something that he suspected his father secretly admired about him) but hated the latter intensely. He would beg and plead and finally scream for his father to let him out of that lonely darkness, but his cries were ignored until it appeared that he had been properly broken. Although they were forbidden, his sisters often crept to his bedside after those ordeals to comfort him and let him know that their father was not a mean or a bad man. He was just trying to make sure that Fereal had all the tools he needed to be a survivor of the world and not someone eaten up by it.

Fereal had it all worked out by the time he was ten. His father's lessons had sunk in well. He knew he was bound for greatness…and he'd even figured out how to indulge his passion for hurting others without his father knowing about it. He had all the tools…intimidation was number one, finding out useful information on a person was another (he was surprised in retrospect how many children feared he would rat them out on a secret that would grant them parental punishment—the things he did to them were often far worse than anything the parents could dish out). Sometimes he would hurt one of his playmates and simply deny that he'd done anything when that kid told an adult.

He'd accompanied his father on a trip to Vietnam when he was twenty. His father had wanted to see some old war buddies who had ended up making a home there for themselves. He hadn't seen them since their days of combat. Fereal had never been anywhere and thought the trip would be good for him.

It had been a huge bore hanging out with his father and his friends listening to him and his friends talk about "the old days." They had planned to stay for a month and a half, and now Fereal was in dread about being in that boring place for that long listening nightly to old men drink and talk about war stories.

With his father's permission he began to explore on his own, finding the local spots where drugs and women were aplenty. A few days in, thugs at a bar had accosted one of the locals that had been helping Fereal with the lay of the land, and Fereal came to his rescue.

The man he saved, impressed by the American's fighting skills, took Fereal outside of the village to meet an old man that everyone knew was "special." Known in his younger days as one of the most brutal fighters of the region.

The old man took a liking to Fereal and they began to train together daily. The days of drinking and womanizing came to an end for him as he spent every ounce of free time with the man. In the space of a month this man advanced every concept of the fighting arts that Fereal had. He'd come to Vietnam thinking he was exceptional, but this little man named Van Troch taught him there was so much more. It was funny to see the reaction of some people passing by on a nearby road as they trained in the field, as Fereal had almost a foot and a half and a hundred pounds on Van Troch. But it was never in doubt who was the master and who was the student.

Fereal told his father about Van Troch and formally introduced them. Fereal had intended to stay and train with this man indefinitely, but wanted his father's approval. His father had granted it after a fifteen-minute conversation with Van Troch. Fereal could not recall a happier moment in his life. He was on the path to becoming his own man, but of all the things he still wanted—still needed—his father's approval.

Van Troch taught Fereal about tapping into his deepest essence, about a secret world of power that existed beyond the simple world of flesh. He sensed the immense darkness in Fereal's personality and taught the youngster that there was nothing wrong with it, that it was a gift to be nurtured. Fereal almost cried when the old man first told him this. He felt like he was not only growing in his martial arts skills but that he was truly becoming his *own* man, not Donald McNaughton's son.

He stayed in Vietnam almost two years before he returned to America. He might not have ever returned if Van Troch hadn't lay down to sleep one night and simply died. Fereal was the one who found the old man lifeless, and when they laid him to rest he could not have cried any harder or felt any deeper pain as if it were his own blood father. There was definitely nothing in Vietnam for him after that, so he simply packed his bags and was home within a week.

He went into police work because he saw opportunities in it. He talked to a recruiter and was told how he'd be starting off at a high five-figure salary and could get a loan on a house without a problem. The side benefits were amazing to him, and he actually enjoyed his job on those rare occasions he got to punish the evil. His proclivity for causing others pain was nothing compared to some of the things he'd seen as a policeman. Some went about it in the world as if it were their sole purpose for living. This was something even *he* could not fathom.

But all of that meant nothing right now. As he eased down the hall toward the living room, he felt his whole life had been centered toward this moment, this showdown. He was shocked at how hard his dick was. He struggled not to just scream and shout deliriously, then he wondered if his reactions were some form of fear he was just refusing to acknowledge. If it was, he was not actively aware of it.

66

Fereal was now near the living room. His senses were completely sharp and alive. He saw at least one body near the entrance, and as he got closer his heart nearly stopped. It was Orlando, his slightly opened eyes rolled back in his head and his tongue lolled out of his mouth. It looked like one side of his head had a huge dent in it and two fingers were missing from one hand. The still-dripping stumps looked as if they'd been cleanly cut with a surgical instrument.

He stepped into the living room and looked around. Handy and Mike Mettigan's bodies lay in different areas of the living room. Israel Baylock was casually seated on one of the sofas looking directly at him, his clothes splotched with blood both fresh and drying. Fereal McNaughton's breath seemed to whoosh right out of him as his eyes widened and his jaw went slack.

"It's the demon," he thought. "The Man-Beast from my dreams. It's him!"

He'd been dreaming about the Man-Beast from the time he'd entered the academy. When he and Orlando had first gotten together, he'd dreamed about him—it—after the first night they'd made hard, brutal love and fell into an exhausted sleep. He dreamed about the hoary demon at least once or twice a year and Orlando would be there to hold him, to talk to him sweetly and rock his sweat-soaked body until he was ready for sleep again.

But those times were gone. There would be no more nights of passion with Orlando Flores. He'd been ready to face that stoically, as he did most traumas in his life, but actually seeing Orlando's lifeless corpse filled him with feelings he didn't understand, much like when his father passed after a long two year battle with lung cancer a few years ago.

Seeing the Man-Beast he had been dreaming about all these years filled him with a feeling that he *did* understand—fear. And Fereal McNaughton was not a man that experienced this emotion often.

"I dreamed about you," Fereal said, his voice low and growling. "So many years I've dreamed about you. You've come here to destroy everything I've built, anything that means anything to me.

"Thankfully there's not much that I care about in this world. That man you killed, Orlando, that was one of the things, one of the people, that…that meant something to me. And now you're going to try to bring down everything I've worked to build for myself."

Fereal raised his SIG Sauer as Israel rose from the sofa. "Do you have any last words?"

Israel nodded yes and said calmly, "Fuck you."

Fereal squeezed the trigger. A loud explosion filled the room, but Israel was not where he supposed to be. Fereal was almost as quick as him, calmly following the blur the heading directly toward him and squeezing off another shot. This one grazed Israel's shoulder, still not deterring him in the slightest.

Fereal squeezed off one more shot at Israel's feet, which missed but actually caused his stride halt for a moment. Then he turned and started bolting down the hallway toward the back room. Perhaps David Hill was right and there was no surviving this man. In case there wasn't, there was one thing he could do to at least avenge Orlando Flores's death. Israel would not be able to stop him, either. And perhaps he might still have what it takes to kill this demon.

67

I once again heard a gunshot, then two, three. I heard the multiple footfalls of someone running down the hall, then, McNaughton was in the room. His face had looked almost sexually ecstatic when he left; now it looked crazed, lightly sheened with sweat. He walked toward me, and when he was right in front of me Israel entered the room too.

He turned to look at Israel and said, "I've got to avenge Orlando—maybe myself as well. But this one is for him first."

Fereal McNaughton put the gun in front of my face and pulled the trigger in three quick successions. Half of my head was disintegrated. He put the gun to my chest and fired off a last shot that went right through my heart. Israel was on him by that time, but I cared about none of that in the slightest.

Just like that, I had been murdered.

68

Israel knew that David Hill was a dead man as soon as he entered the room. A knowing glance flew between them right before Fereal McNaughton made his best friend's head explode.

Israel didn't know if he had ever felt as much pain as he did at that moment. That was the only feeling he had that overrode the anger. It froze him for a single moment, as it seemed like part of him was dying as well. When he realized he was not going anywhere, he was a blur in motion.

Fereal still managed to get off one more shot into David before Israel was on him, dealing the big man a vicious blow to his cheek. The cheek broke but Fereal was too hyped to notice it. Israel threw another punch that McNaughton easily dodged. He hoped that Israel would continue to misjudge how fast he was in spite of his size. He might lure him in enough to finish him off.

He wanted to bring the gun up to shoot but knew that there were over a dozen moves Israel could use to disarm him. Their eyes were locked together, each waiting for the other to move. Both tried to fake the other out into making quick, false moves, but both were too good for that ploy. It momentarily seemed to be a standoff.

He jerked the gun up slightly and fired a shot. It hit Israel almost squarely in the middle of his thigh. He dropped to one knee with a loud gasp and Fereal, sensing his moment, bridged the gap between them to go for the kill.

Fereal stuck his gun in his opponent's face and fired, but even in pain his demon was quick. He narrowly avoided the bullet but the report being so close to his ear caused a shockwave of pain. Israel was temporarily paralyzed in that agony with his eyes squeezed shut, his mouth open in a wide, silent scream. Fereal pointed the gun once again at Israel's face, sensing this was the moment for the kill.

He squeezed the trigger and it jammed. Fereal could not believe it, but he had no time to meditate on it. He dropped the gun and dealt the still-stunned Israel a blow that broke his nose and sent him flying across the room.

He was quickly on Israel, not wanting to give him the slightest chance to recover. He rolled Israel onto his back and sat on him. He wrapped his big hands around his throat and began to choke him. Once again he found himself getting hard.

"I've dreamed about you ruining me all these damn years," he thought. "And now I am going to kill you. I am going to slay my dragon. It's symbolic. Once I do this, I will be unstoppable. I know this now."

"I...don't know...what you're talking about." Fereal was confused at Israel's response for a moment, not realizing he'd been thinking aloud. Israel's throat muscles began to push out and resist even Fereal's tremendous strength. Fereal took one hand off of Israel's throat and with a closed fist hammered the spot on his leg where blood was still flowing steadily from the gunshot wound. Israel grunted loudly and Fereal quickly put the other hand back on his throat, sensing that he was now close to finishing him.

Israel brought his good leg up and over so that his calf was right under Fereal's chin. With all of his might he pushed his calf into Fereal's throat, causing the big man to tumble off of him. They were both back to their feet in a flash, once again faced off and looking for an opening to do the other in.

The room was a fairly large one with both of them having plenty of room to circle like wary animals. Fereal thought of trying to move the battle out of there, but he felt an advantage with Israel being distracted by David Hill's fresh corpse. If Israel had room to focus all of his energy on him he knew he would lose.

He didn't think he had a chance under any other circumstances. Even with his nose broken, blood dripping out of it like a busted tap and a fresh bullet hole in his leg, Fereal could sense his foe's energy and focus were still far beyond the norm.

Fereal's gun was practically between them. He was a little closer than Israel to it, and he knew that if he could get his hands on it he could definitely use it as an equalizer. As he was pondering going for it Israel moved with a speed that he should not have possessed with his wounded leg. He kicked the gun away and at the same time dealt Fereal a backhanded blow across his lips that stunned him. He swung that same hand back as he stepped in and delivered a straight punch that caught the big man solidly in the chest with a bright thud.

Fereal went sailing across the room backward, trying to keep his balance and get his wind back. He failed at both, tripping over himself and falling to floor. He felt a stabbing pain with each breath as he brought himself to his feet. Israel was moving toward him, not with all the speed he could but still fast nonetheless.

Israel fired off a couple of blows that Fereal managed to barely block or avoid. Fereal tried a few kicks and punches back in desperation, but Israel was just as quick in avoiding them and with much less difficulty. This continued for a moment until Israel finally found his mark and delivered a knife-handed chop that caught his opponent hard on the shoulder blade, snapping it in half.

Fereal screamed loudly with the pain. He was not used to pain; he was usually its administrator, not its receptacle. Israel quickly sensed his moment and delivered a straight kick with his wounded leg that caught the big man in his solar plexus. He followed that with a roundhouse punch that caught Fereal on the same cheek he'd broken earlier.

Fereal hit the ground with an almost feminine yelp. He had broken this man's nose, he'd shot him, yet *he* still was the one on the ground writhing in pain. "He's a demon, that's why," he reminded himself. "There is no defeating him. There is only death."

69

Israel was perplexed. He'd been calling David Hill for almost two weeks and he had gotten no response. He had actually gotten through to him once, but right after he said hello he'd received a terse "I gotta call ya back" and then a dial tone. He did not give up though. He didn't even know why he wanted David Hill's friendship so bad, but he did.

He *did* know that he was conflicted about what David had done for him a few days before, standing up to Wade Anderson like he had. He had not really wanted him to do that. He had been learning so much from Mr. Chin and hid his gifts from the world, but sometimes he grew tired of playing the role of the nerd, the kid anybody could pick on or talk about whenever they felt like it. He wanted to show them how mighty he was, and beating Wade Anderson would have been perfect. No one would have looked at him the same ever again. And one thing he had figured out was that the girls seemed to like a man that could defend himself.

At the same time, no one ever stood up for him. And the last person he would have ever expected to do that was the guy who he had humiliated ("Justly," he thought with a smirk) so many years ago. There was no reason for David Hill to stand up for him at all, and yet he did. He believed it was a sign that they should be friends.

At that point Israel thought he should be friends with someone else other than the people in the crowd he currently hung with, most of who were all nerds and bookworms like himself. He sometimes felt above them simply because of all the knowledge Mr. Chin had bestowed upon him. He journeyed places in his teachings that most of them could not even comprehend.

He was sitting in his room and had just finished studying for a test. He had tried phoning David Hill again before he had started his studies; he decided he would try one more time before just finally giving up. It didn't make any sense for him to keep trying to make friends with someone who could care less. It was also beginning to hurt his feelings as well. He did not even know David, so this made him wonder why it was important to him.

He picked up the phone and dialed the digits he now knew by heart. There were several rings before an older female answered, "Hello?"

"Um, hi, I…my name is Israel. I've called a few times for David."

The woman sighed wearily. "I know. He's right here. Hold on for a sec."

Israel could hear her voice in the background against another, more muffled one. "David, you better talk to this boy, he's been calling for a couple of weeks. Why do you keep avoiding him? No, I am not going to lie to him one more minute. David, I don't have *time* for this, you go talk to him yourself."

There was silence for a second, then, a male voice said with an impatient sigh, "Hello."

Israel was stuck. He did not know what to say for a moment. David said once again in an even more irritated tone, "Hello, is anybody here?"

There was one more moment of silence before he blurted out, "Yeah, this is Israel Baylock, uh, the kid you, uh, stood up to that guy named Wade Anderson for, although I don't know if you remember that or not, because a guy like you probably doesn't even register things like that on the event scale of his life even though it was a big deal for me I know football is probably the big deal for you and girls and things like that and I am sure that you have other things in your life that are more important than even this phone call right now and I suddenly feel like a moron for calling all this time trying to get a hold of you, it probably seems kind of gay now that I think about it even though I like girls, don't get me wrong, it's just that maybe for once I might just want to not have all these nerdy people be the sole source of friendship for me, I might just at least know once in my life what it is like to have a cool muthafucka like yourself be my friend, you know what I'm saying?"

There was silence on the other end of the phone. Israel thought about how stupid he must have sounded and cursed himself. He once again wondered why it had been important for him to try to get David Hill to be his friend, and once again he couldn't figure it out. He was getting ready to hang up the phone when all of a sudden his ear was assaulted by a gush of loud, braying laughter.

"Gotdamn," Dave Hill said in between laughs. "That has got to be the funniest shit I have heard in a long time, boy. Did you stop to breathe at all?"

Israel was still at a slight loss of words as he laughed nervously. "Well, uh, I didn't really mean for what I said to come out like, um, how I said it."

"So how did you mean it?"

Israel was thoughtful for a moment. He muttered, "Uh, I guess maybe I did mean it how it came out."

David was still laughing. Israel found himself laughing as well. He said between chuckles, "Fuck you, David Hill," and the laughter between the two of them swelled and grew like a wave breaking toward a waiting shore.

And that was the beginning.

70

Sometimes David and Israel would reflect on how strange their friendship was, although Mrs. Baylock liked to call it *unique.* Both she and Ellena were happy about this new friendship because Israel was happy about it. His fellow nerd buddies could not figure out how he was so tight with the number one jock in school, while David fended off queries about their friendship by saying that Israel helped him study and sometimes even do reports for him. Israel actually did do the occasional report for David. David was definitely smart enough to do his own, but if he had slacked from partying too much with his jock friends or his gangsta buddies and was in a bind, he would help his friend out with just mild chastising following.

They were an odd couple both in school and outside of it when they hung out. David was five eleven and built like a Mandingo warrior, all hard young muscle and sinew, and Israel was a small boy, barely clearing five feet and as thin as a wispy reed. But after a while their friends and the rest of the school just got used to them. In the grand scheme of things, this odd couple was hardly anything worth discussing when all was said and done.

71

One Monday after school David was at Israel's house studying. They were seated at the desk he had in his bedroom going over some algebra homework when out of the blue David said, "Say, Iz, you probably have never had any pussy before, huh?"

Israel looked at David like he was absolutely insane, his face turning beet red. David burst out laughing, almost falling out of his chair.

To Israel women were still a mystery. He knew a lot just by watching the two exceptional ones that he lived with, but outside of his house he knew the average female would never revere him like his mother and sister did. Just as Mr. Chin was showing him the mysteries of the inner world there was so much more to the outer world he longed to know, and the ways of women ranked high on the list.

In between chuckles David managed to get out, "So what's up homie, whaddaya say? Or maybe you like some man booty. Coochie may not interest you."

David burst out laughing again at his own joke. He was blissfully unaware of Israel's evil glare, not knowing how in danger he was of being royally tossed around the bedroom.

David caught Israel's glare and managed to control his laughter. "Yo, baby, it's all good," he said, his hands held up in a surrendering gesture. "I'm just fuckin' witcha."

Israel snorted. "I'd like to see you try being in my shoes for a day. In my world, you don't think too long about girls because they don't think about you. If I was a handsome guy that everybody liked that played football, I might think about them quite a bit, but since I'm not, when I do think about them it just hurts, man."

David hadn't thought about it from Israel's end. He just took such things for granted with his friend because to him they were equals. It was quite logical that most others did not see him that way. He felt bad for teasing Israel the way he did.

Israel shut the math book they were studying from. "Well, I think you can figure out if I'm still a virgin or not, or do I actually have to answer that question?"

"Naw. I guess my next question would be, do you *want* some ass?"

Israel looked at David strangely and said, "Is there something *you* want to tell *me*?"

David did not get it for a second, and now it was Israel's turn to guffaw. It finally dawned on him and he play socked Israel on the arm. When the laughter died down, David asked Israel, "So do you wanna get some pussy or what?"

Israel looked at David strangely. "Look man, there's only so much I am gonna take from you today."

"Naw, nigga, I'm serious. I can hook it up—*if* you want to do it. You been a real good friend to me and you helpin' me with a lot of this school shit too. If you want to make it happen, you just gotta give me the word right now."

Israel was skeptical but definitely interested. He asked, "Who? I don't think there is anybody that would have a genuine interest in a nerdy bookworm like me."

David sighed with a limp smile. "Well, you definitely ain't nominated for best lookin' black man of the year. No, I got a friend of mine that I asked about it just outta curiosity when we were getting high a few nights ago…she said she'd be game, just to see what it would be like. She cool like that."

"So who is it? Is this someone that goes to school with us?"

David Hill nodded his head.

"So are you going to give me a name or what? Quit playing, Dave."

David chuckled. "Okay, fool. It's Melanie Thompson."

Israel's eyes got big. "David Hill, if you are fucking with me, I swear…"

Dave was laughing at his friend's reaction. "Naw, man, I'm fuh real."

Israel could not believe it. Melanie Thompson was a cheerleader, a beauty taller than him at five six. She had long, thick straight black hair that made one think of an American Indian princess that framed a face that had exotically slanted black eyes, a small but slightly flared African nose and lips that were almost as lush as his sister Ellena's and his mother's. Her skin was the color of a Hershey's chocolate bar, dark, rich and smooth. Her body was slim, sturdy and strong—not much in the way of a chest, perhaps just enough for his small hands, but an ass that was a work of art that jutted from her athletic frame as though it were almost a separate entity. He had touched her a thousand times in late night fevered imaginings and could not even fathom what David was saying to him. It was like being told that he had won the lotto.

Israel's logical mind quickly came to the fore once more. He had a confused look on his face as he asked, "David, why would Melanie Thompson want anything to do with *me*? Does she know who I am? You did say the name Israel Baylock to her, right? The short kid with the big eyeglasses?"

"Yeah, I told you I did. Damn! Like I said, she said she would do it just to see what it would be like to do a nerd." David laughed again at the memory.

Israel still looked dumbfounded. David did not want to laugh at him and upset him again. He knew that Israel wasn't like him, did not live in his world and maybe never would. This was a big deal to him. And David guessed it wasn't the act in and of itself but the girl involved, although Israel had never mentioned having crush on her or anybody else for that matter.

Israel was contemplating what he had just been told. He still was shaking his head in disbelief when he said to David, "So if I agree to this, when is it supposed to happen?"

David shrugged. "I dunno, I guess whenever you want it to."

"Um…what's today, Tuesday?"

David chuckled and shook his head in wonderment. He stood up and stretched, letting out a long yawn. "Look, Iz, what about this Friday? Her folks are going out of town for the weekend so her house is going to be empty. The only thing you gotta do is take some weed over there with you, which I'll supply."

Israel was scared but excited at the same time. His conscious mind could not accept that someone as beautiful as Melanie Thompson would want anything to do with him. He almost felt like he should say no because he wasn't worthy.

"No…no, I am worthy," he thought. "I count. I matter. Why shouldn't I find out a little about the world David lives in?"

"David, set it up," Israel said with a confidence and authority that made David Hill look strangely at him. Israel knew he had come off a tad brazen with him and he remembered his promise to Mr. Chin. He did not want David Hill (or anybody else for that matter) to even remotely suspect what he was, what he was still becoming.

"Okay, okay. Let me do that shit right now. Gimme your phone."

Israel went and got the phone off of the bed. He set it on the desk and David picked up the receiver and punched in some numbers. He was silent for a moment, then he smiled and said in a silky, seductive baritone, "Hey, Mel-Mel, what's crackin'?"

Israel could hear her muted voice from the receiver responding. David laughed and launched into a little conversation with her, mostly about their day at school, an upcoming game and some exchanged gossip about other football teammates and cheerleaders. He found their conversation to be rather banal and wondered if this was how most so-called regular teens talked to each other.

Finally David said, "Look, Mel-Mel, you remember what we talked about when we was talking' high the other day?" There was a pause. "No, that's still gonna happen, word! Naw, I'm talking 'bout that little discussion we had about my li'l friend." Another pause. "Uh-humm...yup, now we onna same page."

There was an extremely long pause and then David laughed out loud. "You want me to answer that?" Israel heard a "yes" through the receiver and his best friend continued on, "I don't think you're gonna meet a bigger virgin than Israel Baylock, straight up."

They both laughed at him. Israel felt his cheeks burn with anger. He almost told David to forget about it when David said, "Yeah, he can be there Friday around six. I'll send the smoke with him."

They said a few more words and then David hung up the phone and put it back on the bed. As he sat down at the desk with a satisfied smile he said, "See? It's that simple. Soon you'll be a man!"

"Wow." Israel was a little amazed—both at the fact that this was going to happen and that he felt no fear about it. There was a nervous excitement to be sure, but most definitely no fear.

"So how you feel, bruh?"

"I guess I feel cool. It's just strange. I woke up this morning a virgin, and this evening I find out that two days from now I won't be. It's a little strange."

"So you're not scared about this at all?"

Israel didn't want to admit that he wasn't. That did not fit at all with the person everybody thought he was, although now thinking about it he was not entirely sure that he wasn't scared, either. Still, he said to David, "Yeah, I am just a little nervous, but it's not that big a deal at all, right?"

"Hell naw," David said with a laugh. "Just take ya pee-pee and put it in her wee-wee and you all good, my brotha."

Israel looked at David to see if he was kidding.

"Naw, fuh real," said Dave. "You have to...ya know, ya have to play with her titties and suck on them a little, and play with her pussy a little too. It's not real complicated, like I said. You a smart nigga, you'll figure it out."

David was right on that. To Israel, who admittedly knew not the first thing about pleasing a woman, what David Hill was saying sounded too simple to be true. He would do his own investigation.

72

The next day Israel went and bought a copy of *Penthouse Forum*, a collection of the best letters of so-called true experiences from *Penthouse* magazine, and a thick tome called *The Joy of Sex*. He ditched school to go to a bookstore to get the books and then stayed home all day reading them, absorbing what he thought might apply to him and discarding the rest. Israel was a quick study by nature, and felt fairly confident that when he and Melanie Thompson hooked up he would properly acquit himself.

He decided he would also go to Mr. Chin and ask his opinion. He did not know if this was necessarily the right person to come to for this kind of advice. It did not seem as if Mr. Chin had been with a woman in many, many years, perhaps even since his wife's death. But he was the one person in which Israel confided everything, and decided this time would be no different.

Sitting in Mr. Chin's kitchen that Wednesday, Israel told the old man what was up. Mr. Chin listened intently with a stone face. When he was done, Israel looked at him expectantly and waited for his reaction. Mr. Chin appeared to be thoughtful, considering everything Israel had told him.

"Well?" Israel said after a moment. "Do you have anything to say?"

Mr. Chin was stone faced for only a moment more. Then he burst into a raucous fit of laughter. Israel turned beet red. He had never really seen the old man laugh as long as he had known him, definitely not like this.

"Mr. Chin, I am really tired of people laughing at me when this comes up."

Mr. Chin paused and said, still chuckling, "No, no, no, young man. It is just the situation. You have to see the humor in it. I have never been advised on such matters, it was just part of my teachings. I had planned to introduce this teaching to you later. I tend to forget that each generation advances a little quicker than the last in terms of maturity. I am sorry I did not take this into consideration with you."

Mr. Chin seemed sincere about his apology, although Israel did not really care. He just mumbled, "Uh, no problem. I don't think it's a big deal."

Mr. Chin smiled. "Perhaps not to you, but in my culture it is, as you say, a big deal."

"Okay, well, I am just saying it doesn't matter to me. Especially since you are going to instruct me now, right?"

"No, I am not going to instruct you per se…I am going to offer you a guideline. You see, young sir, every woman is different as is every man, not just in the arena of physical pleasure, but in life. Everyone has a different pulse. There are no two people alike on the planet, male or female.

"If you find this woman's pulse, her vibration, then half the battle is won. The rest will simply fall into place."

Israel completely understood in theory what Mr. Chin was talking about but wanted to know, "When does this instruction begin?"

Mr. Chin smiled. "When would you like it to begin, young sir?"

"Yesterday," Israel replied with a mischievous grin. "But since that time has already come and gone, I guess right now is just as good a time as any."

73

Melanie Thompson was running through several excuses she could use for Israel Baylock, who was due to arrive at her house in an hour and a half. "I'm on the rag," she thought. "I just want to get to know you better first. My parents are coming home early from vacation, they'll be here tonight. I'm too tall for you." She chuckled at this last one.

She was lying on her bed relaxing, having smoked the last little bit of weed she had for the week. She was glad David was sending some over with the munchkin. She would need it if she were going to get through this.

When David had originally suggested getting with his friend, she had thought while she was high that it would be interesting to see how a scrawny little bookworm would react with someone like her. She was sure it would seem like a dream come true to him. But when he actually told her that he wanted her to go through with sleeping with his friend, she was almost in a state of disbelief. Still, she agreed to it. She would agree to almost anything concerning David Hill's wants and desires because she was determined to make him her man.

Not long ago David had taken her virginity after a four month struggle on his part. She had held out as long as she could, half out of fear of the sexually unknown, half because she knew he was a great big ole 'ho' and that his interest in her would surely fade once he achieved his goal with her. He managed to convince her otherwise, but sure enough, after a few hot sessions of sex he had moved on to greener pastures. She had become just another girl from the cheerleading squad that he had fucked.

She cried and had wanted to die initially, not wanting or willing to face facts. She was pretty, one of the most popular girls in school, and every boy wanted her. Everyone, that is, except for the one *she* wanted. But she quickly realized that David Hill messed with girls on *and* off-campus just as pretty as her. If she wanted to get him to see that she was the one for him, she would have to have a different approach.

She figured out that friendship was the best road to take with him. When he saw that she was genuine, he began opening up to her. He told her about the munchkin's sister, a girl named Ellena Baylock that he was stupid sprung on. She was a college girl a few years older than him. When he told her he thought his chances of getting with her were next to nil, she verbally expressed regret on his behalf but her inner heart rejoiced. But his heart still seemed closed off from anyone getting too close to him.

That was all right though, because she was determined to get her man. "David Hill, you will be mine." That was her mantra every day all day, when she sat in class pretending like she was concentrating on her studies, when she was at cheerleading practice going through all the moves by rote, *definitely* as she watched him practice, watched how his teammates admired him and seem to regard him as the team leader more than the coach or quarterback. And during a game, when she watched her heart lead their school to victory, she had nothing but pride in her soul and almost wanted to jump up and down and scream, "Yeah, that's *my* man!"

She sat up in bed and pondered the evening. The only other person she had told about it was her cheerleading mate and best friend Joy Patterson, who had earned that lofty position by being able to keep a secret. Joy, who had far more experience in matters concerning sex than she did (although no one from school would know it; she dated—fucked—strictly college boys, and did that so undercover that the boys at school thought she was a virgin), convinced her not to worry. Virgin males usually had quick orgasms, overwhelmed by the power and glory of hot, wet pussy. But Melanie was not so sure she would be able to get hot or wet. She supposed she would just have to close her eyes and think about David.

She still felt a little like a prostitute, but David wasn't judging her and seemed to be grateful for her doing him this favor, so that was all that counted. Or at least that is what she had to keep telling herself. She hoped he hadn't told anyone else what she was doing for him, but she had asked him not to and she felt their friendship at this point was strong enough for him to honor her request.

She got up and stretched and yawned. She thought she had better find something sexy to put on. She knew that most males are visual creatures so it would be better to wear something as sexy as possible to get him worked up so that he would be sure to cum quickly and she could get his ass out the door and on his way.

Melanie felt herself beginning to stress. Her parents had a full wet bar in the den downstairs. She knew she would probably be paying it a visit before little Israel Baylock's arrival.

74

Israel knocked on Melanie Thompson's door several times. He had walked to her house, which had taken almost an hour and a half. She lived so far from him, all the way up in Windsor Hills, which could almost be called the black Beverly Hills of Los Angeles. He had no choice, though. He could not have his mother drop him off because she knew he knew no one that lived in that area. As it was, he had to lie and say that he was going to spend the evening studying at a classmate's house that lived a scant two blocks away from him.

As he knocked on her door again he began to feel disheartened. He looked at the small, wrinkled piece of paper that he had written her address on and then at the numbers on the wall to the right of the door. He had the correct address all right, unless David gave him the wrong address. Perhaps he had heard him wrong or had written it down incorrectly or…

Just as he was pondering all of this Melanie Thompson opened the door. She was wearing a thick red terry cloth robe. Even with her body hidden, her face was not and Israel thought she was the most beautiful woman in the world, in the universe. He once again almost felt as if he were not even worthy of being there.

"What's up, li'l man," she slurred with a crooked smile.

Israel caught the whiff of hard liquor on her breath, although she did not appear to be sloppy drunk. Israel gave her a shy smile and said almost inaudibly, "Ummmm, hi. Uh, my name is Israel."

Melanie chuckled and said in a throaty, teasing voice, "I *know* who you are, little boy. You're the one helping our star running back pass all his classes."

"Well, uh, he's kinda helping himself. I mean, we just study together."

"Whatever," Melanie said dismissively, although she still had that lopsided smile on her face. "So you want to come in, or what?"

Israel nodde and stepped into the foyer of the house. It was a nice place, a two-story job with cream-colored walls and carpet that was almost tan. He looked at the staircase just beyond the foyer and saw family photos and portraits hanging along the length of the staircase wall. He noticed that there was a mother and father and a brother in those portraits along with Melanie, and Israel wondered someday if he might exist in that setting, either with his mother marrying some worthy fellow ("Not very likely," he thought with an inward chuckle) or perhaps he with a family of his own.

Melanie proceeded to slowly walk up the stairs. Israel stood watching her, unsure what to do. He nervously adjusted his big, thick glasses on his face.

Halfway up the stairs Melanie turned around. "Are you going to just stand there or are you coming up with me?" Her voice was playfully chiding, but Israel did not catch it. He felt like a fool for not automatically knowing he should follow her.

When they got to the top of the stairs she led Israel past the portal of the first doorway to the left. Her room had yellow walls with daisies painted all over them, making the whole room look like a floral patch. Israel had a fairly large bedroom but his paled next to hers. Melanie Thompson's bedroom was the size of the living room and den in his mom's house combined. There was a huge bed in the center of the room that had a Minnie Mouse decorated bed set.

Near the bedroom's window was a huge teakwood desk that Melanie sat down at. There was a pint bottle of Jack Daniels atop it, open but with not much missing from the bottle. Melanie curled a few strands of her long, thick black hair between her fingers. "Do you have the weed with you?"

Israel nodded yes and took a folded up baggie of it out of his pocket and gave it to her. She pulled some Zig-Zags from one of the desk drawers and proceeded to roll a big fat spliff. As she was doing this she looked at Israel. "You're making me nervous just standing there…go sit on my bed." He did so like an obedient puppy as she finished rolling the joint and lit it up.

She inhaled deeply from the pregnant-looking joint and offered it to Israel. He declined it blushing, saying, "I don't smoke, thanks."

She shrugged and said, "More for me." She took another big pull off of the joint and let the smoke roll dragon-like from her mouth and inhaled it into her nose. She then blew out a thick, lazy stream of plume that curled up toward the ceiling and evaporated. She looked at Israel and gave him a sensuous smile.

There was a boom box on the desk. She opened it up and put in a Miles Davis c.d. She liked the contemporary music of the day just as much as any other teenager, but her father had turned her on to Miles and she found his music sensual and mood easing. She asked Israel, "Do you like this music?"

He nodded dopily. "Uh, sure. I don't know much about it, but it's pretty cool."

She laughed mockingly. "I don't think you think that at all. I think you're just saying that because you want to get in these panties." She laughed a little harder and Israel got an embarrassed look on his face. He started to protest, but she read his face. "Relax, li'l man. I'm only kidding with you."

Israel smiled and tried to make it seem like he was going along with the joke, but inside he was thinking, "Damn! I'm really blowing it!"

She took another hit on the joint, looking at him quizzically. She said, "Do you know that I'm doing this only to get closer to David? I love him, do you know that?"

Israel nodded his head yes in a matter of fact way but inside, felt like someone had stabbed him in the heart. She wasn't curious about anything with him, it wasn't like David said at all. He had fantasized about her being his girl for so long. That was the main reason he was there, he thought that in a better world maybe someone like him might have a chance with someone like her. But he was being foolish.

He stood up from the bed. "I'm not a charity case. I'm here because I've always liked you, probably as far back as the fifth grade.

"I'm no fool, I know that a guy like me can never have a girl like you, I just wanted to live in a fantasy for one day and get out of the reality of my life. That's it...nothing more, nothing less. If you want to, you don't have to do anything. I can leave right now."

Melanie sighed. Why did he have to go and make her feel bad? "No, li'l man. Sit down. It's just...I just love him so much, I would do anything for him. I mean, this isn't really me."

"I know. I mean, this logically can't really be *anybody*, I think. I figured what Dave was saying was too good to be true."

"Well, I mean, he didn't exactly lie, we *did* talk about it and I did tell him that I wondered what it would be like hooking someone like you up, but I mean, I was high." Melanie giggled and continued on, "Much like I am now. You say all kinds of stuff when you're high on some good weed, you know?"

Israel smiled wanly and said, "Actually, I don't. I've never tried the stuff before. Been curious, but..." He shrugged. "I guess I'm sorta scared or whatever."

"Is that right? Well look at me. Do I look like I'm losing my mind or acting crazy or anything like that?"

Israel took a good look. Even with that terry cloth robe on, she looked damn good. "No, you look all right to me."

She took a fat puff off the joint that was quickly becoming a roach. She got up and walked over to Israel, not having yet blown out the smoke. When she stood above him she tilted his head up with a sly grin and gestured for him to open his mouth. She then leaned in and kissed him, releasing the smoke in his mouth, and was actually surprised that he kissed her back as if he knew what he was doing. The kiss began to grow passionate, but midway through Israel began to cough out smoke. Melanie chuckled gently at him.

She went back to her desk and sat down again, pulling the robe tighter around her unconsciously. She blew out a little excess smoke. "That's called a shotgun. What do you think?"

Israel felt lightheaded, but not uncomfortably so...he felt a wave of peacefulness roll through him. He was instantly relaxed, no longer nervous at all. So this was what it was all about, this getting high. He was thinking he liked it very much indeed, and gave Melanie Thompson both thumbs up to let her know. Amazingly, he felt like he could not even speak right that second.

She chuckled. "Damn, look what I got started, a dope fiend." They both burst into a raucous fit of laughter that lasted a couple of minutes. The phone rang, which caused Israel to nervously cover his mouth to try to suppress the laughter, as if the police were on the line or something. This made Melanie laugh even harder as she answered the phone.

"Hello...yeah, yeah, he's here." She let out a huge laugh. "Girl, no! Huh?" Israel could hear a loud female voice through the receiver. "Right now? I mean, um, I don't know. Hold on."

She covered the receiver. "My friend Joy wants to come over and get high. I don't really know what to tell her."

Israel grinned. "You can tell her to come on over."

Melanie smiled back a grateful, relieved smile, thinking to herself that Israel was really a nice guy. "Hey Joy, come on over. Hurry up before I smoke the rest of this shit up."

Melanie hung up the phone. She stood up. "I'd better get into some clothes before Joy gets here or she'll get the wrong idea!"

She walked across the room to her bedroom closet and got out some jeans and an orange T-shirt. She threw them on the bed next to Israel and then took off the terry cloth robe. Israel held a poker face as he stared at the object of his desires in a lacey red bra and thong set, her strong, smooth, toned chocolate body so close to him that he could reach out and trace his fingers along her soft skin if he desired to.

She reached down for her T-shirt and paused. She gave Israel a seductive look. "You know, you are such a sweet little guy that I am actually going to give you one more chance to say yes to this. It's gonna take Joy at least fifteen, twenty minutes to get over here."

Israel smiled. "No…no we're fine. You can go on and get dressed."

Melanie shrugged and put on her clothes. Israel watched with a goofy smile. He was disappointed, but the weed was making him forget all of that, taking him to a better place and space in his head. He said tentatively, "Um, could I have some more of that stuff?"

75

When Joy arrived, Melanie and Israel were fairly well fucked up. In addition to rolling another joint, they had both partaken of the Jack Daniels (also Israel's first taste of alcohol—he liked this much less than the weed) and had finished over half the pint. Joy proceeded to try to get catch up to get as high as they were.

Joy sat on the bed next to Israel swigging on the Jack, her feet curled underneath her. Israel knew her as another cheerleader, one of the few David Hill hadn't bragged to him about sleeping with. She was lighter than Melanie, not quite as light as he but close. She had that thick but sturdy build that made him think of his mother and sister, but with a face that had pretty, almost Indian looking features. Her hair was cut closed to her head, looking a lot like the actress Halle Berry's. She was wearing tight butt-hugging shorts and a tank top that showcased an ample bosom.

Melanie currently had the joint and gave it to Joy. Joy took a big puff and passed it to Israel, who could now hit the joint without coughing too much.

"Hey, Israel," Joy said, blowing smoke in his direction. "What's your sister's name?"

"Ellena Baylock," he said, looking at her quizzically. "Why?"

"'Cause I have an, uh, friend that goes to USC that says that damn near every guy up there is chasing after her like a dog in heat. They're not catching, they say she's not giving up anything, but they are definitely trying." She laughed and added, "Even the white boys."

Israel shrugged. "That's nothing new. That's been going on as long as I can remember. Her and my mom both, actually."

"Damn," Joy said in amazement. "I haven't seen her or anything. Is she really that pretty?"

Israel nodded his head.

Melanie did not want to talk about the true object of David Hill's desires. In her efforts to befriend him and come across as someone he trusted, she'd already heard enough about the bitch, perhaps too much. She yawned. "Well, I'm ready to go to bed. What are you guys doing?"

Joy chuckled. "Shit, I'm too high to go anywhere right now. I think I wanna kick it here for a couple'a hours until I feel up to driving again."

They looked at Israel and he said, "I live almost three miles away from here and I walked over. If I could hitch a ride with Joy whenever she leaves and just stay here until then, that would be cool."

"Sure, no problem, li'l man."

Melanie said, "You guys can stay in my brother's room. He's got a big bed and you guys are so small, you should be able to lay on it together without getting in each other's way."

"What about your brother?" Israel asked. "Will he be home anytime soon?"

"Nah, he's on vacation with my folks."

"Okay," Joy said, now feeling a little sleepy. She gestured for Israel to get off the bed with her and said, "C'mon li'l man, let's go catch a nap. You got a curfew or anything, like anytime you have to be home in specific?"

He actually did have a curfew, and the time for it had already passed over an hour and a half ago. Still all he said was, "No, I'm good. Just whenever you're ready to take me home."

"Okay. Melanie gurl, if you're not awake when we leave I'll catch you in the morning."

"Okay, cool." Melanie gave Israel a warm smile. "Thanks, li'l man. You're good people, and any friend of David's is a friend of mine. So maybe we could be friends from now on too."

Israel smiled a stoned smile and once again gave her a thumbs up. Both of the girls laughed.

When he and Joy walked into Melanie's brother's room, it seemed to him to be just as large as the other one. His walls were painted like a forest, all trees and foliage in greens and browns. Israel wondered aloud, "Damn, what does the parents' bedroom look like?" Joy burst out laughing as she took off her strappy sandals and hopped into the big bed in the center of the room.

"Well, you just gonna stand there and look at the walls, or are you going to get in here and get some sleep?"

Israel took off his tennis shoes and got in the bed. It seemed like two seconds later he could hear Joy snoring lightly. A half an hour later he was too.

76

At one point Israel woke up. He was a little disoriented. It took him a second to realize that the darkened room he was in was not his.

As he was trying to remember if he had turned out the light in the room or not. It had definitely been on when he got in bed to sleep. He could hear Joy still snoring lightly.

In the dim cast of moonlight that filtered through the bedroom window, Israel looked at Joy's face. She was lying on her back, one arm behind her head, the other hanging off the bed. She looked beautiful in that light, and watching her full breasts heave high and low with the motion of her sleep breathing began to make him feel aroused. He had been dreaming and fantasizing about a woman all this week, and although the one before him was not the one he wanted, she was not unappealing to him at all.

Israel began to touch her, feeling cotton-mouthed and slightly scared but still driven by firm desire. He began to massage her breasts gently, tentatively at first and then a little more firmly. The bra that she had on beneath her tank top was quite flimsy. He had no problem finding her nipples between the two sets of cloth covering them and rolling them between his fingers. Joy's breathing pattern changed, and he knew she was awake—not quite fully up, but enough to realize what was being done to her. And he could tell she liked it.

He awkwardly, gently pulled her tank top up. She in no way moved to acknowledge him, but he was now in tune with her body and could sense shifts of mood and emotion. He pulled her bra aside to take one of her thick dark brown nipples into his mouth, sucking on it gently, teasing it with his tongue and lightly with his teeth. Now Joy was moaning slightly.

He eventually began to kiss down her toned stomach until he got to the edge of those tight-fitting shorts. He moved to pull them off but was pleasantly surprised when she moved to do it herself. She was surprised at herself as well. This was supposed to be Melanie's thing, to hook li'l man up, but here she was doing it instead as if she were the one called to duty. She thought he was a virgin, from what Melanie had told her earlier. He sure wasn't acting like one, he was touching her like her college boys tended to.

As she removed her shorts and then her tank top and bra as well, he got out of bed. He began to undress as well, and Joy hoped she was not wrong in thinking that he could eat pussy good from the way he was touching her. He was so small, she had to have at least three to five inches on him in height, and he was built like a little toothpick. He did not have his big, clunky glasses on and Joy actually thought he was kind of cute without them.

Other than that, she was thoroughly unimpressed with him until he removed his underwear. Joy's eyes grew wide. She spoke the only words that would be spoken until they were finished: "Gotdamn, your dick is huge. What the hell?"

Israel, who had never seen another man's penis in his life, thought that Joy was being kind to him. He knew that there was nothing remarkable about him, aside from the secrets Mr. Chin was teaching him, and he decided he would give his all into pleasing her to let her know that he appreciated what she was doing for him. As he climbed back into bed, his thick member brushing across her leg like a huge snake, he went back to kissing her from her breasts down to her stomach. When he got past her stomach into the soft patch of her between her legs, his lips found home as if he had done this a thousand times and that is where the moans of pleasure really started.

77

Melanie awoke in the middle of the night to go to the bathroom. She was thankful she had one in her room; the liquor that she had consumed all of sudden seemed to be pressuring her bladder for release. She thought she heard moaning but really did not register it as she bolted to the bathroom, pulled her pants and underwear down in one quick move and sat down and let the urine flow. She sighed deeply in content.

When she finished up and came out of the bathroom, she heard the moaning again. She was sure of it now. She thought Joy was probably having a bad dream but figured she had better check on her anyway.

She walked out of her room and the moaning was louder in the hallway. Melanie's face wrinkled up…she now recognized those moans as sexual. She felt herself getting upset. It would be just like Joy to have taken the li'l man home and brought back one of her little college boys to fuck. She would be the one stuck washing the sheets and having her brother's room back in order before he and her parents got back.

The door was slightly cracked open. She debated whether or not to wait until they were done before she perhaps gave a knock and got Joy to come out of the room to give her the riot act. She decided to take a peek in and see which one of these college boys was bedding her this time.

When she peeked through the door a sight that she would never forget greeted her. Her mouth went slack and her eyes became wide bubbles.

Joy was facing her in the doggy-style position, but her eyes were scrunched closed. There was a light sheen of sweat on her forehead, and she was gripping the top bed spread as if her life depended on it. She even had some of the bedspread between her tightly clenched teeth. She was moaning and groaning as if she were in some place far away from reality that she might never come back from again.

Behind her, looking like a thin stick pounding into all that voluptuousness was Israel Baylock. Melanie felt her breath leave her in a gush. He was facing toward her but he was centered on Joy, looking down at her as he pounded away with an expression of ecstasy on his face that was just as impassioned as hers. Their bodies were crashing into each other with perfect timing and rhythm. The only thing that was so strange to her was how small Israel looked compared to Joy.

After a while he stopped what he was doing and flipped her over effortlessly as if she hadn't had several inches and over ten pounds on him. Joy was panting and writhing as if she could not wait for him to enter her again. Melanie caught a glimpse of Israel's dick and whispered aloud, "Oh my Lord, he is *huge*!" So much so that even though Joy appeared to be wet and ready, he still took his time easing his bigness back into her.

She moaned and gripped his skinny shoulders as he slowly went deeper into her. He was so long and thick that it seemed to take forever. Melanie thought that Israel's dick looked like it did not belong on his small body, like he was a circus sideshow freak or something. When he finally got it all the way in Melanie was amazed; she could not imagine something that size buried all the way inside her.

Melanie was held transfixed by the whole scenario. She watched for the next hour as Israel did things to Joy that she could not have even comprehended two people could do. She knew the phrase "make love" and had thought that David had done that with her, but what she was now seeing was the equivalent difference of watching Pop Warner Football and an NFL game.

At one point Israel just happened to glance her way and spotted her. She was startled, but he seemed not to care that she was there. He gave her an angelic smile, then went right back to Joy and did not look at her again.

Finally Israel began to wind down. Joy was riding him and his mouth opened in a wide *O* as he sucked in a great whoosh of air. She asked him if he were about to cum and he managed to gasp out an answer in the affirmative. She quickly hopped off of his dick and began to jerk it with both hands, and seconds later a thick gush of cum shot out that hit Joy on her neck and breasts. It seemed for a moment like it might keep coming out of him, but then the gushing stream finally reduced to a dribble.

Panting slightly, Israel pulled Joy up and kissed her passionately. Their size difference did not seem so strange now... he seemed very mannish in his actions, and then there was that horse-like appendage between his legs that, even drained of blood and passion, still seemed massive. He was holding her like they had been lovers forever, not like they had met just a few hours ago.

Melanie went back to her room and lay on her bed. She was a more than a little moist and debated whether or not to masturbate, but somehow she thought that would be like cheating on David.

She thought about everything she saw between Israel and Joy right up until the light of the morn spread across the world, crept past the closed curtains of her bedroom window and ushered her into a deep, dreamless sleep.

78

"Damn! So what does this mean now?"

Israel sat up and looked at Joy, who was lying on her back staring up at the ceiling. "Uh, what does what mean?"

"I don't know," Joy said, turning away from him.

Israel was confused. He did not know what to say to her. All of this was new. There was nothing in the books he'd read or anything Mr. Chin told him to help him deal with a moment like he was in now. He thought she would be happy after having been pleased her to the nth power, but now she was tripping.

"Joy, please talk to me. I really don't understand what you're trying to say, and I'd like to."

She seemed to ignore him for a moment, then turned over and looked at him. There were tears in her eyes threatening to roll down her cheeks. Israel was really confused now and at a loss as to whether to hold her or try to say something comforting.

"Israel, you just showed me sex. My mom tried to explain it to me once, and some of these college boys I've dealt with have come close to puttin' it down, but damn, that was like." She tried to come up with an equivalent feeling but could not. "Fuck, it was incredible!

"See, normally if someone had put it on me like that I would be feeling like they should be my man…there's no way in hell I would want to share lovin' that good with someone else, or let them get away if they were single, but I mean, y'know."

Israel sighed. He knew what she was getting at. "Go on."

"Well, you are you. And I am me. I mean, I'm what they would call one of the pretty, popular girls and you are what they would consider, uh, umm...."

"I know, I know." Israel sighed again, suddenly feeling weary. "I'm the nerd, the nobody. Even physically we don't look like we mesh."

Joy nodded her head sadly. One of the tears fell down her cheek as she as she said, "I know that probably sounds so shallow, but..."

Israel wiped the tear off her cheek with one of his small hands. He gave her a game smile. "You know what Joy? I'm used to being a nobody, and I guess I don't expect that to change anytime soon. Definitely not in one night, and I just really appreciate you being here with me like this. You are the first girl I ever slept with, and I don't think I will ever forget you now."

Joy looked at him like he was crazy. "I am?" Israel nodded yes. "The way you just fucked me...no, you've gotta be kidding! I thought maybe the whole virgin thing was just a ploy to get into Melanie's panties."

Israel held up with his right hand with a chuckle. "Swear on a stack of bibles, it's true. Tonight, you have made me a man."

She sat up and hugged her legs up to her chest. She looked amazed as she said, "Wow, I am somebody's first." She chuckled. "Well, you are my first in a way, too."

Now it was Israel's turn to look confused. "How so?"

"Well, for starters, yours is about the biggest dick that has ever been in me!" They both laughed at this. "And no one—and I mean no one—has *ever* made me cum like that. I didn't even know you could have more than one orgasm. No one has ever touched me or made love to me or made me feel as alive as you did tonight, and that's real."

"Wow!" Israel was blushing. "Well, that is something else. I mean, I thought you were kidding when you said my dick was big earlier...but whatever, I'm just glad everything was good enough for you."

She smiled a warm smile. "Sweetie, I don't think it could ever be better. I just feel bad about what will probably happen here after tonight. I mean, I want to see you again like this but I can't. And to be honest, I don't even know how I feel about that right this second."

"Why can't you see me like this again?"

Joy sighed. She really was confused about all of this and did not want him to be confused too. "Israel, it's just...you know what people would think about the two of us together. I hate to say it, it sounds fucked up, but I do care about what they think."

Israel smiled slyly. "Joy, I didn't say let's go out as boyfriend and girlfriend. I asked you why we can't see each other like this again. No one in the world knows about this right now, and no one has to. Ever." He let it sink in with her for a moment and finished, "You follow me?"

She did. And he was right, but still she had to ask, "Can you keep a secret? I mean, if we kept...doing this, would you be able to not tell anybody?"

Israel had to laugh aloud at that one. "Joy, trust me, I can keep a secret better than anyone you know. No one has to know anything. Whatever you decide, no one even has to know about tonight."

Joy thought about it. Her emotions were twisted right now, but she felt like Israel was sincere. She had one last question: "How is it gonna be for you, emotionally speaking? Can you do this?"

Israel felt like telling her rudely that Melanie was the one that he wanted to be having this discussion with, but he said instead, "Joy, please don't worry. I won't say anything to anyone."

Joy nodded her head affirmatively, satisfied. Then she reached for the thick meat that lay still and lifeless between Israel's scrawny legs. It stirred to life in her palm, throbbing and powerful. She looked at Israel, her face clouded in lust, and it was almost disconcerting to him. He never dreamed he could have such power over a girl.

“I want this again, right now,” Joy demanded. “Can you make me feel the way you did before all over again?”

Israel smiled. He said, “Easily,” and leaned in for a passionate kiss…

79

When Joy dropped Israel off that morning, his feelings were divided. He was happy that he had one less mystery in this world to figure out, and happy he had pleased Joy enough for her to want to see him again. He was a little disappointed that it was not Melanie instead, but then he forgot all of that as he remembered he had to go into the house. He knew his mother would be steaming mad, so he just stood in front of the house and just looked at it for a moment before he entered.

Although she and Ellena were sitting on the living room couch waiting when he walked in the door, his mother was not as mad at him as he thought she'd be. They had called around worried and David Hill finally came clean and told them what was going on. He had not gone so far as to give out Melanie Thompson's number, and he had convinced Ellena that she in turn should convince their mother not to go to her house and get him.

It was kind of strange as Israel sat on the sofa and his mother stood above him, pissed off but not too much. It was more as if she were going through the motions of being pissed because that was what she had to do as a parent. She seemed more relieved that he was in one piece, safe and unharmed. By the end of the day life would be back to normal and it would almost be as if it never happened, although his sister would give him knowing winks behind their mother's back that made his cheeks go fiery red in embarrassment.

Later that night, Israel thought about what had happened the night before as he laid on his bed. He was learning so much about life period, and now yet another mystery had been solved for him. And it even looked like he might be having sex on a semiregular basis. He had to laugh at this because he would not have dreamed this possible for him, the way he was and the way he lived.

He had yet to tell Mr. Chin how everything went. He would probably do it the next day. He was really tired. The lack of sleep and the energy expended the night before was catching up to him. He thought of Joy and how good she felt, her soft, silken wetness enveloping his manhood as if it were made just for him alone. He had put his all into her, everything that he had read and been told, and he felt pride each time she had an orgasm and said his name. He could not believe how good it felt once he had his own orgasm. It was like he had ascended into heaven like Icarus, got too close to the blinding but brilliant brightness of the sun and then slowly fell back to earth.

He still wished it was Melanie Thompson he visited these gifts upon and not Joy, but Mr. Chin often liked to tell him that life never usually went how we wanted it to go but often how it was meant to go. He had seen this to be true more often than not. And Joy wanted to continue to see him, even if it was in secret. That would make him the envy of half the school if they knew, even David Hill. He hated to admit to being so petty, but that *did* count for something.

And speaking of David, he knew he would tell David nothing happened between Melanie and him. He would not mention Joy at all, other than perhaps her being there and all of them getting high together, but nothing even close to the truth.

One decision he was slowly moving toward was getting away from LA after high school. He had been checking out his options with different branches of the military and that road was looking a little more appealing to him as just something completely different to do. He wondered how everyone from his mom to his sister to Dave to Mr. Chin would think if he actually went into the armed services...but as he drifted off to sleep he decided that he did not care. He lived in a world of secrets right now, and he would eventually have to shrug them all off and emerge butterfly-like from that suffocating cocoon to become the man he was impatiently waiting to be.

80

Israel and Joy's relationship stayed a secret one, but a funny thing happened to them both as timed passed—they came to genuinely care for each other. Joy still dated her college men, and a couple of them appeared to be quite serious about trying to get her locked in as a girlfriend. But she found herself surprisingly faithful to Israel, and suspected she might be in love with the little boy she affectionately called "man" in their private moments. She had even quit having sex with the boys she dated… she had done it twice after her first encounter with Israel, and initially she had quit because she knew no one would make her feel the way that he did physically, but in the final analysis she ended up caring for him and would not betray him for anyone.

Israel came to care for Joy in the same fashion. Part of him resented the secret nature of their relationship and the fact that Joy still dated other boys, but he always forgot all of that as soon as they came together. They had grown so close that Israel had actually confided in her about his training with Mr. Chin.

They had just finished having sex in his bedroom one day after school. His mother was at work and it would be another three hours before she got home, so they had time to kill. They had already talked about how much they cared about each other and Israel had decided on this particular day that he was not comfortable, holding secrets with her as he had been with everyone else. So he told her his whole history with Mr. Chin from *A* to *Z*.

"Wow," she said, a little amazed but not too surprised at this point. When they were having sex Israel at times handled her physically as if he were twice her size instead of so much smaller than her. She often wondered where he found his strength and agility, and now it was clear.

"Yeah," he said with a chuckle. "That's me, little man kung fu!" They both laughed at this.

Joy was under the bedcovers and Israel was standing up yawning and stretching. He was putting on some fresh underwear as she asked him, "Sooooo, how good are you? Can you really, like, mess somebody up?"

He nodded. "I think so. I'm pretty damn good. Watch this."

He dropped to the floor and did sixty one-arm push-ups with seemingly no problem. He could have done more but got bored with it. He then did a handstand with both hands, also without effort. He then pulled one hand up and was actually doing a one-handed handstand.

He swung his body around in a quasi-flip and landed standing straight up.

Joy's eyes were bugged out and her mouth was wide open. Israel had to laugh. He said, "That's just circus tricks, Mr. Chin didn't teach me that stuff. I just learned it on my own, just to see if I could do it. But I can do that kind of stuff because of Mr. Chin's teachings."

"Damn!" Joy was just shaking her head and looking amazed at him. "You are something else, Israel Baylock."

"Yeah, I am." Israel jumped into bed and gave Joy a long, passionate kiss. He said to her, "And I am going to keep being something else, as long as it pleases you."

She had no answer. She was in denial to herself, but their hearts both beat to the same drummer.

81

One day David was supposed to come over to his house to study. He was very late and Israel was growing impatient. He had not yet opened the history book they were to study from so he wouldn't have to go over the same stuff over again upon David's arrival. He had paged David several times and there had been no answer. He tried again in impatience, and slightly out of worry. David was usually punctual in returning pages from him.

Israel paced his room wondering what could be up when the phone finally rang. He dived on his bed and answered it. His mother had also picked it up, and when he heard Dave's voice say hello to her, he said, "Mama, I got it, thanks."

When his mother hung up Israel snapped, "Goddamn it, I've been waiting to study with you for over an hour now, what the fuck?"

"Dawg, I'm sorry...word, man," David said, his voice sounding weary.

Israel could hear background noise. David was somewhere outside. "Where're you at, man? What's going on?"

"I'm at the UCLA hospital. I'm here with Melanie. They brought her friend here last night, that chick Joy Patterson—the one that was with y'all getting high that one time."

Israel's heart sunk. All of his breath seemed to leave his little body. He was surprised his voice didn't betray him as he said calmly, "Word up? What happened?"

"Well, looks like Joy was fuckin' around with one of these dudes up here in the frat houses and he slipped her something.

Then him and a couple of his homies gang raped her ass ten ways to Sunday. Did her pussy, mouth *and* ass, nigga."

Israel felt murdered inside. Tears formed unnoticed in his eyes as he said in a steady, casually interested voice, "How is she? Is she okay?"

David sighed. "Well, like I said, they slipped her something that knocked her out. I guess while they was bonin' her she woke up and started strugglin'. So they beat the fuck out of her and dumped her ass out in the hospital parkin' lot when they was done. She was damn near comatose all day yesterday, but she done woke up and can talk today. She seems okay so far. Melanie's in with her and her peoples now, but I needed to come out here and take a break. She looked fucked up, cuz."

In that firm man's voice, Israel proclaimed, "I'm coming down there. You need a friend right now. I know that you're being there for Melanie, but no one is being there for you."

David didn't argue. He simply told Israel what room Joy was in.

When they hung up the phone, he let out a loud, piercing scream. His mother came rushing into his room. "Israel, what the hell?"

He ran into her and wrapped his arms around her, crying as if he would never be able to stop. Ms. Baylock looked at her only son in shock for a moment, then began to rock him and stroke his head. "What is it baby, what's going on?"

He could not speak, he was crying so hard. She decided to leave it be. When he could talk, he would tell her what the problem was. Her baby always told her everything eventually.

82

Israel eventually had to tell his mother something. There was a mutual friend of his and Dave's that had been robbed and badly beaten and he wanted to get over to the hospital to see him. Ms. Baylock took her son over to the hospital and offered to come in with him, but he told her not to worry. He would stay for a while and David would drive him home.

He could not get to the room fast enough. The elevator seemed to move in slow motion. His legs seemed leaden as he raced to Joy's room, ignoring the calls of several hospital employees to slow down.

When he got to the room, he stopped for a second to collect himself. He had to get his emotions together. He had to be strong and at the same time not give away any of what he felt for her to anyone else in the room. He promised her no matter what he would never give a clue as to their true relationship to anyone, and a promise from him was gold.

When he entered her room, there was an older woman sitting there that Israel figured to be Joy Patterson's mother. Seated right next to her was Melanie Thompson. Israel looked at the bruised, battered, beaten figure on the bed and found it so very hard to maintain his composure. Her long hair was pulled back into a ponytail, allowing him to take in every contour of her swollen, purplish face. She smiled a dim, secret smile at him, acknowledging that she was glad he was there.

"Hi everybody," he said wanly. A woman who indeed introduced herself as Joy's mother greeted him warmly. He introduced himself in return, telling her that he was a classmate of Joy's and David Hill's best friend. He and Melanie said hello to each other as well.

He wished he could be alone with Joy. There was information that he needed from her. She had been done wrong, and he had to avenge that. There was no way someone was getting away with that. Israel's heart went cold and steely with this resolution.

He asked, "Where is David? Is he here?"

"He's downstairs getting something to eat," Melanie said. "But I'd like to talk to you, would you mind taking a walk with me?"

Israel looked at her cautiously. "Um, sure. Okay."

They left the room and began a slow walk down the hospital hallway. For a moment nothing was said between the two of them. Then Melanie finally said, "I was shocked too when I first saw her. You just don't expect that kind of thing to happen to nobody you know, and I still don't really know how I feel about it."

Israel merely nodded politely, wanting to see where she was going with things before he spoke.

"How did *you* feel seeing her just now?"

Israel stopped walking and looked at her lamely, asking, "What do you mean by that?"

Melanie urged him to keep walking as she said, "Look, I know about you guys. There's no need to try to keep anything from me. We need to be able to talk openly."

Israel nodded in silent compliance.

"So, you still haven't answered my question yet."

Israel looked her dead in the eye. "I feel fucked up. I feel like my heart, my head and stomach all hurt at once. I feel like this mostly because the girl I love is up in that room messed up, but I'm going to feel worse if I don't get some good news about the bastards that did this to her."

Melanie felt bad for the little boy walking beside her. He was almost seventeen, yet he looked as youthful and earnest as a twelve-year-old. But by the same token he had this weird energy that radiated from him that she could not identify. It was really strong, and she suddenly fully understood that all the things that Joy had told her about him were no exaggerations at all.

"Well, a couple of guys have been arrested, but they come from some serious money. Wouldn't surprise me at all if they were already out on bail. Joy's family has money too, they are not poor by any means, but these guys come from *long* money. Two of the white guys that...participated, one's dad runs one of the largest publishing companies in the nation, the other one's dad owns a couple of hotels in Vegas. And the black guy's dad is the CEO of Vigway Family Savings, the largest bank founded and run by African-Americans in the city."

"Melanie, I don't care about any of that. I don't care *who* they are. They've got to pay for what they did to Joy. That's all I know."

Melanie could feel Israel's rage burning out of him. She really didn't know what to say. She wanted Joy's attackers to pay too, but Mrs. Patterson said that these boys' daddies lined up some big money attorneys. She was sure that the burden of proof had to lean against them, but she was still a young black woman and had not seen anything in her life up to that point to convince her that the justice system would be righteous.

"Well, I think the only thing we can do is hope that by the time that all this stuff goes to trial that the police have done their job and everything is as it should be for them to get convicted."

Israel stopped walking once again. "Look, I don't give a rat's ass whether they are convicted or not. I don't even want to chance that. They have to pay. That's it and that's all, and if I'm the only person serious about this, then so be it!"

Melanie was almost frightened by Israel now. She knew he was serious, and although he looked like such a baby his voice, energy and attitude were conveying that he was indeed going to do his best to manifest everything he was saying.

"Yeah, well, David was talking about some of his friends doing something about it."

"No!" Israel said, loud enough to make Melanie jump a little. "I don't want him involved at all, do you understand me? You have to convince him to let the system handle it."

Melanie really had no problem with that. She did not want David involved either.

"Do you know who did this? Do you know who these guys are by name?"

She shrugged. "Yeah, Joy told me. Why do you want to know?"

Israel fixed her with a steely gaze. "Don't worry about that. Just give me the names."

The sight of this little boy should have been funny to her, but it wasn't. He meant business, and it was fascinating and a little intimidating at the same time. She gave him the names of the three boys and the name of their frat house.

"Okay, that's all I need. You didn't say anything to me. In fact, we never had this conversation. Not even David can know, you understand?"

Melanie mutely nodded.

"These bastards are going to pay," Israel said in a cold, iron voice, almost as if he were talking to himself. He looked at Melanie. "You make sure David doesn't get involved. I don't want anything endangering his scholarship attractions, okay?" Melanie nodded.

"Okay. Let's go back to Joy's room."

83

The news about Joy Patterson got around the school quickly. But the stories got more twisted and inaccurate each day. Some would say she was raped, others would say she gave the young men permission to do what they did because she was drunk or on drugs. Some would say it was one person, some would say it was eight. But someone finally saw an article on it in the newspaper and the truth, after almost three weeks of innuendo and inaccuracies, was revealed.

The lawyers for the defendants stated in the article that their clients would be exonerated. They would simply show that Joy Patterson was one of loose morals long before the three boys had gotten to her. This was a shock to most of the students who thought she was a virgin. Even though the article had stated no incidents in particular, everyone ran with it anyway and all of a sudden Joy was a whore that had gotten what she deserved. She thought she was pretty and above the other girls in school…well, she had most certainly gotten hers.

Israel watched all of this happen with a mask on his face that said that it was unimportant to him. He was wondering about what colleges he was going to apply to, so how could all of this matter?

But on the inside he was boiling with a rage so deep he almost didn't know what to do. Mr. Chin gave him many pep talks, the only person that knew what he was going through. The talks helped somewhat, but he still had many sleepless nights, many nightmares in which he saw the boys molesting her prostrate body like a piece of meat while he was helpless to do anything.

His relationship with Joy definitely changed. There were no more passionate trysts, only long discussions of how depressed she was, and how she might have in a way asked for what she got, and how life was quickly getting to be not even worth all of this stuff, maybe it would be nicer if it was just all over. Israel tried talk after talk to lift her spirits, as did her family and friends, but Joy was severely depressed. And the trial hadn't even taken place yet, something that also filled her with fear and dread.

"Israel, my parents think I'm a good girl. I'm already freaked about what they wrote about me in that newspaper article. I'm already freaked out about what they think of me mow. What are they going to think if these other guys get up and start talking about me being…being a slut or something?"

He did not know what to say to that. He knew she was no virgin, but it did not matter to him. But Joy treasured her parents' opinions of her and he knew this was a big deal to and for her.

He wanted so badly to tell her of his carefully constructed plan of revenge, but he decided it was better she did not know. He did not even tell Mr. Chin. This was *his* baby. He knew that since he had never done anything like this before there was a chance he might fail. If he did, he did not want anyone caught up, especially anyone he cared for.

84

Joy's parents received a call a week later. The three boys were all dead. They had been found in a crashed car that had caught fire on impact, burned beyond recognition. They could be identified only through their dental records.

Apparently they had been out for a drive together and the car had run off the road into a ravine off of a stretch of the Pacific Coast Highway some miles north of Los Angeles, halfway to Santa Barbara. The crash caused the fuel line to burst, setting the car on fire. There had been no determination as to whether the boys were unconscious or not while the car burned.

No one could figure out why the boys were headed down that way or why they were even together; they had been carefully advised by their individual legal teams not to associate with each other at all until the trial was over since everyone was preparing their own separate defenses. When the parents were asked if the boys had any friends in Santa Barbara, neighboring Ojai or anywhere as far north as even as San Francisco and the surrounding Bay Area, the resounding response was no. And none of them were informed by their sons that they were going anywhere, never mind meeting with each other against their lawyer's advice.

At this point, none of this did anything for Joy. Her parents ended up transferring her to another school. She changed her phone number and seemed to want nothing to do with any of her close friends, Melanie Thompson included. Israel Baylock was effectively shut out as well.

Israel was depressed and went into a funk for weeks. He sometimes hid his emotions well from his mother, sister and David Hill, but it was hard. He knew for sure where his destiny was leading him and he had now informed everyone of it. He actually did not expect the support that he got from everyone, and he worried. With everything that had happened with Joy he really needed it. But his worrying had been for nothing. They were his people.

Mr. Chin had been the only one to give him any hassle about his decision regarding the military, but ultimately he reluctantly he came around. He told Israel that if he wanted to continue his studies and take himself to the next level that would eventually come with meeting some of his people abroad. Israel told him this was a must and that he wanted to continue his studies until death. Mr. Chin laughed and told him at some point he would have to stop, look around, breathe and enjoy his life outside of training.

Israel smiled and nodded his head politely to what he was told, but he and Mr. Chin both knew that right now he was centered on nothing but getting away. Escape was all that mattered. Freedom was what he thought about every waking moment and every night his eyes closed and his dreams bore him aloft on a magic carpet twined with threads made of fairy dust to better places far, far away.

85

Israel went to the kitchen and quickly found all the things he was seeking. He gathered them up and went back to the room where he had fought for his life and watched his best friend die in. The leg he had been shot in was throbbing and humming, as was the shoulder Fereal McNaughton's earlier bullet had grazed. He'd at least managed to stop the bleeding and bandage those wounds up. His nose was no longer pumping out blood, but still quite sore. But at that moment his aches and wounds mattered not at all.

When he got back he stared at the big man gagged and bound to the chair his best friend had been in earlier. There was nothing but fear in Fereal McNaughton's eyes as he saw what Israel had in his hands. He struggled and tried to scream past the gag but he knew it was all in vain as he was doing it. His demon was about to destroy him and nothing was going to stop that, and he was a fool for ever believing that anything could.

Israel cast a glance over at David Hill's lifeless, almost headless body. He had taken the body out of the chair and propped it against the wall in a corner of the room close to Sean Cudahy's corpse. He thought of the soul that had inherited that body, a robust spirit that perhaps was not the most perfect of men but one of the most real. And he had been an excellent friend and a good father. He had to hold back tears as he thought about the fact that he would never be able to tell him how he was the brother his mother never had and how much he loved and cherished their friendship. And he would probably be the one telling his sister and his nephew that they had lost David as well, a task he did not look forward to not even remotely.

"No, Ellena and Michael didn't lose him. He was murdered," Israel thought as he turned his attention back to Fereal. The sorrow he felt was now replaced by a deep hatred. Fereal could sense this and it caused him to wet himself for the second time since Israel strapped him to the chair David Hill had been in and he himself had affixed so many of his enemies to. He saw the end was coming and judging by the items that Israel was placing carefully at his feet it would not be quick.

Fereal tried to look away from the butcher knife, the meat cleaver, the lighter fluid, shaker of salt and the jug of Clorox bleach Baylock had placed at his feet. He knew that he wanted him to see these items, to think about what was going to happen to him. Fereal McNaughton had tortured and killed so many people in that room, he knew all the tricks of the trade. He knew that he was going to die slowly and painfully.

Israel pulled up a folding chair right in front of Fereal. The only thing between them, were the instruments of his impending torture and death. He had a pen and a notebook pad in his hands. He sighed deeply, pulled the gag out of Fereal's mouth. "Let's not pretend even for one second that I'm going to let you live, okay?"

Fereal said nothing but Israel knew he understood.

"Okay. What's going to determine whether or not I simply put you out of your misery or send you to hell slowly and painfully is if you answer some questions for me. You see, this bullshit is going to end here today. I don't want your fucking cronies hounding my family and me. You still with me so far?"

When Fereal nodded, unable to find his tongue still, Israel continued. "I want the names of all of your buddies involved in this madness. Even the ones who aren't here today and the ones I killed at my sister's house. I am going to ask you specific questions about each of them and I need you to answer them to the best of your ability. Do this, and I might be good enough to grant you a quick death. If I think in any way you're lying to me, I'll be *more* than happy to forget the questioning and spend all night killing you slowly. Is all this clear to you?"

Fereal barely nodded.

Israel nodded grimly. "Okay, let's start with the guys at my sister's house."

He and Fereal's Q and A went on for almost two hours. Israel nodded, wrote on the pad, asked the questions he wanted to ask and, after he committed them to paper, asked some more. His voice was almost pleasant and conversational as he spoke to Fereal.

When Israel was done he had almost twenty sheets of notebook paper completely filled. He could almost admire how thorough Fereal McNaughton was. He had virtually all the information that he needed and certainly had the means to get the little that McNaughton could not provide.

He dropped the pad and pen to the floor and stood up. He turned away from the man bound in the chair and began doing what looked like martial arts or yoga stretches. Fereal watched him for ten minutes before he finally found his voice and asked, "Why are you doing that?"

Israel stopped in the middle of a stretch and turned to face him. Fereal wanted to scream but could not find his voice. There was a toothy smile on Israel's face that read pure evil. He did not even look human to him; he looked at *exactly* like the Man-Beast that had haunted his dreams so long, his own personal satan come to life.

His eyes twinkling with impish delight, Israel said smoothly, "I lied, McNaughton. You're still going to die slowly. It's the least I can do for you and your people trying to kill me and my family and *especially* for killing my friend in the corner over there. Oh, I am going to enjoy myself, so."

Israel picked up the butcher knife and quick as a flash made a cut. When Fereal saw what piece of him fell to the ground he screamed for help, knowing it was futile. A monster was upon him and he was to learn for the first and last time in his life what hell on earth was. And the lesson would unfortunately not be a short one.

86

A funny thing happened to the policemen who worked with Orlando Flores and Fereal McNaugton.

They all knew that the two men were no longer of this world, and this was a blow to their network. They were leaders of the network by default, and now there was a void all of the survivors were scrambling to fill. It just could not be decided who would lead now, although there were a couple of strong candidates.

One thing the survivors agreed on was that there must be vengeance for those that died in the big house on the hill. Fereal's body still had not been found, and to the ego of a policeman this was an affront of the highest order. They came together to plot the demise of Israel Baylock and Ellena Baylock with surgical precision. A flawless plan was conceived that would have both avenged their fallen and also assured the living that no one who had knowledge of their network would live to tell the tale. The men were satisfied that soon things would be back to the way they were, and what happened in the house on the hill was just a slight misstep off the path.

Only one thing would throw them off.

87

Ralph Cantone was a miserable man to his family lately. His wife could not figure it out, simply citing the stresses of being a police officer. In truth, it was because there were a number of schemes hatched by Fereal McNaughton and/or Orlando Flores that had brought in extra money that had become null and void upon their death. It was like the well had gone dry overnight.

As he stepped out on this cold, crisp morning to get his newspaper, clad in only a black terry cloth bathrobe, he was feeling slightly more secure after a meeting with his partners the day before. But he would not feel absolutely sure of anything again until he actually saw money rolling in like clockwork, like it used to.

As he bent down to pick up his newspaper Ralph Cantone paused. There was a pink cake box next to it. He reached for the box, initially thinking that someone must've just wantonly picked his lawn to litter in. But as he picked it up there was slight heft to it, indicating there was something in the box. And it was clearly not cake.

Ralph looked around cautiously, as if he expected someone at six in the morning to be out watching him. It was still fairly dark and not even the joggers were out yet. He opened the box, peered inside, and then dropped it back on the lawn. "Jesus Christ!" he screamed at the top of his lungs.. His robe flew open, revealing his nakedness as he stumbled backward and fell on his behind, but he cared not. He quickly got to his feet and ran into the house.

He was thankful his wife or the kids were not up to see him the way he was now. He was not sure he would have an explanation for them, and certainly would not let them know what he saw in the cake box still out there on the lawn. He went to the kitchen and got the cordless off the charger. Hands shaking, he barely managed to punch out the phone number he needed.

A terse, gravelly voice came on and said, "Yeah, who's this?"

"Larry, it's fuckin' Ralph Cantone, man."

"Yeah, I already know what you're gonna tell me. There was a cake box here at my house too."

Ralph felt like his heart was going to stop. His hand barely managing to keep the phone steady against his ear, he said, "Good Christ! Who the fuck is it?"

The voice on the other end sighed deeply. "It's McNaughton."

That was it for Ralph. His breath left him and his mouth felt dry as the desert. He still managed to croak out, "How do you know?"

"Well, because this isn't the first call I've gotten on this today. Merc Horton got one of McNaughton's feet in his cake box. Terry Jones got a hand in his. Newton MacMillan actually got both fuckin' testicles. And me." He let out a coarse, bitter laugh. "Well, imagine my surprise when I opened up my little cake box and found McNaughton's head in it."

Ralph moaned, unable to believe that someone had gone through all this trouble over Fereal McNaughton. "You're shittin' me, right?"

"Nope. And with it came a note warning us all to stay away from the Baylocks or each of us were going to end up just like ol' Fereal. The frickin' note also said we'll keep receiving these parts until he's either sure we're going along with him or until he makes the move to start killing us off as well."

"What the hell, Larry?" Ralph was pacing the kitchen running a hand through his close-cropped black hair, feeling angry and helpless at the same time. "This is bullshit! I mean, c'mon. We're the LA fuckin' PD. He can't fuck around with us like this."

"Well, normally I'd be inclined to agree with ya, but we're the outside, brother. We are the shadows behind the badge. And when you dance in darkness, if you slip and fall there's nobody to help pick to you up.

"I helped clean up the mess this Baylock guy left at his sister's house and over at the big house. And I am telling you, this motherfucker is somewhere between Bruce Lee and Hannibal Lecter. Friedman—that big Aryan fuck in Dirk Benton's crew—his gut was ripped wide open, like a bear just took a couple of swipes at his stomach and just started rummaging around in his insides. His fuckin' heart was crushed right inside of his chest.

"Orlando Flores's head had a dent in it like someone took a fuckin' baseball bat to it trying to hit a home run. And a couple of fingers were bitten off. Jesus, I mean, who the fuck does that?

"The others he took out were a little less messy, but he did all of it with his bare, fuckin' hands, against men that were armed and hard as nails. Do you understand what I'm saying, Ralphie?

"This guy is a beast. He is a fuckin' beast. And I don't know about anybody else but so far no one knows about any of the shit we've been doing and he doesn't seem to care one way or the other about turning us in or he would have. This fuckin' guy is telling us we are going to either live or die behind this shit, the choice is ours." There was a pause as the gruff voice finished, "I intend to keep breathing. And I am gonna let everybody know today that I am through with all of this revenge business."

"Holy shit, Larry." Ralph was pacing back and forth furiously now. "You really feel like that? C'mon man, part of how we enforce all of this shit is that we let these scumbags know that they can't fuck with us whether we work with them or not! You really wanna just let this guy get away with all of this?"

"Ralphie, I'm not in this to make a point with one guy nobody but us knows or cares about. I am in this to make money. We leave him alone; we can live and still keep these hustles going, even without the nigger and his wetback man-bitch. We try to make a point with this guy, maybe we could get him, maybe not.

But who's to say all of us would even survive him before we got to him?"

Ralph Cantone had to admit that an important point had been made. When he saw what was in the cake box he remembered the icy fingers of fear that had gripped his heart and stolen reason completely away from him. He felt like his badge and all the status it inferred meant nothing, as helpless as a babe in a lion pit. He didn't like that feeling and hoped it would be a long time before he would feel it again, if ever.

The voice on the other line chuckled grimly. "That's what I thought, Ralphie. That's what I thought.

"Now here's what you need to do. Go get that fuckin' cake box off of your lawn and get rid of it somewheres. We're meeting at the big house at two this afternoon. You want to, you can bring it then. We gotta make a collective decision on this thing, but I think that overall we're all gonna come to the same conclusion."

Ralph Cantone nodded dully and clicked the phone off.

He thought about everything he had just heard, and then thought about the many bills that had recently started piling up. Yes, he had to be pragmatic about all of this. If there was a chance he could go back to making the money he had been, why then, that was a chance he would take. As he went outside to fetch the cake box and its sinister content, that was all that was on his mind.

88

The man on the other end of the line, one Larry Feldman originally from New York City, hit the OFF button on the cordless. He put the phone on the coffee table and walked across the spacious living room to the picture window that gave him a marvelous view of Hollywood. He had his hands clasped behind his back. He looked deep in contemplation.

Larry Feldman sighed deeply. "How was that?"

The black man sitting on his sofa hung up the cordless phone he'd been listening to the conversation on and said, "I'm satisfied. He didn't seem to catch on to anything, just like the others."

"So how many more calls do I have to make?"

The black man laughed, but it was a spiteful, harsh sound full of dark intent. "Larry, don't bullshit me. We both know there are another ten on the list. After that I think I'll be motivated to let your wife and kids go."

Larry Feldman was filled with a mix of fear and rage. The fucking nigger had him by the short hairs, but he still felt there was a chance there would be some payback. He just had to get through this. That's all he had to do—get through this moment and take it all one step at a time.

The black man clicked his cordless on. "Okay Larry, enough dillydallying. We got calls to make."

89

At two o'clock at the big house on the hill, all of the men immediately connected to the dark network Orlando Flores and Fereal McNaughton spearheaded were there right on time. A few of them hugged and talked about their families and how things were, and invariably the talk turned to the need to get some firm leadership going so that all the hustles Fereal and Orlando involved them in could be put back into play.

They all milled about in the driveway for a moment, and then Larry Feldman said harshly, "All right everybody, let's move this little party on inside. We got a lot to cover today."

When they were all inside most of the men were going to the conference room, a converted den that most of their meetings took place in. But Feldman stopped them. "No, today we do this in the back room."

There was a lot of grumbling and exchanged glances between the forty men who were there. One of them asked, "Lar, why do you want to meet in there? There are probably not enough seats. 'Sides, that room gives me the creeps. If those walls could talk..."

There were head nods and murmurs of agreement, but Larry's authoritative voice boomed out, "Look, it's important. I got my reasons. Trust me on this, okay?"

The men finally started walking down the hall with no problems or backtalk. Larry was a good man and had been one of the most important pillars of this dark network outside of Fereal McNaughton or Orlando Flores themselves. They had no reason not to trust him.

When they were all in the room, the first thing everyone noticed is that the chair that had once been used to intimidate enemies with was gone. A cake box rested where that infamous chair used to be. Immediately there was bickering among all the men about who could have delivered the box, even though they all knew.

"Dammit," one of the men said, scowling—half in anger, half in fear. "Don't we all have a fuckin' piece of McNaughton? What in the name of Christ could be left?"

Another man suggested, "Well, I know one of us here got his balls. Nobody said anything about getting his cock."

"Gotdamn it, all of you sound like children," Larry Feldman barked. "If nobody else wants to open the damn thing, I will. Can't be any worse than anything we've already gotten."

"I'll open it," said Merc Horton, one of the younger members of their network out to prove himself. He moved forward and kneeled before the box without a trace of hesitation. He casually opened it, a confident smile lighting his lips.

When he had the lid all the way open the smile disappeared. He was not even aware that his mouth had moved, but he'd yelled, "Oh no. God no!"

As the others began to move forward to see what had soured the youngster's confidence and sent it racing in the opposite direction, Larry Feldman made his peace with God. He knew he had done the right thing to protect his family. Hell, all their families. Perhaps in light of all the bad things he had done in his life this made him a hero of sorts.

That was last thought he would have on this earth as the explosion tore the room and everyone in it apart.

90

Israel had parked half a mile away from the big house and hoofed it. Hidden in a nearby bush, he watched the men go inside and then went and stood in front of the house. When he heard the loud explosion he waited patiently, seeing if anyone might run out that perhaps had been out of the room or not close enough to the bomb's epicenter. If so, he would just kill them on sight.

After ten minutes, no one came out.

Israel was still not satisfied. He went into the house, the house that he had come close to losing his life in, the house that his best friend in the world had died in. He saw as he walked down the hallway that the room of death was on fire so he could not get too close. There were a few body parts that had been blasted into the hall that he had to step over to get as close as he could. But smoke was filling the hallway quickly so he had to turn right back around and get back into the living room.

He went to the kitchen and turned on all the gas burners on the stove but extinguished the flames so that only gas hissed out of them. In another ten or so minutes tops, at the rate the flames were spreading, this house would not exist anymore. He felt satisfied that he had completely and thoroughly avenged the murder of David Hill.

He started walking away from the house. He wanted to stay and watch until the house was completely gone, but he knew that was stupid. Someone down the road would surely call the fire department when they saw the smoke, if they hadn't already called from hearing the explosion. It would still take them a while to get to the isolated area where the house was, but still, he knew it would be best for him to be long gone.

As he walked, a thought crossed his mind that made him chuckle. "Fuck these fools." Those were the last words David Hill had spoken to him. Israel had taken them to heart almost subconsciously, and they were now a prophecy fulfilled.

His thoughts turned toward his sister and his nephew. They were still heartbroken that David Hill had been snatched from them, and he knew that they were the only people in this world that felt even worse than he did. A tear formed in his eye as he remembered how he and Ellena tried to explain the concept of death to Michael, telling him that God had called his daddy home to become one of his angels. The boy initially thought this meant that his father would only be gone temporarily, but when he realized it was forever, he began to cry and cry and ask God to bring his daddy back.

Israel would have to be the man for all of them now once again. That was the way it had always been, as long as he had been alive. He didn't mind, really. It was a comfortable role for him and it gave him some sense of purpose for staying in a country that he absolutely deplored. But changes would have to be made to keep them all safe, that was for sure. He was determined to make sure danger never came close to his family ever again.

EPILOGUE

I have to say this—I don't think I could love Israel Baylock anymore in death than I did in life. He was my brother, the best friend I had ever had in the physical world I once called home, and it helped put my spirit at rest to let me know that I had not gone to the next place without being avenged.

Ellena and Michael moved in with her mother. My son slept in Israel's old bed while Ellena moved back into her room. Mrs. Baylock was sympathetic to her daughter, as she knew what it was like to lose a soul mate and feel that empty, hollow ache that comes with knowing you will never, ever in this life see them again, feel them, talk to them, *experience* them. Mrs. Baylock did what she could to comfort her, but it would be a long time before the ache of my loss would dull and throb instead of scream at her every waking moment.

The police were not done with the Baylocks, even though Ellena had quit the force. Ellena had been pulled over several times, basically for nothing, and random patrols would cruise by their house at all times of the day. They made it clear that they hadn't forgotten her and they definitely had not forgotten Israel. Everyone in the 'hood noticed, and the word had started to get around (through a "mysterious source") that the Baylocks were headed for a fall and not to be around them too much. The police would be taking care of them soon.

Israel ultimately decided to take the family back to Dallas, his mother's birthplace. He realized that he could win skirmishes, but ultimately he would lose because he knew he would end up killing one of the officers harassing them and then the whole family would be in danger.

Now all of this means absolutely nothing to me. I mean, I was initially upset that my son would be without a father as I was and that I would never hold sweet Ellena in my arms again. But then a whole other world opened up to me and I had to forget about all of that as my spirit opened wide and soared on to greater heights.

I can only hope that Israel finds some peace and that he, Ellena, Michael and my mother all come to terms with my demise. I wish that I could tell them that I am in a much better place, a place where I am one with everything and that all that mattered to me in the world of flesh means less than nothing here. I am part of the beauty of everything now, and everything is a part of me. And yes, indeed, there *is* a God.

Perhaps they will taste a tiny portion of the nirvana in their lives that I am experiencing now. In fact, I know they will—in the end. I love them all, but I love every speck of dust, every molecule, everything in the universe that experienced life and shares with me the greater experience that I am eternally bound to forever.

They will live their lives, and unbeknown to them there will be more adventures, more they will have to go through for better or worse, and more truths to discover. But none of that means anything directly to me, for this simple reason:

I am dead.

Made in the USA
Las Vegas, NV
02 December 2023

81595446R00177